To Mom 1.

Frannie,

Happy 75th Birthday

Alex McDonald

Sawgrass

By

Alex J. McDonald

authorHOUSE™

1663 LIBERTY DRIVE, SUITE 200
BLOOMINGTON, INDIANA 47403
(800) 839-8640
WWW.AUTHORHOUSE.COM

First published by AuthorHouse 09/20/04

ISBN: 1-4184-9225-6 (sc)

Printed in the United States of America
Bloomington, Indiana

This book is printed on acid-free paper.

Dedicated to my wife Sue and my son, Tony
whose love makes me complete

To mom and dad, Mary, David and John
and all my friends and family who believed

and especially to those men and women who serve honorably on the
front lines of law enforcement and every day risk making the ultimate
sacrifice for someone they will never meet.

FOREWORD

Young Danny Quinn sat on his father's lap, his feet dangling toward the ground. His thumb was in his mouth, he sucked on the fresh cut. His father patted his arm.

"Well, Danny, I reckon that sawgrass taught you a lesson today. Sawgrass is kinda like life. It looks like regular grass but up close, it'll cut you real bad. Life and some folks are like that. They appear to be one thing, but when you look close they ain't always what they appear. You remember that and life will be lots easier."

Danny nodded, tears drying in his eyes. His father hoisted him up and carried him toward the house.

"C'mon son, let's see if your momma has something to put on that cut," his father said quietly.

CHAPTER 1

He could feel it. The rhythmic movement felt so good. He continued moving, pumping up and down. The sweat trickled down his back and face, dripping on the thing of beauty below him. He felt the strain of holding himself up in his elbows and the backs of his arms. He was close now, the tingling beginning in his feet and creeping up his legs and across his back. He felt a tingling in his left hip. It vibrated and squirmed. Dammit! The feeling registered in his brain. He had felt that vibration so many times. He braked and slowed the bicycle, pulling off to the side of the road onto the gravel shoulder. He reached down and pulled the pager from his waistband, pushing the little gray button, stopping its incessant humming.

Danny looked at the readout on the pager. SHIT! They knew where he was and had strict orders not to page him unless it was a dire emergency. He aimed the bicycle back onto the hot asphalt, stroking the pedals rapidly. Only two miles to go until he reached the finish line. One hundred miles on a bicycle and he had almost made it without interruptions. Well, he would finish no matter what. He had pledges to meet. Lots of people pledged money for the charity if he finished this ride and he would. Danny had never quit anything in his life. In Vietnam, he had carried a wounded north vietnamese Major on his back for fifty miles. The other members of his platoon told him to just kill the bastard. When the interrogation team got through with the prisoner, the information they got saved the lives of a lot of American G.I.s .

Danny eased himself off the bike and parked it next to his car. He retrieved the cell phone from the front seat and dialed.

1

Detective Mike Richards answered the phone on the second ring.

"Homicide, Richards," he said with a bit of boredom.

"Mike. Danny, you rang?" Danny asked. "This better be real important."

"Hey, did you finish, I hope." Richards grinned at the receiver. "I know today was important to you. Sorry."

"Yeah, I finished. What is so important?"

"They found our missing cop in an orange grove off Egret Road. I'm on my way out there. The boss wants you there."

The "missing cop" was a city police officer who had been missing for three days. His wife didn't know where he was or why he might have disappeared. Danny had known the guy for about ten years. Had not known him well, but enough to say hello to. Danny felt a jolt in the pit of his stomach. If they wanted him and Richards there, that meant the officer was dead. Danny hated the thought of an officer dying for any reason. It was like a family member dying, whether you knew him well or not at all.

"Gimme the address and I'll meet you there in about forty minutes," Danny replied quietly, a bad feeling already building.

As Danny drove, he considered the possibilities. Either the cop had a heart attack while fishing, or he was murdered or he killed himself. No matter how he died, there would be problems. The relationship between the Sheriff's department and the city police administrators had never been a love match. Not between the officers on the street. They always worked well together. Like all cops, they were brothers who had to depend on each other for survival. Bonds were always strong when you had to rely on another to do the ultimate. Kill for you or die for you. Like soldiers in combat. No matter how much you hated the other one personally, when a cop yelled for help you busted ass getting there. The animosity was between the top brass. Petty jealousies and the perception the other guy was trying to topple your kingdom clouded common sense and good judgment.

He looked out the window to his right. Along the side of the Sawgrass Expressway, the Everglades shimmered in a mirage of heat. Danny hated this road but had to admit it was convenient. He hated it because of what it represented and where it was located. Along the west side was a canal, the flood dike and his beloved Everglades.

Along the east side were houses and condominiums, right next to the road and threatening to leap across the dike and take over the wetlands. This road represented progress but for Danny, it represented overcrowding and the beginning of the end of South Florida wild life and the Everglades themselves. He had grown up in those swamps and loved every inch of them. Too bad no one understood what they meant to South Florida's survival. Marjorie Stoneman Douglass understood. She had fought for the wetlands all of her life. Maybe people would wake up someday.

Danny pulled off the road and drove up to a fence with a sagging metal gate. Parked off to the side was a green and white sheriff's office car. The white-shirted deputy standing next to it was sweating in the heat. His hair was matted to his head. He smiled grimly as Danny rolled down his window. Pointing through the gate he said, "Go down to the second row of trees and turn right. You can't miss them."

Danny smiled and waved, driving through the gate. The road was a tractor track that dug through the knee high weeds past a small irrigation ditch. He turned right between the ten-foot-high orange trees, heavy with green fruit. Too early for the oranges to be ripe. Bees and flies swarmed up from the undergrowth in front of his car, forced to flee the safety of the ground. In front of him, a hundred yards down, he could see more green and white police cars and some unmarked detective cars. Past them stood a green and white van with the words, SHERIFF'S OFFICE CRIME SCENE UNIT painted on the side.

He parked behind the other cars and opened the door. A blast of heat slamming into him, causing him to catch his breath. Detective Mike Richards met him at the car door, his tie undone and hanging limp around his neck. Sweat soaked his shirt under his armpits and down both sides. The back of his shirt was saturated and sticking to his back. His shirt hung over the front of his pants, along with his belly. The gun strapped to his right hip hung down as if wilting from the sun.

"It's not pretty," Richards said grimly, making a disgusted face and wrinkling his nose. "Been here a few days sitting in his car. With this heat he's pretty smelly. Helicopter spotted him from the air while on patrol. Too bad they didn't find him earlier."

Danny glanced up at the green and white helicopter circling almost a mile away. Looking up at the trees that hung over the dead man's car, he knew why they had trouble seeing the car from the air. The little car was almost completely hidden from view. A knot of uniformed deputies and plainclothes detectives stood a dozen yards from the car, talking quietly and glancing at the car as if it were about to jump at them. The driver's door stood open and a forensic detective in overalls, wearing a breathing apparatus on his back, stood in the open door taking pictures with a camera pressed to his face mask. Danny remembered as a teenager shopping for a car. He had dreamed of owning a Corvette. He knew he couldn't afford one but wandered the dealership admiring them anyway. An overweight, middle-aged salesman with thinning gray hair approached him and told him he had just the car for the right price.

"Been trying to unload this piece of shit ever since it hit the lot," The salesman said, opening the door. The smell steamrolled out of the car and struck young Danny full in the face, making him retch.

"Found the owner dead in the car. Been there about two weeks. Damn near melted into the seat. Can't get the smell out of the fiberglass." The salesman grinned evilly at the young man's discomfort. Danny had never felt the same way about Corvettes after that.

Danny walked through the tall grass toward the group of huddled deputies, the grass swishing against his cowboy boots.

"Hey Sarge," nodded an older detective wearing a dress shirt but no tie. Detective Marshall Grimes was the oldest man on Danny's squad and had been in homicide longer than Danny, nearly twelve years. He had forgotten more about homicide investigation than most cops would ever know. Danny relied on him to find the angles no one else thought of.

"Marsh," Danny nodded back, "what do you think about this mess?"

"Don't know yet. But I wish another team had caught this one. You know as well as I do that the shit's gonna hit the fan no matter what."

"Yeah, this one's gotta be done right. The politics are gonna be a fuckin' pain in the ass." Danny agreed.

"How come you're even here? Didn't you have some bike ride to do today?" Grimes smiled secretly.

"Yep. And I finished it. Sorry to disappoint ya." Danny chuckled.

"Fuck me! That means I gotta pay out all that money I pledged. Well, there goes my pension." Grimes smiled back. The entire squad had been pressured into pledging money for the charity ride, so much per mile ridden. The charity would be pleased to get Danny's check.

"Here come the body snatchers," observed one of the uniformed deputies, nodding his head toward the tractor track as he lit a cigarette. A plain white van picked its way along the rut in the grass toward them. The van parked behind Danny's car and two men wearing dress shirts and ties emerged toward the group. Danny smiled at them and said, "Better suit up guys. The body's been there two days in this heat."

"More like three days," interrupted the forensic detective as he approached, pulling off the face mask of his breathing apparatus. His face was red, encircled by the impression of the face mask, sweat ran down his face.

"Looks like he's been there since he disappeared." The smell of death hung around his clothes making one of the newer uniformed deputies take a step back.

"Does it look like a suicide, homicide or what?" Mike Richards asked, glancing anxiously at the victim's car.

"Looks like it might be a suicide. One shot to the mouth, gun still in his hand, suicide note taped to the dashboard." The forensic man answered. "But let's let the ME decide after the autopsy." The forensic man held numerous plastic bags Danny knew would contain all the evidence he had described.

"Ready for us to take him?" asked one of the body snatchers. The forensic technician glanced at Danny, raising his eyebrows. "Sarge?"

Danny returned his look. "If you got enough pictures, is there any reason for us to look ?" Danny hoped not. He really didn't want to look at his former acquaintance in this condition.

The forensic man shrugged and looked away. Danny knew the answer. Of course he would have to look. It was necessary to proper investigation. Danny let out a whoosh of air and headed toward the dead man's car. The smell would hang on his clothes for hours.

He stood in the open car door. The body sat in the driver's seat. Chin resting on chest. The front of his shirt was caked with black dried blood which pooled in his lap. Rivulets of dried blood tracked down his face from the top of his head. The blood seemed to have run out of his mouth. His left hand was frozen in a grotesque fist, as if gripping an invisible gun. Danny sighed and walked away.

Mike Richards walked Danny to his car. Danny was really feeling the strain of exercise now. His legs were stiff and he placed his hands on his hips, stretching backwards to relieve the stiffness in his lower back. They watched as the body snatchers wrestled the body from the car, heavy from lividity and settled bodily fluids.

"I need to go and get some rest. Notify the wife and I'll catch up with you in the morning," Danny said quietly. He hated to dump that job on his partner. It would be difficult to tell the wife of one of your own he was dead.

"Yeah, OK. I'll see you at the office in the morning." Richards nodded grimly.

Mike Richards turned the car onto the palm tree-lined street. He and Grimes scanned the house numbers, trying to find the right one. Locating the house, they drove into the driveway and parked. Richards switched off the engine and they both sat quietly looking at the house. It was typical

South Florida architecture, one story stucco. The house still had jalousie windows, typical of older homes. Two palm trees stood together in the front yard in a circular cutout in the grass. Wood chips covered the ground around the base of the trees. An open fisherman style boat, Richards guessed about twenty feet long, squatted on a trailer on the side of the house, covered by a blue tarp.

Richards glanced at his companion and sighed. "Well, let's get this done."

"Man, I fuckin' hate this part of the job. No matter how long I've been doing this, I never get used to it. The way they stand there with that "you're lyin" look on their face and then start crying and screaming. Man, I fuckin' hate this." Grimes opened his door and hoisted his bulk out of the car.

The door was opened by a short, middle-aged woman, dressed in jeans and a t-shirt. Her hair was pulled back and held by a red cloth band. She was thin and the strain of the past few days showed on her face. Richards held up his badge.

"Mrs. Conrad?" Richards asked quietly. "I'm Detective Richards, Sheriff's Office. This is my partner, Detective Grimes."

"You found him didn't you?" She said with a whisper.

"Yes, Ma'am. I'm really sorry to tell you we found your husband. He's dead." There was no other way to say it but straight out.

"Won't you come in?" she asked, turning to let them in.

Richards could see she was fighting to maintain control of her emotions. Typical veteran cop's wife. Years of dealing with her husband working screwed up shifts, never knowing if he would come home again, had taught her how to keep control. She ushered them into a neatly kept house. The living room had terrazzo floors. Not too many of those left. The typical Florida house now had ceramic tile or carpet.

Richards and Grimes sat next to each other on the edge of the over stuffed couch, the kind that swallowed you up and made it tough to get back out. Mrs. Conrad sat facing them in a recliner chair. She looked Richards straight in the eye. He liked that. But she had been a cop's wife for a long time and she had been through the wringer more than once.

"I need to know everything, Detective Richards," she said, a slight quaver in her voice.

"We found him in his car. Parked in an orange grove. He died from a gunshot wound."

She looked away for an instant, tears brimming up in her eyes. Grimes shifted uncomfortably in his seat.

"Why would anyone kill my husband? Was it someone he arrested in the past? Have you considered that possibility?"

"Yes ma'am. But it appears to have been suicide. There was a note."

She gasped and placed her hand to her mouth. The look of disbelief was suddenly replaced with a look of certainty. "My husband did not, I repeat, did not kill himself, Detective Richards."

"It's early in the investigation. We'll know more when we have time to look into it." Richards said reassuringly.

"Well, I suppose I need to call the family," she whispered, standing to show it was time for them to go. Richards could see she was losing the battle to maintain control. Both detectives rose and she ushered them to the door. Richards placed his hand on her arm.

"Let me know if you need anything. I'll let you know what we find out." He could see tears filling her eyes, threatening to overflow. As she closed the door behind them, they could hear her begin to sob uncontrollably.

Enrique "Ricky" Madeira sipped his drink and let his eyes slowly roam around the crowd at the pool. Across from him a group of young men and women clinked their glasses and laughed at the antics of one of their group. In front of Ricky, a very full breasted woman floated on a raft, her sunglass shielded eyes tilted toward the sun. A short distance behind Ricky, a large muscular man with dark sunburned skin sat at the bar. His mustached face never moved, but Ricky knew under the sunglasses, the eyes never stopped looking for signs of a threat. Jose was Ricky's constant companion. He had saved Ricky's life more than once, here and at home in Colombia. Jose's muscular arms swelled under his brightly colored Hawaiian shirt.

Ricky loved the pool side of this bar. All across the patio the women paraded their bodies looking for a sign from the men. Hoping to rope a rich, handsome lover who drove a fancy sports car and lived in an expensive house. One who owned one of the go-fast boats tied to the floating dock beyond the pool. Someone like Ricky.

Ricky smiled to himself and stroked his long black hair, worn in a tight ponytail on the back of his head. An attractive brunette in a G-string bikini passed him for the fifth time and smiled down at him. Ricky smiled back, admiring her for the umpteenth time. The dayglow-green bottoms of her bathing suit disappeared into her firm round bottom. The top barely contained her firm breasts which jiggled when she walked. She stopped and grinned a white-toothed grin.

"Hi," she cooed, her voice a soft subtle stroke. "May I join you?"

7

"Please," Ricky replied, patting chaise lounge beside him.

He saw Jose start to rise out of his chair and waved him off. She folded her long legs under her and glided into the chair. She moved with the grace of a dancer and Ricky guessed she was probably a stripper from one of the local nightclubs.

"My name is Carla. What's yours?" she waved for another drink to the shorts clad waiter.

"Ricky. Do you live around here?" He smiled at her with his come on smile. The waiter approached and set her drink on the small table next to her.

"Please allow me," Ricky said to the waiter, pulling a wad of bills from his pocket and flipping through the hundreds for a five. He saw her looking at the bills in his hand and smiled inwardly. Yes, this would be the one. She sipped her drink through a straw and showed him her best lewd grin.

"I live in town. Down near the beach. How about you?"

Ricky waved his hand north down the Intracoastal Waterway. "Down that way." He thought, this day would turn out all right after all, as he admired her body.

"That's a very nice neighborhood," she replied, obviously impressed.

"Do you like boats?" Ricky asked.

"I love boats," she answered putting the emphasis on the word love. "Do you have one around here?"

"Come, I'll show you," he replied getting up and waving his hands toward the dock.

Jose rose and Ricky nodded at him imperceptibly. Carla followed him down to the dock and smiled when she saw the red and gray Scarab, Ricky's pride and joy. She accepted his hand and stepped down into the cockpit. Ricky followed her into the driver's area and fired up the engines which let out a roar and then a deep growl. Heads at the pool turned at the sound. Jose glided up and untied the lines. Ricky raised one eyebrow at him, their signal to meet at the house. Jose had seen this move dozens of times. It never failed. Jose admired Ricky's ease at picking up women. There was no jealousy. Jose was unquestionably devoted to his boss. He would give his life for Ricky, if necessary.

Ricky idled under the bridge and cleared the NO WAKE sign, then pushed the throttle down hard. The boat seemed to leap out of the water then settle. Ricky nestled down in the driver's seat which wrapped around him like a glove. Carla stepped over to him and stood next to his side. He slid his arm around her and cupped her buttock with his hand.

The house was a masterpiece of architecture. Every room had Italian marble floors. The rear of the house was glass from floor to ceiling, allowing an unobstructed view of the Intracoastal Waterway. Boats glided past, family boats with husband and wives and their kids, the kids lounging on the bow or standing at the wheel, their fathers right behind them, helping them steer for the first time. Boats with fishing poles sticking up from the sides, having just returned from chasing dolphin or marlin or whatever would bite in the ocean. Occasionally a go-fast boat like Ricky's would rumble past, pissing off the owners of the houses along the route. Many of the people along the waterway had sold out and moved, because of those boats, roaring past in the night, rousting them from the peaceful sleep of the rich.

Ricky lay on his back on the bed in the second floor bedroom which overlooked the pool and the boat dock, his head thrown back and his teeth clenched. Carla knelt between his legs, manipulating him with her mouth. His penis was rock hard and the feeling of her warm mouth sliding up and down was driving him crazy. He rolled her off and turned her on her back. Holding her legs in the crook of his arms, he entered her quickly. He began to thrust inside her, faster and faster. Her head was thrown back, her neck craning to go farther backward, and she matched his thrusts with her hips, pushing back against him. He grunted against her neck in unison with her moans. He felt the orgasm rising in him, starting in his toes and rolling up his legs and back in a rising wave. He released into her with an explosion as she climaxed with him, gripping his penis in spasms.

He lay on her heaving breasts for a while, catching his breath and letting his heart slow down, then raised himself up and moved off, stretching out next to her on the sweat soaked bed.

Ricky lit a cigarette from the pack on the night stand as she walked to the bathroom, shutting the door behind her. He heard the shower come on, as he blew smoke toward the ceiling fan and smiled. This one was good. He would have to keep her around awhile. He remembered his first one, as a teenager in Medellin. He was around fifteen. Her name was Conchita or something like that. They met while they both worked in the coca fields, cutting the plants for transport to the processing lab. For weeks they smiled secretly at each other, slowly progressing to holding hands and finally resulting in a sweat soaked, grunting, adolescent first try in the jungle beside the field. She was scared her momma would find out and refused to speak to him after that no matter how hard he had tried.

He had bragged to his friends as they sat in the bunkhouse at night, regaling them with stories of how much of a man he was, but never naming the girl so as not to ruin her reputation, or have her parents find out. Especially her father. He was a squat man with arms like wood, covered with scars from many knife fights with other coca cutters who tried to cheat him out of his few dollars pay in a card game. One eye was intersected with a scar that removed his eye but left a white line from his hairline to the corner of his mouth, leaving the eye blind but showing a little white sliver. Ricky and the other boys were deathly afraid of him. He could not readily remember her name but he remembered her body, bronze, smooth with firm small breasts. Nipples like dark fruit to be tasted.

A light tap on the door to the bedroom caused him to rise. He listened at the door for an instant and recognized Jose's whisper. He opened the door and Jose looked around him to make sure the woman was not in earshot.

"The police have found our friend's body," Jose whispered in English. Ricky nodded and replied,

"Bueno. Yo Entendo," (good, I understand) Jose nodded and slid away soundlessly. Ricky admired the way the man moved so silently for his huge bulk. As Ricky closed the door, he heard the shower stop. He wondered if she would be ready again and smiled.

CHAPTER 2

Danny sipped his coffee and reread the article again. Five small lines on page two of the local section. They couldn't print more since the investigation was so new. The reporter quoted an unnamed source in claiming the death was suicide. Danny hated the way they made up what they didn't know. Unnamed source. Right! It had to be the Public Information Officer, the stocky ex-reporter the new sheriff had brought with him after the election. The rank and file deputies disliked him almost as much as they disliked the new sheriff. Most of them had voted for him after they believed the campaign promises he made. After taking office, he had destroyed their hopes and dreams of being treated as he promised them by restructuring the department into what most of the cops considered a social services agency instead of a police department.

The new sheriff believed in the current, politically correct philosophy, the political buzzword of the nineties. The idea came into being when the traditional methods failed to lower the crime rate. Those who did the job knew the problem wasn't the methods of the police but that the system broke down at the court level. Too many appeals, too many legal loopholes and no one spending any time in jail. There was no deterrent. Most cops kept their sanity by believing the problems with the system wasn't their fault. Their job was to put bad guys in jail and do their part to the best of their ability. If the courts let them out, then that just meant they would be there for the cops to arrest again. But the new regime expected the employees to not arrest bad guys, but to get involved in the causes of crime, such as broken homes, juvenile delinquency and the other social ills the bosses, who had forgotten what it is like in the streets, claimed was the root of all evil in society. They expected the deputies to take under-privileged kids to pro football games and basketball games on their own time as volunteers, which the kids got into for free. Most cops didn't have the money or the time to take their own kids to professional sports games, between working shifts and off duty details to make extra money to support their families, much less take someone else's kid to a game. Danny was glad he didn't have school age children of his own.

Danny heard the shower start up and swallowed the last of his coffee. His wife was up and showering to start her day. He walked into the bedroom quietly and noticed the bathroom door was open. Glancing in, he could see her in the shower through the partially opened curtain.

He loved to watch when she didn't know he was. Even after all these years of marriage, she was still beautiful to him. No other woman even interested him. He leaned against the bathroom door and smiled. He watched her breasts sway as she bent down to soap her calves. He slipped off his robe and stepped into the shower when her back was turned. She turned, startled to see him standing naked behind her. She smiled up at him, her wet hair plastered to her forehead. As she moved to him, he slid his hand around her soapy waist. He pulled her to him and could feel himself becoming erect against her wet belly. She leaned away and looked down at him, smiled and gave him the smile that always aroused him.

"Well, good morning to you too", she grinned and he pulled her close again.

Trevor Daniels pushed open the double French doors and stepped out onto the patio surrounding the pool. He flopped open the newspaper as he lowered himself into the plastic chair, placing his cup on the patio table. Daniels liked to rise early, before the day became too hot, and sit outside with his first cup of coffee of the day. A large gray fishing boat drifted past in the canal, its engines idling deeply. The skipper stood on the flying bridge, dressed in a tee-shirt and shorts, a Navy baseball cap perched on the back of his head causing his white hair to protrude out from underneath. He waved when he saw Trevor on the porch. Trevor waved back and thought how nice it would be to be retired and go fishing every day.

The man was a retired Navy Admiral who lived farther up the canal. He loved to fish and spent his days piloting his boat off the beach, reliving his lost Navy days. In a few short years, if things worked out, Trevor would retire too, but at an age young enough to have fun. Not that he didn't have plenty of money already. As President of First City Bank, his salary was more than most people could spend in a year. It had helped buy this house for almost half a million dollars. The two-story house stood at the intersection of the New River Canal and a side canal which meandered through a very elite, expensive area of Ft. Lauderdale referred to as Sailor's Bay. Directly across the New River from the Daniels' house was an area known as The Riverfront.

Five years ago it had been a stretch of boat yards and vacant lots strewn with trash and debris, home to vagrants and winos. Then the city stepped in and refurbished the waterfront. Spending millions of dollars, they transformed it into a brick walkway that followed the seawall to trendy restaurants and waterfront shops. Now, it featured Oktoberfest and other events sponsored by the city. The Riverfront drew families to wander and enjoy the scenery. Behind the waterfront stood the Center For the Performing Arts and the rejuvenated downtown area with high-rise office buildings, the local newspaper building and even Trevor Daniels' own bank.

Daniels' mind wandered to the meeting of the night before. The Corporation he had formed with a group of investors and friends was doing well. But, Daniels didn't like having to deal with Madeira. Daniels thought of Madeira as a pig, but a necessary one. He had the connections they needed to keep things running smoothly. He thought of Gina. She had been good for business and good for Daniels. They met at a party sponsored by some charity his wife was involved in and hit it off immediately. Daniels didn't care about her drug past. When she told him she was interested in making big money, Daniels knew he had found his connection. Her part of the business was to make introductions. She brought him Madeira. Madeira had the things they needed to make the deal work, as long as they could keep him under control. Gina also filled Daniels' other needs too, one of the things at which she was most adept.

Danny spent the first fifteen minutes trying to find a parking space at the Public Safety building which housed the Sheriff's Department. It also housed the administrations of the County Fire and Rescue, Civil Defense, and other county agencies. Danny entered the building and followed the hallway into the atrium through which the public also entered. The atrium was five storys tall, like the building. In the center was a low wall with plaques in memory of the deputies killed in the line of duty. The floors and walls of the building were brown marble and on one side of the atrium was an escalator which moved continuously between the lobby and the second floor which housed the Criminal Investigations section. Like other Sheriff's Office sections, it was secured by a locked door guarded by a coded keypad. Since this was a county facility and not exclusively a Sheriff's Office facility, certain sensitive areas were protected by such keypads. Like the fifth floor offices of the Organized Crime Division.

The OCD housed the investigations division which handled narcotics and other sensitive investigations. The OCD was also guarded by a receptionist behind a glass enclosure, who buzzed visitors into another locked door, after inspecting their credentials. OCD was so secure that the recent capture of a juvenile from the neighborhood, in the act of stealing a computer from an OCD office, had the bosses completely stumped. The self proclaimed rap singer said he just walked in when no one was looking. It didn't surprise the real cops who never understood the wisdom of putting the building in the middle of a crime-ridden ghetto the cops referred to as the Danger Zone. They also didn't understand the reason OCD had been moved into the building from their former office, disguised as a real estate office. Bringing the undercover officers, whose very survival depended on their not being recognized as cops, into the public building where victims, witnesses, people paying fines and the like, were likely to see the undercover officers, made no sense. Did the bosses think drug dealers didn't get traffic tickets and couldn't possibly recognize a future business associate as the long-haired cop they had seen at the Sheriff's Headquarters while paying their fine?

Danny punched in his code to enter the CI section and smiled at the receptionist seated at the front table. The CI section was one large room, roughly half the size of a football field with glass windows along three sides. Offices for Lieutenants and above were along the windows giving them a view and some sunlight. The rest of the room, which the detectives called the "Rat Maze," contained prefabricated cubicles, eight by ten feet for lowly investigators and ten by twelve for sergeants. The only problem was the creators of the building apparently never thought investigators working the same case might want to talk to each other without having to yell over the cubicle walls. The detectives didn't mind not having window offices so much since sniper fire in this neighborhood was not uncommon and the detectives snickered that sniper fire was the best way to create openings and allow for upward mobility. So, being the creative geniuses they were, the first order of business upon moving into the Rat Maze had been to tear down the cubicle walls and redesign the areas for the different divisions. Robbery was along the west wall, Sex Crimes and Major Crimes along the back, Fugitive in the middle and Homicide had their own section in the corner. At least they could see each other and discuss the progress of investigations. It was still a Rat Maze but at least the families of rats had group cages.

Danny sat at his desk and checked his messages. Finding nothing important, he waited for his team to assemble. The Homicide division was broken up into two teams, each with five detectives and a sergeant. Each team took turns being on call for anything occurring after working hours. Danny's team was on call this month.

In an attempt to cut down on paying overtime, the policy stated if a detective was called out, his working hours started then and ended eight hours later, no matter what time it began. Two of Danny's team had been called out the night before at four a.m. and would work until noon, leaving him two bodies short. However, unlike his counterpart on the other Homicide team, Danny actively worked cases with his people. The other Sergeant let his people do the work while he reviewed reports and wrote memos. The other team preferred that system anyway since the detectives proclaimed their Sergeant had the God given-talent to screw up a wet dream.

Voices outside the Homicide cubicle signaled the arrival of the team which had been called out at 4 a.m. They entered the cubicle with the look of people who had been dragged, half awake, out of their beds to witness the violence human beings were capable of inflicting on other human beings. Detective Kay Matthew's dark hair was in disarray and she had a red-rimmed, bleary-eyed look. Dressed in faded, but tasteful jeans, a pullover and a green wind breaker with "DEPUTY SHERIFF" in gold letters on the back, she flopped into a chair and smiled wearily.

"Morning Sarge," she grumped, "I hope at least you slept well."

"You look terrible," Danny grinned, "Where's the Latin lover?" referring to Matthews' partner, Raphael Fernandez.

"He'll be in here in a second. Said he had to stop off in the little rafters room."

It was a standing joke among the team that Fernandez was Cuban born and in reality had probably been born on a raft between Cuba and Miami as his parents fled Castro. Fernandez kept the joke going by bringing in pieces of old wood occasionally and placing them by his desk, claiming he was going to find a girl to share the plank with.

"What happened to get you out of bed so early in the morning?" Danny asked. He had been called at 4 a.m. by the patrol Sergeant to advise they had a homicide and get authorization for homicide team to respond. Danny always wondered what would happen if he said no.

"Shooting at the Jamaican bar on the Boulevard. Ex-boyfriend shows up at the bar and runs into suspect, his ex-girlfriend. An argument ensued and the boyfriend left. Ex-girlfriend goes out to her car. The victim slash boyfriend is parked across the street and makes a U-turn to drive past suspect. She removes a two inch, five shot thirty eight from the vehicle's trunk and as victim passes in his car, she fires one shot. Bullet passes through the passenger window, which by the way is darkly tinted, misses the passenger and strikes the victim in the neck, passing through and severing the carotid and jugular. Victim stops and jumps from the car running around in circles. Two uniformed deputies just happen to be around the corner and hear the shot. They respond and find the victim bleeding to death. One deputy talks to the victim, unsuccessfully, until he croaks. Said he looked like a fountain with blood shooting out both sides of his neck. Died before Rescue got there. Suspect arrested at the scene. The weapon was recovered and after Miranda, the suspect gave a taped confession." Matthews closed her notebook.

"And we tried to hire her as a firearms instructor!" Fernandez grinned as he bounced into the room. His energy was boundless and no matter how tired he was, he seemed to always be in fast forward. Danny marveled at him every day. Sometimes, just being around him made Danny tired.

"Any problems with the arrest, search and seizure, anything?" Danny asked.

"Nope. Everything's clean and neat," Raphael replied dropping into a chair next to his partner with a thud.

Danny looked at Matthews and noticed the look she was giving her partner. He had recently wondered if they were more than just partners. Not that it mattered, it was not unusual for opposite sex partners to become involved personally in the tight knit, dependent on each other, world of cops and robbers.

"Okay. Finish up what you need to on this one and the rest of us will hold down the fort for the day." Danny leaned back in his chair as they rose to leave. Matthews rose wearily as Fernandez nearly leaped out of his chair. Matthews frowned at her partner.

"How do you put up with him all the time?" Danny asked her. She just shrugged.

"It's because of my many talents," Fernandez grinned, lewdly twirling the end of his thick black mustache with his finger.

"Move it or lose it," Matthews growled, pushing him out the door with her hand.

Mike Richards entered the team area with a coffee cup in one hand, and a stack of papers in the other. He dropped the papers on his desk and smiled at Danny. He hadn't tightened his tie yet and as usual, it hung loose around his collar.

"And how do we feel this morning?" he asked.

"I'm a little stiff and sore but not bad." Danny answered.

"I don't know how you can ride a hundred miles in one day. It would take me a month. And I would still have to quit."

"It's all in your mind," Danny replied.

"And a sick mind it must be." Richards chuckled.

Before Danny could form an answer, Detective Marshall Grimes and his partner, Leon Carter, entered the team area. Carter was the only black homicide detective on the department and maybe the largest human being. Carter, the ex-college football player, had tried out and made the Miami Dolphins but had to retire in his third year due to a knee injury and subsequent surgeries. He now concentrated on body building and had arms the size of mid-sized tree trunks. Bad guys didn't mess with Leon Carter. When he had worked in uniform, in the beginning of his career, his uniforms had to be tailor made since normal sizes wouldn't stretch across his chest or his arms.

The detectives gathered in front of Danny's desk. It was his responsibility to delegate the assignments in the investigation. He had a hard time believing the suicide theory, but the case had to be fully investigated whether it was suicide or homicide.

"How did it go with Conrad's wife?" Danny asked Richards and Grimes.

"About like you would expect," Richards shrugged. "She's been a cop's wife for a long time. She knows the game. She doesn't want to believe her husband ate his gun."

"I don't know if I believe it either," Danny replied. "But either way, we play it all the way. Mike and I will cover the autopsy. Marshall, you and Leon check with the Crime Lab. See if the pictures are ready and anything else they've come up with. Then start on Conrad's background. Mike and I will stop at the personnel office and pick up the file. Kay and Raphael are already on a case from overnight. Tomorrow they can join in the fun." Danny shifted in his chair and adjusted the big automatic on his hip when it caught the arm of his chair. He also had a small revolver in an ankle holster in his left boot, a habit he got into in the military. A lot of detectives carried ankle guns or left their guns in desk drawers but Danny always carried both guns where he could get to them in a hurry, if necessary.

"Make sure your reports are up to date daily on this one, guys. The political fallout may get uncomfortable and I need to be on top of everything in case anyone has a question." As if on cue, the phone on Danny's desk buzzed, the homicide division secretary's voice interrupting the conversation.

"The Lieutenant would like to see you, Sergeant Quinn." Danny rolled his eyes toward the ceiling and rose from his chair.

"Let the shit begin," Richards observed sarcastically as the meeting broke up and Danny headed out the door toward the Lieutenant's windowed office.

Danny paused outside the glass front of the Lieutenant's office and watched the Lieutenant, bent over his desk, writing. Danny liked the boss, Lieutenant Greene. He was young for a Lieutenant and something of a hero. Greene had been wounded years ago and still continued to pursue the suspect until he died in a hail of police bullets, but not before wounding four deputies including Greene. Before coming to the Detective Bureau, Greene had been a uniformed Patrol Lieutenant. When one of his deputies was killed by a suspect with a shotgun, who barricaded himself in his house, Greene had sprinted across open ground to drag the wounded deputy to cover only to find he was already dead. Danny had to respect a supervisor who cared enough to risk his life for his men.

Danny knocked on the door and entered at Greene's wave.

"Morning, Dan," Greene said as he waved Danny to a chair.

"Mornin' Lou," Danny nodded, using the abbreviation reserved for Lieutenants the men liked.

"Sorry to take up your time, Dan. What's new on the officer case. You know there will be shit over this one." Greene frowned.

"Haven't really had time to get very far into it yet. The wife insists it wasn't suicide. We'll know more when the autopsy is done."

"Make sure you keep close touch with me and keep me updated. I know for a fact the police chief has already called the sheriff," Greene said.

Danny figured that had happened. Since the current police chief was the one who took over the City Police Department when the sheriff, the former city police chief, was elected to his current position. In Florida, the sheriff was still considered the same as the old style southern sheriff. He was chief law enforcer of the entire county. He also had the authority to hire and fire anyone he pleased. When he took office, he immediately replaced many of the top people with his own cronies from the Police Department. Ranking officers like Greene had been lucky to survive the slaughter, especially since the new Major of the Detective Bureau was one of those cronies.

"Don't worry, boss. I won't leave you swinging in the breeze with the new higher beings." Greene chuckled and waved Danny out the door.

Mike Richards parked outside the Medical Examiner's office. He and Danny traded looks. Richards knew Danny hated the place. He had grown up in the southern tradition of sitting up with the dead. In the South, when a person died, a family member was with the body all the time until the burial. Danny had sat in the funeral home with his parents after their deaths.

They entered the building through the double glass doors and were greeted by the receptionist. She sat at her desk behind a low partition. The partition had a swinging gate which allowed access to the rest of the building. Beyond her desk were two large solid steel doors leading to a hallway. The hallway had offices for the pathologists on each side and ended at an airtight door leading to the autopsy rooms.

Danny smiled at the receptionist as they pushed through the swinging gate.

"Who's on today?" Mike Richards asked the receptionist in whom he had a more than passing interest. Richards was a consummate ladies' man which had caused his wife to walk out on him a year ago. He still had trouble dealing with her leaving and drank to ease the pain.

The receptionist smiled wearily. "Dr. Berkowitz will be entertaining you today." Berkowitz was one of the top forensic pathologists in the country and taught at the University of Miami Medical School.

"What a treat," Richards replied, winking at her.

They pushed their way through the airtight door to the autopsy room. Berkowitz was bent over a body on the table which Danny and Richards recognized as officer Conrad, deceased.

Berkowitz was over six feet seven inches tall and his neck was elongated, making him look like a giant stork, causing the homicide detectives from around the county who frequented the ME's office to nickname him Ichabod, after the fictional character. Berkowitz was bald on top with a reddish fringe of hair around his gleaming skull. He glanced up and, upon seeing the detectives in the doorway, bellowed toward the corpses scattered around the room on the steel tables.

"Look alive, everybody, we have visitors." Berkowitz giggled at his own joke. Homicide cops weren't the only ones with a morbid sense of humor.

"Good morning, Doc. What do you have so far to report this fine day?" Richards asked as they approached the table.

"Just got started." Berkowitz had removed the top of the dead man's skull and was examining the inside. As he worked he grunted and frowned, occasionally talking to a microphone hanging in front of his face.

"Projectile appears to have caused severe damage to the upper palate of the mouth and traveled upward through the sinus cavities penetrating the brain. Projectile passed through the brain and exited through the top of the skull and is not in evidence in the area of the wound." Berkowitz glanced at the detectives.

"He was found sitting in a car, is that correct?" Danny nodded. Berkowitz grunted and returned to his examination of the brain.

"Projectile is probably in the headliner of the vehicle." Berkowitz shifted his position over the table and pushed open the dead man's mouth. He leaned closer and peered into the mouth, probing with a steel instrument. He adjusted the overhead light so it shone into the mouth. He continued to poke and probe all the while muttering to himself. Finally he straightened up and looked at the detectives.

"Well, gents, this man did not commit suicide."

"Doc. You better be able to justify that decision. This one is political," Danny replied.

"Oh, there is no question. The wound proves it. You see, when a person shoots himself in the mouth, he puts his mouth around the gun like this," the pathologist formed an O with his mouth. "This occurs because the person expects the shot. A person who is shot in the mouth against his will unconsciously sticks out his tongue into the barrel, possibly believing he can stop the bullet from coming out. This man's tongue was stuck into the barrel of the gun. The end of his tongue is missing."

"Is that your professional decision? That it was murder?" Richards asked, glancing at his partner.

"Absolutely, no question. My report will show the cause of death as murder."

"Thanks, Doc." Danny smiled and turned to leave. Berkowitz pouted.

"Are you leaving so soon? It's really dead around here with no one to talk to." Berkowitz giggled. Richards rolled his eyes as they pushed through the airtight door.

Detective Leon Carter was always uncomfortable visiting the Forensics Unit. He spent his entire life worrying about his health. He ate every two hours. Small meals to fuel the huge muscles he lovingly spent so much time developing. He always felt unclean after entering the Forensics building.

The Forensics Unit was housed in a one story building which had been condemned by the Health Department years ago, but the Forensics Unit remained. The main Crime Lab was in the county courthouse across the street. Every member of the Forensics Unit suffered some type of health problem at ages younger than those types of problems would be expected to turn up. Two of the detectives suffered mild cases of skin cancer. Three suffered heart problems. Two of those three died suddenly in their mid forties of massive coronaries.

The place always had a slight unidentifiable chemical smell. Leon believed the chemicals and other substances permeating the building had caused the health problems. He feared catching something just entering the building.

Marshall Grimes and Leon Carter pushed open the door of one of the offices and were greeted by one of the Forensics detectives, a half-eaten sandwich protruding from his mouth. Leon cringed. The Forensics man waved them in and removed the sandwich, plunking it down on the desk among piles of paperwork.

"I guess ya want the file on Conrad," the Forensics man shuffled through the files on his desk. He withdrew the file from the stack and flipped it open.

"Let's see now. Weapon was a 2 inch Smith and Wesson, model 60, five shot .38 revolver, one shot fired. Entry wound was in the mouth, the rest you get from the ME. Weapon was test fired and found to be functional. The cylinder was loaded with thirty eight caliber hollow point ammo. Department issue. The spent cartridge was under the firing pin. Uh, okay fingerprints." He flipped to another page.

"We found numerous fingerprints in the vehicle and on the weapon. Mostly Conrad's. Mrs. Conrad provided comparison prints. Some of the prints in the car were hers. We found one print that we can't ID, we ran it through AFIS and got no match. It was a right forefinger."

AFIS was the automated computer into which every fingerprint of any person arrested in the county was entered. In the old days, it took hours for a fingerprint technician to visually compare prints against possible suspects. With AFIS, it took minutes for the computer to compare the fingerprints at a crime scene with every fingerprint on file in the computer.

He closed the file and handed it to Grimes. "Pictures are in the file."

Grimes and Carter rose to leave as the Forensics man took a bite of his sandwich. Carter shuddered and suddenly felt his stomach do a flip flop.

"Listen, ma'am," Danny said to the receptionist in exasperation. She liked the southern accent and looks of this tall, well built sheriff's detective in front of her but she wasn't about to do anything to jeopardize her job.

"We need Officer Conrad's personnel file for our investigation, and it is public record. You cannot withhold it from us." Danny was getting irritated, something he didn't do often.

They had been in the personnel office of the City Police Department for over an hour. The personnel receptionist had told them numerous times they would have to wait for her supervisor to return from lunch. It seemed it may never happen. Danny wondered if the supervisor was one of those who went to lunch and ran errands, coming back when it suited them. An older woman approached the counter. She had white hair, nicely coifed, and wore a business suit outfit, a bow tie around her collar. She reminded Danny of his first grade teacher.

"Can I help you gentlemen?" she asked as she approached. Danny held out his badge and ID card for her inspection.

"I'm Sergeant Quinn from the Sheriff's Office. We're investigating the death of Officer Conrad. We need a copy of his entire personnel file."

"Let me check on this," the supervisor turned on her heel before Danny could protest and walked to a desk. After a minute she returned from a whispered conversation on the telephone.

"Do you need all of the file?" she asked sweetly. Danny nodded. "That will take a while. It's a big file, Officer Conrad had been here for many years."

"Thank you, we'll wait," Danny replied. Danny turned and sat in a gray metal office chair against the wall. Richards sat next to him in an identical chair. His legs were stretched in front of him, head back against the wall as he dozed.

On the way back to the Crystal Palace, the nickname the cops gave the Public Safety building, Richards thumbed through Conrad's personnel file. The file was at least eight inches thick and filled with Officer Conrad's entire life with the police department. Commendations, reprimands and all personal data, family, test results when Conrad was originally hired, all the way to the date of his death. Richards read to Danny from the file.

"Ten years in patrol. Two years in traffic investigation as a traffic homicide investigator. Four years in the detective division, worked property crimes. Three years in OCD. Worked smugglers. Hmmm, that's interesting. Listen to this, after three years in OCD, he requests a transfer back to uniform patrol and the graveyard shift. Kind of a backward step in his career. Transfer denied."

"Not necessarily," Danny replied. "Lots of guys spend their entire career in uniform. They like the action and having no two days the same." Many people, spouses and family included, couldn't understand that. They believed uniform patrol was a place to start a career, not spend a career. Even other cops sometimes looked down on a guy who lived for patrol. They were considered by some to be unmotivated and perhaps a little lazy. But Danny understood. He liked uniform and if he hadn't gotten into homicide, he would have been one of those dinosaurs on patrol for an entire career.

"Been married for twenty years to his wife and has a son who is nineteen. Damn, that must be some kind of record for a cop, staying married all those years. Especially to the same woman." Richards marveled at it. Cops were notorious for multiple marriages. Too much temptation with women throwing themselves at cops all the time. They probably believed cops were fairly stable and brave and strong so they were attracted to them. And many cops were fair game for a good looking woman who would do anything for a stable relationship. Police work can put a strain on even a good marriage.

"OOPS, sorry," Richards said suddenly, realizing Danny and his wife had been married that many years and Danny had never strayed. Danny still loved his wife as much today as when they first met. Another police record.

Danny and Richards passed through the metal detector in the lobby of the courthouse by flashing their badges at the security guard. They took the elevator to the eighth floor and walked down the crowded corridor to room 854. The courtroom had light gray carpeting and light gray walls. The rear of the courtroom was filled with wooden benches on both sides. Along the right wall, behind a low wooden partition matching the wood of the spectator's benches, were rows of padded chairs on pedestals reserved for the taxpayers who served as jurors. The jury box was empty. The front of the courtroom was dominated by a high wooden desk where a bored, silver-haired judge leaned back in his swivel chair and gazed at the ceiling. A young, fresh-faced Public Defender was reciting some obscure case law from a thick brown statute book.

Danny and his partner had been diverted from their return to the Crystal Palace when Richards' pager beeped at them. Richards had called the number on the cellular phone and been told to report to the courthouse, *ASAP*, by the Prosecutor. The Prosecutor informed them a suppression hearing was scheduled to begin as soon as they could get there. However, as usual, immediately meant when the wheels of justice ground snail-like to their turn, which could take hours.

Two hours to be exact. Danny was finally called to the stand after Richards testified. During Richards' turn in the witness seat, Danny was forced to wait outside on a hard wooden bench, since the defendant's attorney had invoked "The Rule".

The Rule, as it was called, meant all the witnesses scheduled to testify had to wait outside and not talk to each other so as not to hear what each other said. In actuality, it was a way for the defense to make the witnesses look foolish in front of a jury by not telling the exact same story. The defense could then claim someone was lying and therefore the defendant was innocent. Most juries were laymen and unable to realize not everyone had the same perspective or angle of sight or were in the same place at the same time. It was then up to the Prosecutor to point out to the jury the basic facts in each witnesses' testimony regardless of different viewpoints.

The case involved the murder of a young woman by her ex-boyfriend. She had been shot in her doorway when she answered the bell. Her ex-boyfriend saw her earlier with her current beau and made good his threats to "kill her black ass" if he caught her with another man. He also promised to terminate any new suitor's misbehavior. There were numerous witnesses and luckily one of them knew the new boyfriend and where he lived. The detectives immediately headed to the new boyfriend's residence and encountered the shooter driving in the area. They stopped the ex-boyfriend and removed him from the car at gun point, over his protests that they were "fucking with me 'cause I's black." A search of the car turned up the gun after the boyfriend admitted to its hiding place.

"Sergeant Quinn, when you removed my client from the car, did you search him?" the defendant's attorney asked.

The attorney was not a county-paid Public Defender, but a high priced attorney known for defending drug dealers, which proved to Danny the rumor that the ex-boyfriend was a drug dealer in the neighborhood.

"Yessir, we did." Danny smiled at the scumbag lawyer.

"And what did you find?"

"Originally we found nothing."

"And did you search my client's car?"

"Yes Sir, and we found nothing either," Danny replied, anticipating the next question.

The lawyer frowned and examined his notepad. He didn't like being upstaged by a lowly cop.

Danny loved to fuck with lawyers.

The lawyer seemed to regain his train of thought. "What happened then, Sergeant?" The lawyer spat the Sergeant title.

"We then went back and removed the suspect from the police car and began to search him again. As we were searching him the defendant stated, and I quote, "tell me what you're lookin' for and maybe I can hep ya." I then stated we were looking for a gun. The suspect replied, quote, 'Oh I gots it.' I was so surprised I asked where and the suspect replied, again quote, 'Under the back seat.' We removed the back seat of the vehicle and found the gun wrapped in a towel." Danny recited quickly so as not to give the lawyer a chance to interrupt or object.

"And had my client been advised of his rights at that point?"

"No Sir, it was a spontaneous statement." The Prosecutor who remained silent at his table during the testimony, winked and smiled at Danny.

"Any more questions of this witness, Counselor?" the judge growled at the defense attorney, leaning over the bench to glare at him.

"No, your Honor," the attorney replied, walking around the defense table and sitting down.

"Thank you Deputy, you are dismissed." The Judge smiled down at Danny.

As Danny walked through the courtroom toward the door, the defense attorney was requesting the gun be thrown out as evidence since his client had been interrogated without benefit of his constitutional rights to remain silent and have an attorney present. As Danny left the room, he heard the Prosecutor begin his argument.

"Your Honor, this was a Res Gestae statement made by the defendant without interrogation." Danny closed the door, cutting off the remainder of the words.

Richards met him in the hallway.

"We have been summoned," Richards said, matching Danny's stride toward the elevators. Danny had turned off his pager while in the courtroom since this particular Judge didn't allow pagers in court and would find anyone in contempt of court who forgot to turn theirs off. The usual fine was fifty bucks which the lawyers could afford but cops couldn't.

"And who requires our presence now?" Danny asked sarcastically.

"Greene. Major Dick is in his office. Apparently pacing in anger."

Major Dick was Major Richard Stevens, who liked to introduce himself as Dick. He probably didn't realize his title and the name Dick created great glee among the troops. Stevens had been one of the cronies that left the City Police Department as a Lieutenant and arrived at the Sheriff's Office with the new rank of Major. The cops liked the promotion. They thought it appropriate since they considered him to be a "Major Dick."

This was turning out to really be one of those days, Danny thought as the elevator door closed.

CHAPTER 3

Moses Hammond didn't look like a cop. He looked more like a high school Social Studies teacher. At five foot six, one hundred thirty pounds and wearing glasses, Moses was rarely recognized for being a cop. Moses had been a legend in the department before transferring to OCD. Police legends are usually made while doing something heroic or loony or knocking the shit out of a guy you weren't expected to be able to knock the shit out of. Moses became a legend because of his size. Moses worked for many years in uniform and occasionally had problems being taken seriously by the bad guys he was trying to arrest. The day Moses became a legend had started out normally. He handled the usual calls involving intoxicated idiots who proved how much alcohol affects judgment, numerous false burglar alarms and the usual bullshit calls that irritated cops because it wasn't really their job but made the taxpayers feel like they were getting their moneys worth.

Moses was dispatched to a family disturbance. The report indicated a man had beaten his wife severely enough to cause their young son to call the police, which he had never done before because his parents argued all the time anyway. But this time, he called.

When he arrived at the house, he was confronted in the front yard by the husband, who was very drunk, and angry about the police butting into his affairs. The husband was six foot eight inches tall and almost three hundred pounds of solid muscle. Moses tried to talk to the husband who became more angry by the second. Moses tried his best soothing voice, then a more forceful tone, neither of which had any affect on the husband who, by now, had yanked off his shirt and thrown it down on the freshly mowed lawn, his voice rising and his eyes becoming more enraged. Then the husband made the fatal error of balling up his fists and threatening to kick Moses' ass.

Moses drew his department approved *Nunchuka* sticks, two short sticks attached in the middle by a string and made popular in Kung Fu movies. Moses softly told the husband to calm down and back off, to which the husband replied he was not taking orders from a "runt nigger playing cop." He then charged toward Moses with his fists raised. By the time the first back up unit arrived, the husband was sprawled on the grass handcuffed and suffering so many bruises and contusions he looked like he had been beaten with a weed whacker. He was whisked away to jail for assault on a police officer and Moses became a legend.

The story was told in the coffee shops and district stations all over the county. The unspoken question of Moses' ability to defend himself had been answered in grand fashion.

Moses fidgeted in the seat and wished he could turn on the air conditioner in the car. The heat blasted through the open window and he was soaked with sweat. He fought the urge to scratch his chest where the tape, holding the hidden microphone in place, burned his skin. Moses couldn't allow the unconscious habit of scratching the tape since he might do it when the target was around and be made as a cop. The target was thirty minutes late and Moses was unhappy. He had half a mind to grab his nunchukas from under the seat when the target showed up and replay the front yard dance with the angry husband.

Moses noticed the target's car pull into a parking space three cars down and he glanced at his partner Jean. The little Haitian cop sat frozen in the seat next to him, staring straight ahead. Neither the heat nor the sweat that glistened on Jean's face seemed to bother him. Moses nudged him and pointed with his chin toward the target, walking toward their car. He spoke quietly for the benefit of the backup team monitoring the body bug from a car across the highway.

"Target is approaching, wearing faded blue jeans, and a golf type shirt, blue in color, black male, six foot with a mustache. Named Andre Baptiste."

Baptiste was Haitian by birth and used mostly Haitian teenagers and adult males to run his drugs, which was the reason Jean was so important since he spoke Creole from birth and Moses spoke none at all. Baptiste also spoke Creole and generally conversed with his employees in that language when he didn't want the customer to know what he said. Things like "kill him."

Baptiste leaned in the open car window on Moses' side.

"Hey, Mon. Nice to see you made it."

"Yeah, nice of you to finally show up. You're fuckin' late muthafucka." Moses replied, trying to establish a dominance and show Baptiste not to fuck with him.

"Sorry, Mon. Couldn't be helped. Had some business problems to take care of." Baptiste spoke with the musical sounding accent of the Islands.

"Let's get this shit over man." Moses climbed out of the car and walked around to the trunk. He placed the key in the lock and hesitated. He turned and squinted at Baptiste.

"You do have the agreed amount?" Moses asked.

" T'ree keys as ordered." Baptiste answered, glancing toward his own car.

Moses turned the key and the trunk opened. Inside was a gym bag stuffed with money. Baptiste' eyes smiled in satisfaction. He reached down for the bag but Moses stopped him. Moses lifted the bag.

"When I see the product, you get the green." Moses smiled into Baptiste' face. Baptiste just shrugged and led the way to his car. Baptiste opened the trunk and stepped back. Moses leaned down and examined the contents of the brown shopping bag. Inside were three square packages wrapped in plastic wrap and then partially covered with duct tape. Moses punctured one open in a small square with his pocket knife withdrawing a small triangle of white powder. He dropped the powder into a small plastic tube, adding a pink color liquid. The mixture instantly turned a radiant blue. Moses looked up at Baptiste and smiled.

"That's good coke." he said for the tape recorder in the van.

"Of course, Mon. Only the best for my betta customahs," Baptiste replied.

Moses lifted the grocery bag from the car, leaving the gym bag in the trunk.

"I'll call ya, man." Moses turned and walked back to his car. He waited for Baptiste to start his car and leave the parking lot. Moses leaned down toward his chest and spoke to the microphone.

"Do we have a good strong signal?"

The headlights on the van flicked on and off, indicating the homing device in the gym bag was working properly. A blue Camaro, parked next to the van, backed out and entered traffic going the same direction as Baptiste. Over seventy five people in the restaurant ate their lunches and never even knew a large drug deal had just happened right in front of their cappuccino and croissants.

Trevor Daniels entered the outer office of the executive suite. The doors to the offices on this floor were ornate carved wood. A large oriental rug covered nearly the entire floor of the outer office. Around the perimeter of the oval-shaped outer office a desk stood guard in front of each door leading into the private offices of the corporate officers of the bank. These desks belonged to the private secretaries of each officer. Their job was to screen visitors, take private correspondence, handle phone calls to each individual officer and perform the other duties required by their bosses. No phone calls made it this far without going through a gauntlet of operators and lower executives. Unless you had the private number.

Rose Hinton, Daniels' secretary, watched him approach and shuddered. She hated the man. She had been his private secretary for a year and dreaded every day at work. But a single mother of two small children didn't have much choice. Her husband had run off with a co-worker and left her to make her own way alone, and to pay off the bills he had run up with extravagant expenditures and drinking habits. Trevor stopped at her desk and leaned over her shoulder.

"Any messages?" Trevor asked as he discreetly slid his hand around her waist and brushed the bottom of her left breast with his thumb.

"Just this one," Rose replied, handing him the pink message slip and gritting her teeth to keep from screaming. Daniels released his grip and turned to enter his office, closing the door behind him. Rose glanced up and caught the eye of another secretary seated across from her in the outer office. The other secretary looked away.

Daniels plopped himself down in the thick leather chair behind his desk and dialed the number on the slip. The phone was answered on the third ring.

"Hello." Gina Morelli answered, out of breath.

"Hello, baby," Daniels smiled at the phone. "I wasn't expecting to hear from you today."

"Hey Trev. I need to see you. Can you meet me for a drink later?" Morelli asked, drying her hair with a towel.

"Sure. What time?" Daniels asked.

"Say about six. Top of the Pier?" Morelli replied referring to the rotating restaurant and bar on top of the PierPoint Hotel.

"No problem. I'll see you then," Daniels answered.

"Okay, see ya' then." Gina hung up the phone.

Trevor Daniels smiled at the receiver. He would have to tell his wife he had a late business meeting. It wasn't unusual for Daniels to have meetings after hours. The meetings of the Sawgrass Development Group were usually conducted when the directors finished their office hours. But tonight, he would be meeting with his favorite director. And probably get a room at The Pier for a couple of hours.

Gina Morelli hung up the phone and bit her lip. This was going to be a tough night, telling Trevor she didn't want to see him anymore and she was quitting the Sawgrass Development Group would be difficult and possibly dangerous but she had to get out now, before it drove her nuts.

Moses Hammond punched in his entry code and entered the office. Being a detective with the Sheriff's Office Organized Crime Division gave him the opportunity to make full use of his non police appearance. His talent for the job had landed him an assignment to the DEA Narcotics Task Force. He was still getting his paychecks from the county but at least he didn't have to report to the Crystal Palace where every dirtbag in the world would recognize him. Moses completed the evidence forms and photographed the three kilos of cocaine he had purchased from Andre.

The markings on the packages showed clearly on the Polaroids. He copied the markings into the notebook he kept in his desk drawer. The markings were important since every drug operation used their own codes to identify the customers to whom the drug was destined and to keep track of the origin of the drug. Moses wrapped red stick-on evidence tape around each package, making sure he covered the holes he had cut. He placed the packages in an evidence locker, sealed it and headed to the Operations room.

The DEA Operations room was a veritable electronics fantasy world. It contained communications equipment to talk to the agents on the street. The room was covered on all four walls with electronic maps hooked into the computer system. The computer could track any homing device in the southeast United States on a large map of the DEA units area of operations. With a push of a button, the computer would zoom into the exact street and then the exact house where the tracking device was located. The computer saved a lot of surveillance in their cars. Rolling surveillance was difficult since cars could get lost in traffic or the bag containing the tracking device could be discarded without the agent's knowledge.

The operations room also contained a complete video studio to copy surveillance tapes and audio tapes, and could, at the move of a toggle switch, zoom in on any part of any surveillance tape making it easier to identify a defendant for the jury during court proceedings.

Moses stood behind the technician seated at one of the maps, tracking the device Moses and his team had placed in the gym bag given to Andre.

"What's going on with our friend?" Moses asked the technician. The technician pointed to the screen that displayed a residential street in Southern Fort Lauderdale. "He took it to this address and went to ground. Hasn't moved for hours." The technician sighed.

"Fuck me." Moses cursed. They had hoped Baptiste would take the money directly to whomever he got the drugs from. They knew Baptiste didn't have the funds to purchase the drugs outright and then resell them. Many times, the supplier would give drugs on consignment to regular customers. The drugs would then be sold, after the price was increased to allow the dealer to make a tidy profit, and then the cost of the drug would be paid to the supplier, who also made a tidy profit. Moses knew for a fact Baptiste bought all his drugs on consignment. Based on the volume of cocaine Baptiste sold on the street, they knew he had a good supplier, possibly the group that imported the drugs into the country. Probably Colombians. Moses had worked his way up to Baptiste's level after two years of buying larger and larger amounts of cocaine. He started the climb by buying cocaine, made into crack and sold on the streets. Baptiste reportedly, according to informants, bought his drugs in powder form from someone with an unending supply. He and his cookers then made the cocaine into Crack. Through distributors the drugs were given to runners who delivered it to team leaders. The team leaders then supplied the drugs to street level dealers, like teenagers, who were paid a salary to sell it on the street. Profits then reversed direction and climbed the ladder back to Baptiste. They were now at the point that Baptiste would hopefully lead them to his supplier. Unless he had discarded the gym bag and took the money elsewhere. There was a surveillance team watching his every move in case that happened. Now Moses would have to wait, something he hated to do.

Moses Hammond was the son of a preacher. His father, the Reverend Moses Hammond, Senior, led the congregation of the Blessed Mountain Baptist Church for twenty years until he died suddenly in his sleep from a massive heart attack. The Blessed Mountain was a Southern Baptist church of the type found in black neighborhoods all across the South. It was home to a choir of drums, guitars and tambourines and singers that sang with all their hearts and souls. The music could be heard across the neighborhood. Clapping, singing and twanging of guitars and the shaking of tambourines echoed for blocks. Until Moses' mother put her voice in full blossom. His mother was the lead singer of the choir and her singing combined the roots of soul music and the magic of one filled with the Holy Spirit. When Moses' mother sang Amazing Grace, it seemed as if the entire neighborhood stopped to listen. Even the drug dealers on the corners and the prostitutes ceased their actions to listen.

Moses loved to listen to his mother's voice. Even around the house she seemed to hum gospel songs constantly and calm the entire family with her melodies. Moses hated the way people used their childhood circumstances as an excuse for their actions. Growing up, Moses had no more than other children. They lived in a small house provided by the church and his mother had to work as a domestic to help keep the family going. The pay for a preacher in a small ghetto church didn't go very far. Moses had been what is now referred to as a "Latchkey Kid" letting himself in the house after school and taking care of his younger brother and sister. Moses' father spent most of his time at the church and was rarely home. Moses had not attended college but worked hard in high school and got very good grades and loved to read. He would immerse himself in the biographies of famous people and leaders of government, dreaming of being a famous war hero someday. He had actually hoped to go to Vietnam and fight for his country, but his graduation coincided with the end of the war and Moses missed it. He always felt a little guilty about not going and fighting for the many young black men in the neighborhood who didn't come home or came home without body parts, crippled or unable to reach back and return to reality. So he became a cop. He believed he was doing something for his people by keeping them safe from the animals that roamed the streets of his neighborhood. He was unsuccessful in the case of his younger brother who had become addicted to drugs and ended up being shot to death by a rival dealer who felt Moses' brother was on his corner.

Moses was single, but not by choice. He had once had a fiance who, after three years of dating and talk of marriage, suddenly decided the life of a cop's wife was not for her and fled from his life. Moses couldn't blame her. The life of a cop's wife was difficult at best and took a very strong, self assured woman, which Moses always wondered whether she was. So he didn't blame her but he sometimes wished she understood. Being a cop was not a job, it became a way of life. It changed your personality and your perspectives.

"Moses, your target is moving," announced the phone on his desk and Moses rushed to the Operations Room.

"He's moving South on I-95," The technician pointed at the map.

"Is the surveillance team still with him?" Moses prayed they were.

"OPS to team one." The technician said to his headset.

"Team One," replied the voice of the surveillance team leader.

"Do you have the target in sight?"

"Ten Four," replied the team leader. "Southbound on the I, passing the Hollywood Blvd. Exit."

"Ten Four," smiled the Technician.

Moses sighed with relief. Baptiste had kept the money in the gym bag and had not found the bug. Now they only had to wait until he arrived at the stash house, hopefully.

Baptiste took his time getting to his destination. He stopped for lunch. He visited a girlfriend apparently, spending two hours doing what they could only speculate about. Moses and the technician provided sound effects, while Baptiste was in the woman's house, getting so carried away that other members of the task force, who wandered past the Operations Room, stopped to join in the fun. At one point, fifteen narcs were laughing in hysterics as one of them moaned and groaned at the top of her lungs yelling "Oooh Oooh Baby, it's so small, try harder."

Baptiste finally stopped at a residence in a lower class neighborhood of single family homes displaying broken down cars and unkempt yards, the kind of neighborhood where the residents didn't question the odd comings and goings at the small white stucco house with the windows covered up with blankets.

"Team One to OPS," the team leader's voice came over the radio speakers.

"Team One, Go."

"Target has entered the residence with a blue gym bag. Verifying this is your package, Ten Four?"

The technician glanced up at Moses and he nodded.

"The package is verified," the Technician informed the team leader.

"Ten Four. Copy the address." The team leader slowly gave the address of the house as Moses wrote it down. Moses thanked the Good Lord of his father's fire-and -brimstone sermons. Sometimes, things worked out.

Twenty minutes later the surveillance team informed them Baptiste had left the residence without the gym bag. Now, the surveillance team would watch the residence to see what developed. The team would photograph everyone who came and left and write down tag numbers of every car. A nondescript white van moved unnoticed into position within sight of the residence. The van was equipped with video cameras, long range directional microphones, and the latest audio recording equipment. On the roof was an air vent. When the vent was raised, it looked like a normal air vent, but was actually a periscope which allowed the surveillance team member sitting in the van to watch the house. There was also a telephoto lens-equipped video camera capable of zooming in so close one could count the pimples on a suspect's face from two hundred yards away.

Armed with the address, Moses headed to the fourth floor computer room. The computer room was located in the intelligence division of the DEA headquarters. The computers were linked to real estate, telephone, cable television, public utilities, and the databases of all other public entities. In the computer room, the agents could cross check tax records, bank records and any other record linking the world together. The magic of computers made the drug war much easier and saved lots of man hours which, in the past, had been required to track drug networks and their players.

Moses crossed the computer room, headed toward his favorite wizard. Dana Barbieri was the wizard of wizards. She could literally make a computer do things its creators only dreamed about. And she was very pretty. She was not the egg head type and if you met her in a bar you would never know she had an IQ of over 200.

"Morning, Dana," Moses smiled at her as he pulled a swivel chair next to her console.

"Hey you. How goes the game?" Dana smiled a bright smile.

"Same game, different day," Moses replied, placing the address in front of her.

"You need the usual run?" Dana asked, scrutinizing the slip of paper.

"Please ma'am," Moses was always polite to a woman, something he learned from his father. He would never be accused of sexual harassment.

"Give me two hours and I'll let you know how many times the toilet gets flushed this month."

"Thank you ma'am," Moses said, rising to leave.

"You're welcome, kind sir." Dana winked at him as he turned and left.

Trevor Daniels was greeted by the Maitre' d as he stepped off the elevator.

"Good evening, Sir." The Maitre'de bowed slightly with a tip of his head. "Would you like a table?" Trevor spotted Gina seated by a window.

"No, thank you, I see my party." Trevor walked past him, crossing the thick carpet. The restaurant sported a subtle but classy decor.

Gina smiled at him as he approached. She was seated by a window overlooking the marina. In the distance was Port Everglades, beyond that, the Atlantic Ocean. The sun was setting in the window and gave Gina's dark curly hair a reddish glow. The setting sun reflected in the water of the marina, giving it a shiny orange tint, making it look like molten lava.

Trevor smiled at Gina after ordering a martini from a waiter.

"Well beautiful, haven't heard from you for a while." Trevor glanced down her blouse.

"I know. I've been avoiding everyone. I needed some time to think." She looked at her glass as she swirled the wine in it. "I need to get out, Trev. I can't do this anymore."

"Is there a problem?" He looked out the window at the marina.

"Listen. It's not anything specific. I just need to go away for awhile. I met someone a while back. He was a very kind man but wouldn't approve of what I was doing. So I broke up with him. I've thought a lot about this and I've decided I want to try to have a normal life. O.K.?" She glanced hopefully at him. Trevor smiled as if smiling at a frightened child.

"It's not a problem sweety. It's not like we own you or anything. You've done well and the business has done well with your help. So don't sweat it. Do what you have to do." He sipped his martini and looked her straight in the eye. "I mean that. Don't worry about it."

She let out a sigh of relief. She had been afraid there would be trouble over this. She was afraid of Ricky and hoped Trevor could control him.

"What about Ricky?"

"Ricky won't be any trouble." He hoped.

CHAPTER 4

Danny and Mike Richards entered the Criminal Investigations Division heading directly to the Lieutenant's office. As they approached they could see Lieutenant Greene and their Captain in a heated discussion with Major Dick.

Major Dick Stephens was tall and stocky. His hair had thinned on top to the point that he had three hairs left, which he kept long and combed over the bald spot on top of his head. He wore gold rimmed glasses and had a very thin salt-and-pepper mustache, reminding Danny of a molting caterpillar. He wore a checkered suit coat, polyester pants and thought he was the best dressed commander in the department.

Well, everyone needed a dream to hold onto, Danny thought. The conversation between the commanders ceased immediately as the detectives entered the office. Captain Barton sat upright in a chair in the corner. A tall, distinguished black man, he carried himself with an air of quiet confidence. Barton was very soft spoken, to the point his men lovingly called him "Mumbles."

He was a thirty year veteran of the Sheriff's Office and had survived five sheriffs but wasn't sure he would survive this one. The men loved working for Barton since he stood behind his men and believed as long as you did your job you should be left alone to do it. Barton was obviously angry and Danny didn't blame him. Most ranking officers, like Majors didn't get involved in the day-to-day operations of their personnel. That was the job of the Captains and Lieutenants. Majors were supposed to go to staff meetings and write memos and basically stay out of the way unless they were needed.

But not Major Dick. He was always violating the chain of command and taking action and getting involved in investigations and snooping around trying to find a detective taking too much time on his lunch break, or reading the morning paper at his desk before starting his day-to-day investigations. He had publicly made the comment county deputies weren't half the cops city officers were.

Major Dick glared at the two detectives as they entered and pointed to a chair in front of Green's desk.

"Sit down Gentlemen," he snarled at them.

Danny glanced at Green who slightly shrugged his shoulders in resignation.

"I'll get right to the point. I understand you have been spending a lot of this agency's time investigating an obvious suicide. Even to the point of requesting the personnel file of the victim." Obviously the buddy network was still alive and well in the city department.

Danny sat silently. Richards shifted uncomfortably in his seat. Danny waited for the next question. The silence lingered and with it rose Major Dick's anger.

"Well. What do you have to say?" Major Dick's voice rose in anger.

"We are conducting a standard investigation into a death, Major. I don't understand what the problem is." Danny glanced at Captain Barton who studied his shoes with great interest.

"This is a suicide, Sergeant. Do you make a habit of wasting time and man hours investigating obvious cases? Because if you do, maybe we need to find a different position within this agency for you and get someone who knows how to do your job the right way." Dick paced back and forth behind Green's desk.

Barton shifted in his chair and sat upright.

"Bullshit! Danny is one of the best homicide detectives in this state." Barton said so quietly they had to strain to hear him. Major Dick silenced him with a withering glare.

"Major, we don't know yet if it's actually a suicide or not. The wife says not and the ME agrees. The end of the victim's tongue was amputated by the bullet." Danny tried to control his temper.

"His tongue? You mean to tell me that because the end of his tongue is gone he didn't commit suicide? Is that the entire premise for prolonging this investigation?" Dick asked incredulously.

"Yes sir." Danny waited.

"And because the wife says her husband didn't kill himself you are going to spend your time following bullshit leads? Have you ever known a surviving spouse to believe her loved one was weak enough to eat his gun?" Dick's face was turning red.

Danny bristled at the suggestion Conrad, or any cop who took his own life, was weak. Suicide among the ranks of police officers wasn't uncommon and didn't mean they were weak. The stresses of seeing man's inhumanity to man day in and day out could get to anyone. Especially someone who joined the profession to ostensibly help their fellow man. After discovering the system didn't let them accomplish that end, the frustration could build up to the breaking point.

"We have already gotten pressure from the police chief, and the city insurance company and the mayor to close this investigation and the sheriff wants it completed. Do you understand?" Dick stood over Danny's chair and frowned down at him. Danny understood. The city didn't want to have to pay Conrad's wife the insurance money owed her if her husband's death could be proven not to be a result of his official duties. Suicide benefits were much less and the city wanted a break in the cost.

"Yessir." Danny sighed. Major Dick left the office and slammed the door so hard he almost cracked the glass of the enclosure. After his departure, a silence hung thick in the air. Finally, Barton stirred and rose from his chair. He walked toward the door and stopped behind Danny's chair.

"Well, that was fun," he said quietly. He put his hand on Danny's shoulder. "Do what you have to do."

Danny smiled up at him sadly. Danny was not about to close this case until he was sure Conrad had, in fact, killed himself. It would be unfair to a good cop and Barton knew it.

Danny propped the phone against his shoulder and waited for Dr. Berkowitz to answer the phone. He had been on hold for five minutes, listening to some inane muzak intended to soothe waiting callers. It didn't work. Danny hated muzak. He would have preferred country music.

"Daniel. So how are you?" Berkowitz had a habit of making every statement a question.

"Not good Irving. I need your help." Danny answered. He was trying to figure out a way to keep the case going. "The political shit is getting deeper."

"And why am I not surprised?" Berkowitz chuckled over the phone. "What can the Medical Examiner's Office to do assist it's favorite Irish son?"

"I need to prove this wasn't a suicide."

"What about the tip of the tongue? That proves it." Berkowitz sounded a bit miffed that his opinion was being questioned.

"Not good enough. They don't think it's conclusive enough."

"They, meaning Stephens?"

"You guessed it."

"That mensch. He couldn't find his gluteus maximus with both hands." Berkowitz liked to use medical terms in place of profanity whenever possible. Danny knew when Berkowitz was drunk, he swore like a sailor.

"Doc, do what you can to help. Re-examine the body. Maybe you'll find something we missed."

"Very well. I will put all my considerable faculties to work and show that moron what is what," Berkowitz replied.

"Thanks." Danny smiled as Berkowitz hung up. If there was something more to find, Berkowitz would find it.

Danny looked at his team, assembled in his office. Matthews and Fernandez looked more functional than they had after their late night call out. A day off to rest had worked wonders. Richards and Carter were present. Grimes had called earlier and asked for a few hours off but wouldn't give a reason, just stating it was personal.

"Alright folks. The brass and the city are pushing for a conclusion and they want it to be a suicide. I disagree and so does Dr. Berkowitz. He is convinced Conrad was murdered and I trust his opinion. So, we are going to do our usual thorough investigation until we prove otherwise. Kay, you and Rafael do the usual background. Bank accounts, debts, etcetera. Look for a motive for someone to kill or a good reason for Conrad to eat his own gun. I want to know about Conrad's work history. Mike and I will do some background. Talk to friends, other cops he worked with. Mike and I will talk to Mrs. Conrad again, and coordinate with Forensics. Questions?" Danny waited. No one had questions.

"What does Forensics have so far?" Danny looked at Carter.

"The gun was a .38. Ammo was Department issue. Nothing unusual there. They printed the car and the gun. Mrs. Conrad was kind enough to provide comparison prints. Most of the prints in the car were hers and her husbands. But, and this could be something, they found a print they can't identify."

"AFIS?" Danny asked.

"Nothing. Whoever it is, he or she has never been arrested in this county or even this state. They are going to run it through the FBI next."

"Okay, Mike and I will follow up on that." Danny looked around at their faces and could see they were anxious to start.

"Let's get to it," Danny dismissed them.

Danny Quinn and Mike Richards glanced at each other for the fiftieth time. Richards let out a sigh and glanced at his watch. They had been waiting almost thirty minutes. They were in the Organized Crime office of the City Police Department.

The OCD unit was housed in a warehouse district and was indistinguishable from the other buildings in the area. Most of the businesses in the area were auto repair shops or shipping warehouses. The building had been picked for this reason. It would not attract attention to have long-haired, dirt bag types coming and going at all times of the day and night since most of the other buildings had people coming and going all the time anyway. Not one of the other business owners suspected their neighbors carried guns and badges. And no one paid much attention to their neighbors anyway. Every other building in the area had at least one mangy, vicious-looking dog tied up in front to protect the employees and property.

Finally, the door to the small office opened and a tall, lean man entered. His blond hair hung to his shoulders. He had a wispy blond mustache, an earring, diamond stud - no less, perched in his right ear lobe. Behind him shuffled a short, dark, Italian looking man wearing a black tee shirt with a skull and crossbones emblazoned on the front. His beard was so thick and dark it almost hid his face, making him look like a demonic vision, of the type seen by mental patients and winos suffering from D.T.'s

The tall blond sat behind a desk and smiled at the detectives. The demon sat on a credenza behind him and constantly scanned the wall behind their heads. Danny wondered if the demon was the devil that the preacher in the church he had grown up in warned him about. The blond man held out his hand and shook each detective's hand in turn.

"Gents, I'm Sergeant Johanssen. Sorry to keep you waiting so long. We had a dealer we were talking to. This is Dominic Basso," he nodded at the demon seated behind him. The demon suddenly smiled and his teeth were so white they lit up his entire face like a sun lamp. Danny wished he had worn his sunglasses.

"No problem Sarge," Danny cleared his throat. "Apologize for disrupting your routine. We're investigating the death of Officer Conrad and we need some background. I understand he worked for you in OCD"

"Yeah. He worked for me for two years. Dom was his partner. But I don't know what we can do to help. I thought Conrad committed suicide?" Basso shuffled his feet and looked at the ceiling.

"We're not sure. Did Conrad ever do anything to make you suspect he was depressed or suicidal? Any marital problems, anything like that?" Danny glanced from one to the other.

"Nope. Conrad was a good cop. We were shocked when he disappeared and even more shocked when we heard that he was dead. Dom, did you notice anything?" Johannsen turned to Basso.

"Conrad was a good partner. He was quiet sometimes but nothing unusual. He seemed to be in love with his wife and talked about his family but never anything negative. I don't believe he killed himself either." He nervously glanced at Johannsen.

"Anything that made you think he was dirty? Did he have a girlfriend or mention any financial problems?" Danny focused on Basso's face and thought he saw something there. A faint glimmer.

"Conrad was clean. He didn't show any more than passing interest in other women. You know, he would admire a fine looking woman like any other guy, but no, nothing like having any strange on the side." Basso looked at his hands as he opened and closed his fists.

"I don't think we can help with anything guys. And I resent the implication one of my people was, or is, dirty." Johannsen said coldly.

"We didn't mean anything by that, Sarge. We don't think anyone in your unit is dirty but we have to ask all the questions," Danny smiled his best ass-kissing smile.

"Sorry, I didn't mean that the way it sounded but I hate the thought any cop is dirty. But you know how it is around here. When you work around dope dealers with lots of cash, the temptation is always there. Internal Affairs is always snooping around trying to find something amiss in OCD. They think all dope cops have to be dirty." Johannsen leaned back in his chair, obviously appeased.

"If you think of anything, call," Quinn and Richards rose to leave. They shook hands with the two narcs and picked their way through the warehouse office. When they were out of earshot, Danny leaned toward Richards, speaking out of the side of his mouth, "Did you notice?"

"Uh huh, I did," Richards answered quietly.

"Sit outside for a while?" Danny opened the outside door.

"Definitely," Richards grunted.

They didn't have to wait long. Basso exited the warehouse and shoved his sunglasses on his face against the bright sunlight. He walked toward a blue jeep Cherokee. Quinn and Richards met him at the driver's door.

"Anything you want to tell us, Dom?" Quinn asked quietly.

"Not here. Meet me at the gas station on the corner." He glanced around nervously. Quinn wondered if it was real or just a habit that many dope cops develop.

Basso's Jeep was parked behind the gas station when they arrived. The two homicide cops climbed in and shut the doors. The dark tinted windows protected the occupants from prying eyes.

Basso turned in his seat to face them. The sunglasses covered the rest of his face and made him look even more fierce. Danny wondered if his specialty was interrogating suspects. Looking at his foreboding face made Danny want to confess his indiscretions.

"I know this seems like secret squirrel shit guys. And I don't have anything earthshaking to tell you. But Johannsen can be a prick sometimes and I don't need him on my ass. Conrad was clean and the unit is clean, but we don't believe he killed himself. We have been told the company line is suicide. Probably so the city can save money on death benefits. Y'know how these pencil-pushing assholes in the finance office are, anything to save a buck. But, my gut tells me it was a hit. I don't know why anyone would hit Conrad, but I've seen enough hits to know that this one smells."

"We have no reason to dispute the suicide theory yet. And nobody seems to be able to give us reason Conrad would be a murder target. We're gonna keep digging though, so if you think of anything or come up with a motive, there's my pager number, call anytime." Danny handed him his card.

"If I find anything," Basso paused and glanced at the card. "Something about this whole thing sucks."

"Yeah, we know. It sucks every time a cop falls, for whatever reason." Danny opened his door and got out of the Jeep. Richards followed.

CHAPTER 5

Doctor Irving Berkowitz held a sandwich in one hand and with the other he poked and probed the body of Officer Augusts "Gus" Conrad. The body had been cleaned with formaldehyde and smelled slightly of the chemical, but the stench of deteriorating tissue still lingered. Berkowitz didn't notice either smell. He had grown so used to it he had trouble smelling anything.

For twenty years he had been a pathologist and still found his work fascinated him. He entered Medical School with intention of curing the sick and helping the infirm. But when he attended the required pathology class, he knew he had found his niche. Handling dead bodies didn't bother him. He could turn off his humanity and be objective. The trick was not to consider them humans. Not to think about the fact this was, at one time, a living, breathing, loving person with a family and friends. If you thought like that the job would drive you crazy.

Berkowitz had a special way to unwind when the job got to be too much. He loved fast cars and tinkered with them whenever he could. His garage contained a Corvette, two Porsches and a vintage 1957 Chevy that could turn 13 seconds in the quarter mile. When the job got to be too much, Berkowitz would drive, fast. Late at night, he would get out on the Interstate when there was no other traffic and go as fast as he could go. The Highway Patrol had once clocked him at over one hundred twenty miles an hour in his Corvette. They didn't catch up to him until he reached Palm Beach. After explaining who he was and what he was doing, they let him go with a stern warning. Cops understood the need to unwind. After three incidents with the troopers, Berkowitz began to limit his drives to the race track but sometimes the track wasn't open when he felt the need. The last time a tall, muscular trooper, with a buzz hair cut, told him in no uncertain terms that he would one day end up on his own slab. So Berkowitz behaved himself after that, most of the time anyway. He was going to go for a drive after this case was finished, he was beginning to feel the strain.

Berkowitz examined the x-ray of Conrad's skull again. There was a distinct track the bullet had taken from the mouth and through the brain. He placed a ruler over the X-ray and with a wax pencil, he traced the bullet's track from the top of the mouth to the top of the head. The line ran to the left of center. Usually, when a person shot himself in the mouth, the bullet tracked in a straight line upwards or toward the back of the head. But this track seemed to run from the right to the left. Berkowitz called over his investigator and pointed at the x-ray.

"What does that say to you?" Berkowitz stepped back to allow the investigator to get closer to the film.

After several minutes the investigator straightened and looked at Berkowitz with a frown.

"Kind of strange. Looks like the gun was held to the right, causing the bullet to track at an angle to the left."

"Yep, that was my thought exactly," Berkowitz reached for the file. He flipped to the crime scene photos and examined them. He beckoned to the investigator with one finger. He pointed to the photo he held in his hand.

"Which hand is the gun in?"

"Left hand. Shit!" The investigator frowned at the photograph.

"Exactly, my dear boy. There is no way this bullet was fired by a gun held in the left hand." Berkowitz turned to the corpses lying on tables around the room.

"Guess what everyone, we have a 'who done it' on our hands." Berkowitz turned back to Conrad's body. The investigator thought Berkowitz was one weird mother fucker.

Why, Berkowitz wondered, would one sit in a car and allow someone else to put a gun in one's mouth and pull the trigger? Well, of course they wouldn't, there had to be some way to restrain the victim. But apparently there had been no visible sign of a struggle in the car. So how was it done? Berkowitz loved a good mystery. He decided there had to be something he had missed the first time. Something on the hands or arms. He retrieved a magnifying glass from his desk and began to inspect the arms of the corpse. He started with the wrists since that would be the most logical way to keep the victim from grabbing the gun. Nothing. He carefully inspected the fingers and the fingernails, still nothing. Dammit! It had to be here somewhere. He began to work his way up the arms with the magnifying glass. The forearms were clean as were the elbows. I must have been wrong, he decided, and almost stopped

Suddenly, there it was. A slight discoloration on the bicep of the right arm just above the crease of the elbow. He examined it carefully and then checked the left bicep. In the exact same spot was a very faint discoloration. Berkowitz snatched up a scalpel from the instrument tray. On both arms he cut a square of tissue that intersected the discoloration. Each sample was four inches long and two inches wide.

Very noticeable, Berkowitz thought, I better make a note to remind the funeral director to cover those cuts for the family's sake. Berkowitz placed both hunks of skin into the tissue cleaning machine on the counter next to the microscope. In eight hours the tissue would be ready to place in the paraffin wax cubes for tissue shaving.

Berkowitz glanced at his watch, noticing it was past midnight, too late to call Quinn now. Besides, he thought, it was a week night and there would not be much traffic on the Interstate and his Corvette was waiting.

Berkowitz arrived early at the lab. The building was empty and he was still pissed off at the Highway Patrol. The trooper that stopped him last night had absolutely no sense of humor. He had glared at Berkowitz under the stiff black campaign hat as Berkowitz smilingly explained who he was and why he had almost burned up the radar when he flashed past. It took the patrol car almost four miles to get close enough for Berkowitz to notice the flashing blue lights in his rear view mirror. Besides, Berkowitz had stopped and waited for it to catch up, sitting in his Corvette by the side of the road as the trooper marched, red-faced, up to the driver's window, which was already down. Berkowitz didn't even mention the stumble he made as he approached. He didn't even laugh as the trooper picked himself up off the ground and examined the tear in the knee of his tan uniform pants. Berkowitz had produced his Medical Examiner's badge and offered to examine the knee for injury. Obviously, he didn't know Medical Examiners were medical doctors first and ME's second, as he jumped back when Berkowitz bent down to examine for a wound. What had the trooper called him - a fucking corpse cutter? Berkowitz decided the cop was fresh out of the academy in Tallahassee when he started to pull out his ticket book. Good thing the other trooper showed up when he did since Berkowitz had no intention of signing any ticket. He knew the other one and received a stern warning, which he didn't mind.

Berkowitz removed the skin samples he had dissected the night before from the tissue cleaner. Inserting a small hook, similar to a fish hook, into the ends of each hunk of skin, he hung it across the top of the tissue holder. The tissue holder was a square receptacle made of stainless steel. The sample hung in the center of the square. Berkowitz carefully poured melted paraffin wax into the holder so the tissue hunk was suspended in the paraffin. While he waited for the wax to harden, he poured himself a cup of thick black Cuban coffee.

When the wax had hardened, Berkowitz removed it from the tissue holder and inserted it into the tissue shaver. The tissue shaver had a blade as thin as a hair that spun so fast it was almost invisible. The shaver was controlled by a computer allowing it to be programmed to cut any thickness desired. Berkowitz programmed the shaver and waited as the machine hummed and cut a cross section. Berkowitz placed it on a microscope slide and inserted it in the microscope. The microscope's viewing screen enlarged the object twenty times. It was also equipped with a camera so the picture could be preserved for court presentation. Berkowitz squinted at the picture on the view screen and there, big as life, was the answer.

The tiny capillaries of the skin had been ruptured and bruised by pressure being exerted against them. Berkowitz punched a button and color pictures, eight by ten, slid out the end. Berkowitz gathered the pictures and checked to make sure they were clear.

Mike Richards had spent his evening knocking down an entire fifth of bourbon and now he was paying for it. When he arrived home the day before he discovered his wife had been by for a visit. When she left, so did most of the furniture. She had been kind enough to leave the television from the bedroom, a black and white set that was almost as old as Richards himself. She also left his recliner in which he spent the evening with his bottle. Richards knew he had been a fool. He had been blinded by the women who literally threw themselves at men. Richards used those women to fulfill a need within himself he couldn't explain or define. But now, he was realizing his mistake. He had finally discovered he loved his wife and didn't want to lose her. The note she left made it clear as far as she was concerned, it was too late. She had contacted a lawyer named Cohen that would be contacting Richards soon, he could rest assured.

His head pounded and the Alka Seltzer didn't help this time. He felt as if his tongue was swollen and covered with a fuzzy film he couldn't get rid of, even though he had scrubbed it with his toothbrush until it almost bled. Food was out of the question and even the smell of his coffee was causing his stomach, which was already jumping like a frog on a hot plate, to jolt and grumble. He answered the phone on the first ring since his head hurt too much to let it ring again.

"Homicide," Richards groaned as a sip of coffee tried to force its way back up.

"Good morning, Michael. How are you today?"

"Don't fuckin' ask." Richards leaned his head on his hand and wished the room would stay still.

"Rough night, I guess. Is Daniel around?" Berkowitz grinned at the phone and Richards' misery.

"Nope. Should be in anytime though, Any message?"

"Yes, as a matter of fact, I have good news for you boys. I have been able to determine, through my scientific and pathological skill, that our Officer Conrad was, in fact, murdered. And probably by two perpetrators." Berkowitz always used really big words when he was especially proud of himself.

"What?" Richards raised his head in surprise and was rewarded with a stab of pain.

"That's correct. When you boys get a chance, stop by the office and I'll show you what I've got." Berkowitz was a little more subdued, realizing the kind of shape Richards was in.

"I'll tell Danny as soon as he comes through the door."

"See ya later," Berkowitz hung up.

As Richards hung up he wondered if he could figure out a way to kill lawyer Cohen and not get caught by Berkowitz. Maybe Berkowitz would even help.

Danny entered the office and dropped his briefcase on his desk with a crash making Richards squeeze his eyes shut from the pain.

"You don't look so good," Danny examined his partner's face with a frown.

"I'll be fine after a while," Richards replied. He glanced up. "Berkowitz called. He's got something for us. Says Conrad was murdered by, and I quote, "Two perpetrators"."

"Irving's up early." Danny replied.

"Well, some people have no life," Richards groaned.

"Let's go see what's up," Danny chuckled.

Richards didn't speak on the ride to the ME's office. He sat in the passenger's seat with his head against the headrest, eyes squeezed shut behind his sunglasses. Every movement of the car made his head swim. When they entered Berkowitz's office, he picked a chair and slumped into it, propping his chin in his hand.

"Okay Irv, amaze me." Danny grinned at Berkowitz who beamed at the compliment.

Berkowitz handed Danny the tissue cross section photos.

"The first thing I noticed was the track of the bullet. It tracked from right to left, which would indicate the gun was in his right hand, if he shot himself. However, the crime scene photos show the gun was in his left hand, which, again, if he shot himself, would mean the bullet would logically track from left to right. Also, I checked. Conrad was right handed." Danny raised his eyebrows at that statement.

"Then," Berkowitz continued, "I decided that no one would sit quietly while a gun was placed in his mouth and fired. I checked his arms and wrists and found very faint marks across the upper arm, just above the elbow. Both arms. We missed them the first go round because we weren't looking for them. Those photos," Berkowitz pointed at the pictures in Danny's hand, "are cross sections of the marks. As you can see, the minute capillaries are ruptured. That is indicated by the tears in the cell walls. Therefore, I believe Conrad was seated in the driver's seat and one person was seated in the rear seat, behind Conrad. That person put a strap, approximately three inches wide, over his head and across his arms and chest, pinning him to the seat. The marks indicate the width of the straps. A second person, in the front passenger seat, then stuck Conrad's own gun in his mouth and fired. Ballistics matched the bullet to Conrad's gun." Berkowitz sat back with a satisfied look.

Danny smiled. "Irv, you are a godsend. This is a great job. I knew it all along. Now, the question is. Who and why."

"I think we can safely assume it was either someone Conrad knew or felt comfortable enough with to allow them into his car and go for a drive."

Danny rose and crossed the room to where Richards was dozing in his chair as Berkowitz watched.

"Bad night?" Berkowitz asked quietly.

"Bad marriage, good bottle." Danny answered as he shook his partner awake.

Danny's pager hummed on his hip on the ride to Conrad's house. Richards was dozing in the passenger seat. Danny reached around his knee and retrieved the cellular phone from the floorboard and dialed the number to his office. Kay Matthews answered on the first ring.

"Matthews."

"You rang?" Danny asked, swerving the car around a stalled milk truck in the street.

"Yeah, I found something interesting, Sarge. I ran Conrad's name through the bank computers and checked bank accounts all over the county. Nothing showed up under his name. Then when I cross referenced by social security number, I found an account under a different name but same social security number. Get this, there's over one hundred thousand dollars in that account."

"One hundred grand?" Danny whistled, "That's a lot of cash for a cop. Have there been any recent deposits or is it just his mad money he's been putting in over the years toward retirement?"

"There have been two deposits over the life of the account. Each for fifty thousand dollars. I checked the dates against his personnel file and the first deposit was one month before he asked for a transfer out of OCD and the second was two weeks later. The other thing is, why would he put the money under another name if it was for his retirement?"

"Unless he was dirty and the money was a payoff," Danny replied, deep in thought.

"Yeah, unless.." Matthews considered it.

"Okay. Thanks." Danny hung up the phone.

He wondered why everybody, even Conrad's partner insisted he was clean unless Basso was taking money too. And why didn't Conrad hide the money better. Using his social security number wasn't smart, unless he figured no one would think to reference social security numbers.

Danny knocked on the front door of Conrad's house and heard a rustling from inside, a faint voice telling him to wait a minute. The door was opened by a woman in her mid fifties, with silver blond hair pulled back into a bun. She wore faded blue jeans that looked as if they had seen better days. Her tee shirt was tight across her chest and was damp with sweat.

"Yes, can I help you?" The woman asked with a wary look. Danny showed her his sheriff's star.

"I'm Sergeant Quinn. Is Mrs. Conrad home?" Danny wondered who this woman was since he knew it wasn't Mrs. Conrad. They had met once at a police Christmas party.

"I'm her sister. What can I do for you?" The woman asked, inspecting his badge.

"I'm sorry to disturb you. I'm investigating Gus's death and have some questions, if it would be possible."

"Come in, Sergeant," the sister waved him inside.

She led him through the dining room to a brightly lit sun porch in the back of the house. The porch was separated from the rest of the house by sliding glass doors which stood open. The porch was enclosed by jalousie windows and had indoor outdoor carpet, faded by the Florida sun. Mrs. Conrad sat in a large, old brown armchair in the corner. She was reading a paperback, her glasses perched on the end of her nose. Danny thought she had aged thirty years since he last saw her. She looked up and smiled sadly when he approached.

"Dan, how are you?"

"I'm fine. But how are you doing?" Danny sat in a stiff backed chair beside her. He could see she was trying to be strong.

"I have good days and bad days." She glanced down at her hands, clenched in her lap. She forced them open and tried to relax her fingers.

"I know this is a bad time for you but there are some things I need to ask." Danny saw a flicker of anguish in her eyes. She nodded slowly.

"The police department and the city say Gus killed himself. They have tried to get me to accept an offer of half of his death benefits. The city lawyer says they're being generous at that. He says they don't have to give me anything in the case of suicide." She glanced away quickly and frowned.

"Dan, did Gus kill himself?"

"No. He did not. The Medical Examiner found proof Gus was murdered." Danny saw a cloud of fear cross her face.

"You're not in any danger we don't believe. But, now I have to figure out why anyone would kill Gus. Do you have any ideas?"

She shook her head. Her sister stood beside her and put an arm around her shoulders.

"Mrs. Conrad." Danny began carefully, this was going to be tough to ask, "We found a bank account under a fictitious name under Gus's social security number. Did you know about that?" The look of shock on her face gave him his answer.

"Sergeant Quinn. How dare you insinuate what I think you are insinuating?" Her sister snapped at him. "My brother-in-law was a good cop. I can't believe you people. Don't you ever give up trying to smear a good man?"

"I'm very sorry, but I have to ask all the questions in order to figure out what happened. I don't believe Gus was crooked and everyone we have talked to agrees. But the account does exist and it causes some concerns in the investigation." Danny turned back to Mrs. Conrad. "What about your son? Would he have anything to add or know some of your husband's friends?"

The tears suddenly welled up in her eyes and overflowed.

"My nephew is in the state prison, Sergeant," her sister answered for her.

"Why?" Danny was taken aback.

"Possession of narcotics," Mrs. Conrad answered, regaining her composure. Danny glanced from the sister and back to Mrs. Conrad, his look asking the question.

"Dan, I'm sure it comes as no surprise to you that cop's kids have it rough sometime. Shunned by other kids 'cause their dad is a cop. Police Officers tend to be authoritarian at home and kids rebel. Gus Junior rebelled in a big way. He started hanging around with the wrong crowd. The harder Gus tried to make him shape up, the worse it got. My son started using drugs in high school. Counseling didn't help. Eventually, he moved out and it broke his father's heart. Two years ago, my son was arrested for possession of three kilos of cocaine."

Danny didn't know what to say. He knew it was true the children of some cops had it tough. Sometimes cops couldn't leave the job at work and became demanding at home. Psychologists called it the "police personality". It was hard to get away from the need to be in control of situations off the job. Something as simple as not being able to sit in a restaurant without facing the door to watch for danger, to becoming a tyrant at home. It was the reason police families had some of the highest divorce rates of any profession.

Danny rose and took her hand. He smiled at her sister.

"If you need anything, please do not hesitate to call me."

"Thank you Dan, I will." She smiled softly.

Trevor Daniels sipped his drink, and surveying the scene before him. He smiled at the antics of his best friend, Rich Martelli, the owner of Martelli Realty and Vice President of the Sawgrass Development Corporation. Martelli was fondling a large-breasted redhead and trying to pull her top off. Unfortunately, Martelli was too drunk to be successful. He fell off the couch during the attempt. The redhead helped Martelli to his feet and led him, staggering toward one of the bedrooms.

Daniels walked out the back door onto the porch. Jeff Grayson was seated on the porch, cleaning a scoped rifle. He looked up at Daniels and grinned. Grayson's forearms bulged as he wiped the barrel of the rifle with a silicone rag. Grayson was blond and sunburned from years in the sun, working on roofs of houses and buildings he erected. Grayson was the building contractor for Sawgrass Development. His job was to see the projects were completed on time. He was stocky and muscular from a life of wielding a hammer.

"I see you had a good hunt," Daniels remarked to Grayson, nodding at the dead wild boar hanging on a rack in the back yard.

"Yeah, that son of a bitch. We were sitting in a hammock all morning and didn't see nothin'. Then we decided to go back to the halftrack and eat. That fucker walked right out in front of us while we were eating. One shot and he hauled ass into the grass. Took up almost an hour to find where he went down." Grayson grinned.

"Well, I guess we better fire up the grill for dinner," Daniels replied.

Daniels glanced up at the sound of a car engine. A black BMW with tinted windows drove into the yard. Ricky Madeira eased out of the passenger door as soon as the car stopped. He was dressed in jeans and his hair was pulled back into a ponytail.

"Hello, Trevor." Ricky greeted Daniels as he stepped up onto the porch.

"Hey Ricky. Glad you finally made it. C'mon in." Daniels led the way into the house.

Jose followed Ricky up to the house. He stopped, glancing warily at the boar hanging in the yard and at the rifle in Grayson's hand. Grayson smiled at him and laid the rifle on the floor beside him. Jose made Grayson nervous. The son of a bitch never smiled and always seemed about to attack. Grayson believed Jose would happily kill all of them if Madeira snapped his fingers, but Grayson also believed Madeira would kill them himself if he had any reason whatsoever. Grayson rose and led the way into the house ahead of Jose. He hated having Jose behind him but knew from experience Jose would stand outside all day before he would let anyone walk behind him.

Jose glanced around him before he entered the house. He hated this place. It reminded him too much of the prison camp back in Colombia before Madeira got him out.

The house was a wood frame structure standing on forty-two hundred acres of Everglades, fifteen miles west of the city. The property was owned by the Sawgrass Development corporation. The area around the house and yard was fenced. A hand painted sign on the gate proclaimed it *Sawgrass Camp*. The yard around the house was mowed short but the rest of the property was natural Everglades with sawgrass and dry woods. The owners used it as a hideaway on weekends to hunt and cavort with the host of women impressed with their playboy lifestyles. The wives had never been allowed here.

Trevor handed Madeira a drink and settled down in a chair in front of the fireplace.

"What's new with the next load, Ricky?" Daniels asked.

Madeira glanced toward the bedroom where they could hear the redhead and Martelli laughing. Madeira didn't like talking about business with the sluts around. Ricky considered these men to be fools. They knew nothing about discretion and tended to talk too much. Ricky knew that was dangerous and could get them all put away for a long time. Daniels chuckled at Madeira's discomfort.

"Relax, Ricky. They can't hear us. Besides they are having too much fun to notice."

Madeira shrugged.

"The load will be here on schedule. We have everything set."

"Good." Daniels sipped his drink. "Then relax and have fun. Steve will be here in an hour or so. He says he has some fine ladies coming this weekend."

Ricky set his glass down and headed for the door.

"I can't stay. I have some friends coming to the house tonight." He jerked his head toward the door and Jose followed.

"That mother fucker worries me." Grayson muttered after they left.

"Yeah, but he's necessary." Daniels agreed with a frown.

CHAPTER 6

The surveillance team leader sat bolt upright as the garage door slid up. He tapped the agent in the driver's seat and pointed toward the Cadillac easing out of the garage. The agent started the engine of the van as the Cadillac coasted down the driveway. The team leader grabbed the radio microphone.

"Team One to Team Two." He keyed the mic.

"Team Two, we see him," replied the second surveillance team agent.

The surveillance van fell in a half block behind the Cadillac. The Camaro followed at a discreet distance. The Cadillac reached the main road and turned right into traffic. The agent driving the van tried to sneak into traffic behind the Cadillac but didn't see the pickup truck bearing down on them. The impact slammed the van sideways across the intersection, causing the agent driving to hit his head on the driver's window. The glass of the window exploded, showering them.

The agent in the swivel seat in the back of the van was propelled across the rear compartment, bouncing off of the surveillance camera post, shattering his shoulder and opening a gash in his forehead which spurted blood across the electronics equipment. The driver of the pickup was thrown to the floor under the dashboard, knocked unconscious. The pickup and the van melded together and came to rest against a concrete telephone pole. Both vehicles blocked the entire intersection, blocking in the Camaro. The agents in the Camaro leaped out and sprinted to the van, the lead agent already radioing for an ambulance.

Moses Hammond gave the computer technician a big grin as she handed him a stack of computer printouts.

"House is owned by Sawgrass Development Corporation. The President of Sawgrass Development Corp is Trevor Daniels, Vice President of First Bank of Ft. Lauderdale. Sawgrass Development is a corporation that owns lots of rental property in the area and also builds numerous shopping centers, malls, office buildings, etcetera."

Moses glanced over the printouts.

"Thank you ma'am. This is a big help." He bowed slightly. The technician bowed back and they both laughed.

Moses walked down the hall toward his office. As he passed the communications room, the operator hailed him from inside.

"Bad news Mo'," the operator sighed. "The surveillance team lost the mule leaving the stash house. They had a wreck."

"Damn! Anybody hurt?"

"Two agents in the hospital and the driver of the pickup that hit them. Don't know yet about the pickup's driver, but the agents are pretty badly banged up. The camera operator is headed for surgery with fractured skull and shattered shoulder. The other agents should be okay."

"Good. At least nobody got killed. Whose fault?" Moses asked.

"Looks like our guys. Seems like they pulled out in front of the pickup."

Moses nodded and headed for his office. He had a status meeting with the Special Agent in Charge in twenty minutes.

DEA Special Agent Arturo Diaz was Puerto Rican, born in San Juan. At age ten his parents moved him to New York to escape the mean streets of San Juan, only to find New York wasn't much better. His father drove a truck in the garment district and his mother found work as a seamstress.

Arturo had a strict upbringing and had not been allowed to hang out on the streets like a lot of his friends. His parents had instilled in him a strong work ethic. He had been a straight A student all through school and was a good college prospect. Unfortunately, his parents had not been financially able to afford college and not many scholarships were handed out to the kids at P.S. 151. So Arturo joined Uncle Sam's Army. He excelled in the military and was assigned to the Military Police section for three years. Following the M.P.'s, he entered the Criminal Investigations division and found he liked being an investigator. He attended military college and, after leaving the Army, he joined the DEA. His first assignment had been an eradication team in Colombia, burning down Coca fields and trying to stop cocaine at its source. His next assignment had been home to Puerto Rico where he had infiltrated a Colombian drug ring smuggling cocaine through Puerto Rico and into Miami. His work in Puerto Rico had been noticed by the DEA Management and his promotion to Special Agent In

Charge of the Ft. Lauderdale office had been a dream come true. Diaz was not only a supervisor, but had done his time as a street agent and undercover agent. This gave him the ability to understand what his agents had to do and the risks involved. His knowledge of undercover work was evidenced by the scar that started at his left ear and tracked diagonally down the front of his neck past his collar. A street thug in San Juan had found him out and tried to cut his throat. Arturo had ended the thug's misdeeds with four bullets as he held his throat together with his other hand. Diaz was well respected by his agents. He had no problems accepting local officers assigned to the Federal Task Force and considered Moses one of the best he had. Diaz reviewed the reports Moses had placed in front of him. He looked up finally and studied Moses.

"Well Moses, where do we go from here? The surveillance team lost the mule. We don't know for a fact he was taking the buy money to his boss but we can probably assume he was."

"I think this guy is more than a mule. He's probably a cell boss. Surveillance photos show him at the stash house most of the time. Others that came and went were probably transporters." Moses shuffled through the photos in the file.

Both of them knew how the drug trade worked. Drugs were smuggled into the country by the most surreptitious route. The smugglers had tried many methods. Sometimes, they recruited people to transport drugs hidden on their persons or inside their stomachs. The transporter, or "mule", as they were called, would swallow condoms filled with cocaine and then fly to the United States on commercial flights. Unfortunately for the smugglers, sometimes the condoms broke and the "mule" died of an overdose. This method was usually not financially feasible since the amount of drugs the "mules" were able to carry was fairly small. Smugglers had even tried sewing condoms of cocaine under the skin of a dog on a commercial flight. An alert Customs Inspector had noticed lumps in the dog's abdomen and x-rays revealed the cause. This action caused an uproar with the media and animal rights activists, more uproar than the death of a human "mule" the week before. At least the dog survived. In order to be financially beneficial, the amount of drugs had to exceed the risk involved.

Once the drugs arrived in the country, they were placed in a house or warehouse for distribution. The drugs were then packaged in smaller amounts and distributed to different stash locations. This distribution was usually handled by a "Cell Boss". The Cell Boss was usually in charge of three or four stash houses. Large organizations had three or four cell bosses, each responsible for numerous stash houses. Distributors purchased the drugs in kilo amounts and distributed the drugs in smaller amounts to their equivalent of a cell boss who distributed it to the street dealers. The money was delivered by the cell boss back up the chain to the head of the organization after being laundered through legitimate means.

Andre Baptiste was a distributor. Moses had worked his way up the chain to Baptiste.

"Which way do you think we should go?" Diaz asked Moses.

"We can go two ways. We can see if Baptiste will take me to the cell boss and I could buy from him directly or we can try to turn Baptiste. If I can get as far as the cell boss and make some buys, we could try to turn him.

"What about this Sawgrass Development Corporation? Do you think they are legitimate and don't know their property is being used as a stash or are they involved?" Diaz glanced at the reports on his desk.

"I don't know yet. They just popped into the picture," Moses replied. Diaz glanced at the Intelligence Division agent seated next to Moses. He shrugged.

"Do you think Baptiste trusts you enough to take you higher and do you think he can be turned?" Diaz folded his hands in front of him.

"I think he will take me higher. And we may be able to turn him if we got after him through Immigration. I know he is illegal and doesn't want to go back".

Diaz nodded in agreement.

"Okay. Moses, I want you to stay under. If we take Baptiste down and until we take him down, I want you to stay in your role. We'll spring you on Baptiste during debriefing if we need to."

"Greg," Diaz addressed the Intelligence Agent, "follow up on this Sawgrass Development. Follow the paper trail. Deposits, money transactions, bank accounts. Check into their finances and the First Bank angle. See what pops out."

The agents rose to leave.

"Moses." Diaz said with a look of concern, "No chances. Back up always, from here on in. I don't want you getting careless. These are bad ass mothers. Don't get hurt, understand?"

Moses nodded.

Moses paged Baptiste and punched in the phone number of his cellular phone. He gave out that number since he was the only one who had access to it and no one would accidentally give away his identity. The agency had phone lines that were answered with a "hello" instead of "DEA" to protect the undercover's identities but more than once the operator had forgotten which line she was on, from force of habit. Those dealers were never heard from again. He also used his cell phone in case Baptiste had

Caller ID. Dealers had ways to trace phone numbers. A cellular number told them nothing.

Moses answered the phone on the first ring.

"H'lo."

"Hey, mon. You called me from this numbah?" Moses recognized Baptiste's Caribbean accent.

"Andre. Moses. I need some more blow, man. We cooked up all the rest and I need more." Moses prayed Baptiste wouldn't get suspicious.

"You used it all already? You got some hungry customers up there mon."

Moses had used the cover story that he was buying the drugs in South Florida and transporting them to Jacksonville and Tallahassee.

"I don't know, you seem to be using lots of product." Moses heard the suspicion creep into Baptiste's voice. He was ready.

"Andre, haven't I been a good customer? My people have been doing lots of business. We are ready to expand to Daytona and St. Augustine." Moses crossed his fingers.

"How much do you think you need?" Baptiste seemed to be going for it.

"Fifteen keys." Moses knew Baptiste could not handle fifteen kilos and would have to take him to his supplier, hopefully the cell boss.

"Fifteen?" Baptiste was incredulous. "That's a lot of weight. I don't know. You know I don't handle that much at one time."

"Well, maybe you could help me out somehow." Moses waited.

"Let me make a few calls and get back to you tomorrow." Moses breathed a sigh of relief.

"Don't take too long, Bro. I can't wait too long or I'll have to take my business somewhere else. An' I like working with you."

"Tomorrow, promise." Baptiste hung up.

Special Agent Greg Bolton smiled at Rose Hinton. He had a charming smile, she thought. Bolton held his identification our for her inspection.

"Special Agent Bolton, DEA We would like to see the bank president please."

"May I ask what the reference is?" Rose Hinton inspected the badge and identification card. Nice picture but it didn't do him justice.

"I'm sorry ma'am, it's confidential." Bolton smiled.

"Well, the president isn't in. The head of the Board of Directors is here. He oversees the entire operation. Will that be okay?" Rose was dying to know what this turn of events was about. Maybe that pig Trevor was finally going to get his.

"That would be fine, ma'am." Bolton smiled at her with that dazzling smile. She thought she would melt.

"Have a seat and I'll tell him you're here," she grinned, pointing to two leather chairs in the outer office.

They didn't have to wait long. She returned in less than five minutes. Bolton was used to waiting much longer. Normally, when someone heard the DEA wanted to see them, they called their lawyers first. They were escorted into the spacious plush office of Trevor Daniels Sr. which overlooked the New River. Trevor Daniels Sr. was seated behind a large mahogany desk. Behind him the skyline of Ft. Lauderdale loomed in the window. He rose as they approached the desk and extended his hand.

"Welcome gentlemen. What can I do for you?" Daniels liked to get right to business.

"Mr. Daniels, we're investigating some property owned by Sawgrass Development Corporation, which I believe is connected to this bank." Bolton said as they took seats in front of Daniel's desk.

"My son is president of the bank and also on the board of Sawgrass Development. Is there some problem?" Daniels' eyes narrowed.

"No Sir, not really. The property came up during an investigation of a drug smuggler we arrested six months ago. We were going to seize his assets according to the RICO act and wanted to clarify ownership of the property before it was seized." Bolton lied, carefully watching for a reaction from Daniels.

"Well, I can certainly see how careful you must be, what with the newspapers questioning the government's use of RICO," Daniels smiled warmly. "I can assure you gentlemen if the property is listed as owned by Sawgrass, then the property is solely owned by the company. What I know of my son's policies, as to property ownership with the company, they own the property outright. Whomever this person is, he does not have any claim to the property other than as a renter."

"Well, we thank you for your time. That certainly clears up any questions in regards to seizure or forfeiture of that particular property." Bolton and his partner rose and shook Daniels' hand.

"Feel free to call on us anytime, fellows," Daniels smiled as they left.

On the way through the outer lobby, Bolton gave Rose Hinton his warmest smile.

When Bolton returned to the office, he headed straight to Moses' cubicle. Moses was reading the surveillance notes on the stash house. He looked up as Bolton entered and nodded to a chair.

"What's the deal?" Moses asked, dropping the notes on his desk.

"The president of the bank is one Trevor Daniels, Jr. He is also on the board of directors of Sawgrass Development. He wasn't available. We interviewed his father who is chairman of the board at the bank, also named Trevor Daniels. Senior. He claims any property owned by Sawgrass Development is solely owned by the company. Anyone in the house is strictly a renter.."

"You didn't let on what we had going, did you?"

"No problem" Bolton looked hurt that Moses would even ask.

Moses nodded. "I've called Andre and he is working on the deal I asked for. We'll see."

Bolton smiled and rose to leave. He stopped and looked at Moses carefully.

"Mo', be careful with these guys. I got a feeling that this is a bad group. Don't push too hard. For your own safety."

"Thanks man."

Andre Baptiste looked nervously at Ricky. Jose loomed behind Andre and made him nervous. He was afraid of both of them. He knew Jose would kill him if Ricky gave the word. He also knew Ricky would kill him himself if Andre made him angry. He firmly believed Ricky liked to hurt people. Andre knew Ricky's nickname "El Cuchillo", which was Spanish for "the Knife", was well deserved. Ricky always had a knife clipped in the back of his waistband. The knife was a double-bladed, fighting knife and was razor sharp. Baptiste had once seen Ricky slash the face of an employee who made him angry. Andre never wanted to make Ricky angry.

"Do you trust this man?" Ricky asked quietly, suspicion in his voice.

Andre glanced at the men in the room. Alejandro Castellon, the Cell Boss he dealt with, sat mute in the corner. Watching.

Andre cleared his throat.

"I don't have any reason not to trust him. He has been a good customer so far. His crew seems to be doing well upstate." Ricky sat quietly for a long time, contemplating. He glanced at Castellon who nodded slightly.

"Very well. Tell him you need three days to obtain fifteen kilos." Ricky turned to Castellon. "Set it up."

CHAPTER 7

Danny glanced to his left and caught a glimpse of the sunrise between the condos. He loved this time of the morning. The sweat ran down his cheeks as he pedaled steadily. It was worth it to get up before the sun rose and do his morning bike ride. It helped him clear the sleep from his brain and focus on a case.

As Mike Richards drove, Danny sat quietly , deep in thought. He was trying to put the ends together to form a complete circle. The Medical Examiner had shown Conrad was murdered, not the victim of a suicide. That meshed with what everyone connected with Conrad, had insisted and they had been right so far. They also insisted Conrad had been clean. But there was the secret bank account. If Conrad had taken money from drug dealers, why had he used his own social security number but a different name? Conrad was a veteran cop. He must have known that if an internal investigation had started, they would have cross referenced the social security number. Was he just being sloppy or had he assumed he had covered his tracks so well no one would ever be suspicious? Had he been killed by rival dealers or his own people. If he was dirty, but was he? And who had been in the car? Friend or foe? He must have known his passengers or he would not have allowed them in his car. Or had they forced their way in? It would seem to make sense that if they had abducted Conrad, he would have been in the passenger seat, not the driver's seat. Danny couldn't seem to get the facts to form a circle instead of bouncing around in an uneven line. He closed his eyes and began to doze.

The drive to the Martin Correctional Institute took them a little over an hour. The prison perched next to the Interstate and was visible from the road. It was a cluster of one story, tan buildings surrounded by two fifteen-foot high chain link fences. The fences were topped by spirals of razor wire. The inner perimeter fence and the outer perimeter fence were separated by thirty feet of open ground, shooting lanes for the guard towers which towered forty feet above the ground at each corner of the compound. The towers were similar to airport control towers. The tops were glass enclosures that gave a 360 degree view. Around the outside of the tower was a walkway. On each walkway was a guard, dressed in the tan and brown uniform of State Corrections, armed with a high -powered rifle. Danny wondered how good the guards were with those rifles.

Outside the perimeter were mobile homes clustered together. Some had bicycles in the yard, or bass boats, indicating the correctional officers who lived there had their families with them. At the end of the compound, near the Interstate, was a ten position pistol range for the guards to practice, in view of the prisoners' exercise yard, presumably to dissuade thoughts of escape.

Richards parked in the visitor parking lot, next to a nondescript white van with a screen behind the front seats. Prisoner transport, Danny thought. He stretched his arms above his head to ease the stiffness in his back from the morning ride. Gonna be one of those days he just couldn't feel rested. Damn.

They entered through the double glass doors and approached a guard in a glass enclosure. Surrounding the guard's chair were banks of television screens showing every inch of the complex covered by security cameras. The guard's blond hair was pulled back and cut short and she wore no makeup. The shoulders of her uniform shirt were taut across broad shoulders and large biceps bulged from the bottoms of her sleeves. Body builder, Danny thought, but not so muscular so as not to be feminine at the same time. She pressed a button in front of her and a metallic voice asked through the speaker on the counter, "May I help you gentlemen?"

Danny fished out his wallet and held his credentials up to the glass for her inspection.

"We're here to interview Augustus Conrad. I called ahead and set it up." Danny said to the speaker as she examined the badge through the glass. She nodded and pointed toward the thick glass door to their left.

"Step through the door when it opens. On the wall you will find lockers. After the outer door closes, please deposit any weapons, handcuffs, ammunition or impact weapons in the locker and keep the key. When the inner door opens, you will be met by an officer who will escort you." She said it mechanically as if she had repeated it a thousand times.

They turned and the outer door slid open soundlessly. After they were inside, the door slid closed, enclosing them in a glass cubicle. Danny tried to remember the instructions in order. They placed their guns in the lockers embedded in the wall and pocketed the keys. A small, black officer approached the inner door and waited. The inner door slid open and the officer turned, telling them to follow.

They followed him down clean white corridors, then through a large open day room filled with long tables. Here and there prisoners sat at the tables reading. Two of them were embroiled in a heated game of poker. They followed down another corridor and entered a small interview room. At one end was a two way mirror. In the middle of the room was a gray metal table bolted to the floor. The chairs were also bolted to the floor, which kept the chairs from being used to change the attitude of belligerent prisoners or interviewers who pushed too hard.

"Wait here," the black officer said, closing the door.

Richards sat in one of the chairs.

"Friendly folks," he said, glancing around the room.

Danny shrugged and leaned against the wall. They waited twenty minutes. The door opened and Augustus Conrad entered. He looked very different from the last time Danny had seen him. Of course, he had been ten years old at the time. His hair was shaved short and his face, clean shaven. Both upper arms sported crude tattoos as did the back of his right hand. They were homemade and had obviously been collected over the years. He glanced around like a caged animal. He was dressed in a white t-shirt with the word PRISONER stenciled across the back and chest.

Conrad glanced at Danny and Danny felt a slight sadness. A cop's kid gone bad. His eyes were expressionless except for a suspicion he didn't try to conceal. He glanced around the room and his eyes rested on Richards. Danny could feel the contempt Conrad had for them. He wondered how to approach this interview. Conrad was obviously a veteran at being interrogated. Probably all of his life.

"Hello, Gus." Danny smiled at him, trying to lighten the mood. "I haven't seen you for a lot of years. I'm sorry it has to be under these circumstances."

Conrad stared at him and there was no indication he remembered Danny. Danny pointed toward one of the metal chairs.

"Have a seat and let's talk." Danny said.

Conrad shrugged and flopped into one of the chairs. He reached into his sock and extracted a pack of Marlboro's. He lit one and eyed both detectives warily.

"What the fuck you want, man?" Conrad asked, finally breaking the silence.

"We want to ask you some questions about your father." Danny spoke quietly, trying to keep the tension down.

"What about him? He's dead. And I didn't kill him. I was in here." Conrad sucked in a long drag of the cigarette and blew the smoke toward Richards. Danny sensed Richards beginning to rise up and quickly shook his head at him. Richards relaxed back in his chair. Danny knew how he felt. He wanted to slap the hell out of Conrad himself.

"We know that, Gus. We want to know if you have any idea who did?"

Conrad shrugged and began to wipe an imaginary spot on the floor with his foot. Danny decided to change tactics.

"Tell me about your arrest." Danny tried to make eye contact but Conrad looked away.

"I got busted. So what. Ain't the first time. Fuck it."

"Do you think your arrest has anything to do with your dad's death?" Danny waited. Hoping the mention of a connection would cause some reaction from Conrad. Nothing.

"Did you know your dad had a secret bank account?" Conrad looked up quickly in surprise, then caught himself and dropped back to the sullen silence.

"That makes him look like he might be dirty. Taking bribes. Was your dad involved in your drug business?" Danny asked.

"Squeaky clean, super cop Gus Conrad?" Conrad smirked. "Not hardly." Danny let the silence hang in the air. Sometimes, if you let them think for a second, they start talking without realizing it.

"Look man, I got caught with three kilos of blow. The people who owned it weren't happy about losing that much weight. And I got life with no chance of parole for at least twelve years. They tried me under the federal law. They really think that law will stop business. Or stop people from doing business. Ain't gonna happen. Too much money to be made. As to my fuckin' old man, he didn't do dope. He didn't take money and he thought I was shit. So don't come up here trying to get me to flip on the people who owned the blow by using my old man. I got nothing more to say. I got twelve years to do and I want to live long enough to get out of here." Conrad apparently realized he was talking too much. He went silent and looked out the window.

"If you think you're in danger here we can get you moved to another facility. Maybe somewhere closer to home?" Danny knew he was losing him now.

"Fuck off asshole. I got nothin' more to say." Conrad got up and stood by the door, waiting to be dismissed.

Danny sighed and knocked on the door, signaling the guard Conrad was ready to return to his cell. Danny touched Conrad's arm as the door opened. He looked into Conrad's eyes.

"If you need anything or someone to talk to, call me." Conrad glanced away and tried to put on his best disgusted look. He failed.

The same guard escorted them to the glass cubicle where they collected their guns from the security lockers. Danny waved at the blond body builder as they passed her window.

Danny took the wheel for the drive home. They rode silently for a while, both lost in thought about the reasons a kid goes bad. Finally, Danny turned toward his partner.

"What's your theory on all this?" He respected Richards' opinion and more than once Richards had solved a case by looking at it from a different angle.

"Well, we know the kid didn't do it. He's been in a cage. Conrad was a veteran cop Given the suspicious nature of cops, he wouldn't let somebody in his car he didn't know. Not without a fight. He was driving, so he picked them up, presumably from another location. They went to a private place to talk. Question is, what about? Were they people Conrad Senior was in business with? Or was it to talk about junior? Everybody seems to be convinced Conrad Senior was clean but what about the bank account? Real, or a smoke screen to make him look dirty? Either it was pre-planned or the discussion took a turn for the worse. Either way, the asshole in the back seat throws something over Conrad's head and pins him to the seat and asshole number two grabs Conrad's gun, sticks it in his mouth and blows his brains out. I would love to know who the unknown print belongs to." Richards fell silent.

"Where do we go from here?" Danny asked, to keep the conversation going.

"Maybe the bank account. See who's signature is on the paperwork to open the account. Compare it to Conrad's signature. See what pops up." Richards looked at his partner questioningly.

"Sounds like a plan." Danny smiled. The smoke screen idea was a good one. He hadn't thought of that.

Detective Kay Matthews tapped her fingers on the arm of the chair and waited. They had been waiting for almost an hour. Her partner fidgeted for the thousandth time. Finally, the Accounts Director approached and smiled. She held a white envelope out to Matthews.

"I'm sorry it took so long, officers. We had to verify your court order. And then it took some time to find the original account papers." Matthews opened the envelope and scanned the paper. It was a copy of the original paperwork opening the account with Conrad's social security number but a different name. The signature was legible and clear. Just what they needed. Matthews thanked the Accounts Director and slipped the envelope into her jacket pocket. Her partner fairly leaped out of the chair and headed toward the door. Matthews sighed. His exuberance pleased her when they were in bed but sometimes he drove her crazy. She caught the Accounts Director watching Fernandez leave and mentally agreed with her. Yeah, he wasn't bad to look at.

"Well, it's obvious the signature on the bank account is not from the same person as the one who wrote the suicide note. The angle of the letters is slightly different and the loop of the letters is different. See." The handwriting analyst pointed to the computer screen. Matthews could feel Fernandez' closeness as he pressed in behind her to look over her shoulder.

"I don't see the difference," she said finally, squinting. The analyst pointed to the screen. The signature and the suicide note were next to each other on the display.

"The width of the E and the A are different. The spaces between the letters are also inconsistent. People tend to write the same way all of the time and space the letters evenly apart. It's done unconsciously." The analyst pressed a button and lines appeared, running down the screen from top to bottom, dissecting the letters. He pointed again.

"The angle is different here. The letters on the signature lean at a ten degree angle to the left. The letters on the note lean to the right at a twenty degree angle from center." The analyst punched another button and a third set of letters appeared, a sample of Conrad's writing from an old police report.

"This writing is different still." The analyst looked up at them. "Three different people wrote these words."

"Conrad wrote the report. We know that for sure, but who wrote the others?" Fernandez frowned at the screen. The analyst cocked his head to the side.

"Find me some writing to compare and we may be able to say for sure."

Danny removed the holster from his belt and placed it on top of the kitchen cupboard with the gun. He went to the bedroom and removed his work clothes and changed into jeans and a T-shirt. He pulled his boots back on and sat on the edge of the bed. He was tired and knew he should go for a ride or work out for a while but he just didn't feel like it. He returned to the kitchen and placed dinner in the oven. It was his turn to cook. He and his wife shared the household chores, not out of any set agreement, but because Danny felt she worked just as hard as he did and that they were a team. He had learned that from his father, among other things. Danny's father had worked hard all of his life but still helped his mother around the house. Danny's father saw nothing unmanly about pushing a broom or dusting a lamp. He was a strong, hard man who had a very gentle side when it came to his wife and son. Danny had grown up living on the edge of the Everglades in a wooden house which stood next to a small pond. Beyond the pond was endless River of Grass. He and his father tended a small farm and subsidized their meager income with hunting and fishing. Danny had accompanied his father on his hunting trips for alligators since the age of nine. Danny's father would pole the small wooden canoe while Danny searched the dark water for the gleaming red eyes that reflected the light Danny wore on a band around his head, similar to a miner's light. Danny would then shoot the alligator in the eye with a .22 caliber rifle. The alligator would spin and thrash its tail, sending geysers of water spraying over them until it fell silent, lying motionless in the black water. They would quickly snag it with a large grappling hook before it sank and tow it to shore. When they had harvested enough for the night, they would take them to a clearing, a mile from the house, so as not to be too close for the Game Wardens to become suspicious, then clean them, saving the light-colored belly skin for sale to the dealer who would come around once a month in a beat up old pick up truck and collect the hides. Danny's father taught him not to ever kill anything for sport but to use everything you took. They sold the belly skin to help pay the bills and used the meat and hides for food and other necessities. But Danny learned other things, too. He learned to respect nature and live in harmony with it. His playmates were the Seminole Indian boys from the nearby Big Cypress Reservation. They would spend hours exploring the Sawgrass and hammocks. Danny learned how to wrestle and capture alligators alive. He and his friends would crawl on their bellies toward an alligator sunning itself then pounce, wrestling it into submission.

Danny also had a deep love for animals he learned from his father. He was always bringing home an injured bird or animal and putting it in one of the many small cages in the yard until it was healthy enough to be released back into the wild. His mother referred to it as "Quinn's Zoo".

Danny also learned how to survive in the wild. He learned how to cut the heart from the cabbage palm for food and which parts of the Sawgrass were edible. He loved the days in the Everglades. When he was sixteen, the family moved farther north to Clewiston, on the southwest edge of Lake Okeechobee and his father took a job with one of the sugar cane companies, driving loads of cane to the processing plant. Danny had explored the lake in a small skiff his father had gotten him in trade from an old fishing guide on the lake.

Danny was seventeen when his world crashed down on him. His parents left on a bright, moonlit night to drive to Naples to visit friends on one of the few times they took time off. Crossing Alligator Alley, they met a drunk driver head on. The drunk, a salesman from Tampa headed to Fort Lauderdale from a sales meeting in Naples, walked away from the crash with cuts and bruises but Danny's parents died instantly, pinned in what was left of their old Ford truck. Danny went to live with a family friend on the Reservation and was once again where he loved to be. Danny had no trouble being the only white kid among the Seminoles with his dark Irish eyes and jet black hair.

Two weeks before high school graduation, Danny and his best friend stopped at an exhibit table set up in the hallway of the high school and talked with the Army recruiter. They had no interest in the other recruiters at the other tables since Danny's father had served in the Army in the Second World War. Three weeks later, they enlisted and headed for boot camp in Georgia. Danny caught the eye of the Drill Instructors and especially the rifle range staff for his natural ability with both the rifle and the pistol. His years of hunting had given him a keen eye and steady hand. His work ethic and physical skill also raised some eyebrows. Danny enjoyed boot camp, unlike the other recruits, and showed the survival instructor, a grumpy old master sergeant with a voice like rocks thrown at aluminum, his knowledge of woods and swamps.

One week prior to graduation from boot camp, Danny was summoned to the commandant's office. His heart pounded as he reported to the colonel, mind racing, trying to figure out what he had done wrong. The colonel was a tall, thin man whom the recruits marveled at during his morning run. First for being up before they were and second because he seemed to run forever.

"Private Quinn," the Colonel cleared his throat and looked up from his desk as Danny stood at attention. He pointed to a chair. "Be seated, son." The Colonel smiled benevolently.

"Private, I have a proposition for you. Your instructors are very impressed with your performance. They have recommended you for additional training, if you are interested. Or, you can go into the infantry and go directly to Vietnam."

Danny felt himself begin to relax. He had hoped to go to an infantry company with his friend Oscar and go to Vietnam. But his father had always told him to take any education he could get.

"I'd like to serve my country in Vietnam, Sir. But I'd also be very interested in the training."

"The training won't be easy, Private. And I can assure you that you will see your share of combat." The Colonel tried to hide a smile. He liked this kid.

"Thank you Sir." Danny rose as he was dismissed.

The rest of Danny's boot camp squad went their separate ways after graduation, some to further specialty training while Oscar and others directly to Vietnam. Oscar would return home in less than a month, in a body bag. Danny remained at Fort Benning and completed Army Ranger School. Two days after completing Ranger school, the most physically and mentally demanding thing Danny had ever done, he was on a bus to Quantico to the Marine Corps Sniper Training Course. Danny spent six weeks at Quantico, perfecting his shooting and wilderness survival skills, much of which was already covered at Fort Benning. Then he returned to Fort Benning. He had been in the Army almost a year and had only been in two states.

Danny arrived back at Fort Benning and reported to the Colonel. He was given the weekend to rest and go into town if he wished. Then he was told to report to the head of the Ranger School.

The head of the Ranger School was a tough, hard-looking Major who seemed to be looking everywhere at once. Suddenly, his eyes would stop darting around and drill straight into your soul. It was enough to make you sweat in the middle of a blizzard.

"Private Quinn. Welcome back to the real military. I hope those Jarheads at Quantico didn't spoil you." The major grinned.

"No Sir. I tried not to get too friendly with them," Danny replied, wondering what his military career would hold for him now.

"Good, glad to hear it. Private, you have been chosen to be part of a special unit. You have excelled in your training and it has not gone unnoticed. Now, you are to join your team. You'll find them in the barracks at the end of the path by the motor pool. This is your squad leader, Sergeant Ross." The Major waved his hand toward the door and Danny suddenly noticed someone had entered the room, silently, as if he just appeared. He was dark and muscular. A large black mustache nearly covered his face. He nodded at Danny. Danny noticed his eyes were without emotion. Ross motioned Danny to follow and led him from the office and down a wooded path behind the motor pool.

"Private Quinn, you got any idea what Uncle Sam has in store for you?" Ross asked as they walked. Danny noticed Ross moved fluidly, like water flowing, as if his feet didn't touch the ground.

"No, Sir," Danny answered, trying to keep up with Ross.

"Well, now you will find out. The Squad you are assigned to will continue for more training and then the fun begins. But understand this, it will not be a picnic and everything we do is top secret. Therefore, you can never tell anyone. Not your sweetheart, if you have one. Not some piece of ass that you shack up with. Nobody. Understood?"

"Yessir, Sergeant."

Two days later, the team left Fort Benning and boarded a plane without knowing where they were headed or why. The first stop was Japan. They spent four months learning Aikido and Judo from a small, squat Japanese Master who spoke no English but taught through an interpreter. In the beginning, Danny was afraid he would die before they finished school. He had never hurt so much or had so many bruises on his body at one time. The classes lasted nine to eleven hours each day. When the students made a mistake in technique or movement, the master would mutter in Japanese and swat the student across the back with a rattan stick. The students learned quickly to minimize their mistakes.

After Japan, they traveled to the Philippines and learned stick and knife fighting from a skinny Filipino who had an amazing number of tattoos and scars. The scars were the result of a lifetime of proving himself in gang fights growing up in Subic Bay. After the stick and knife classes, they remained in the Philippines and were trained in the use of pressure points by a Chinese instructor who was the size of a ten year old girl. The places on the body they learned to poke and strike could knock a man unconscious with a light touch or kill with a firmer strike. Interspersed between the martial arts classes, the squad practiced their rifle and pistol skills until they had mastered them, and then some.

One morning, the squad was startled awake by Sgt. Ross, screaming at them to get their sorry asses out of the rack, terrified they had overslept. Ross grinned at their discomfort and informed them that class was over. Tomorrow they would leave for Vietnam.

Their arrival in Vietnam signaled the end of normalcy and the beginning of endless days hunting other human beings and killing them. Danny's team was assigned to a fire base near the Au Shau Valley. Their job was to search out and terminate the enemy leaders in the area. And they did it well. Through the use of long range sniping skills or sneaking into Viet Cong strongholds, guided by local American sympathizers and silently killing the commanders and officers of the Viet Cong, they tried to cause confusion among the enemy.

Danny refused to rationalize the reasons for it, or allow the act of cutting a man's throat as he slept affect him. He looked on it as a job to be done until he could go home. And everyone he killed, he felt was retribution for Oscar.

Danny didn't mind Vietnam. The heat and the bugs and being damp most of the time reminded him of his days in the Everglades. The team members received their assignments from Sgt. Ross who apparently received his orders from the man in the khaki clothes that visited frequently. Danny suspected he was CIA but could never confirm it. Not that it mattered.

Danny became very good at his work. He had the natural ability to move silently and appear at the least expected place. The other soldiers in the fire base nicknamed him Shadow. One minute he was nowhere to be found and the next he could be standing beside you. He still did it unconsciously, much to his wife's dismay. More than once she had been startled by his presence in the room when she had not heard him come in. Danny had done much of his work alone in 'Nam since it was easier for him to get in and out of tight spots without worrying about his partner's safety along with his own.

Danny heard the key turn in the front door and realized his wife had arrived home. He rose and greeted her at the door. She smiled at him as he took her purse from her shoulder and stood aside to let her pass. She leaned up and kissed him softly.

"Hi you," she said, looking into his eyes. She could always tell when he had been with his memories. But she knew not to ask. They were his memories and his alone.

"Hi gorgeous. How was your day?" Danny asked, following her into the house.

"It sucked, like always." She laughed. She really hated her job but couldn't quit since the pay was so good. She had good days and bad like every other working stiff.

She sniffed the air and grinned.

"I smell something good."

"Dinner will be ready soon. Why don't you get comfortable."

Danny watched her walk down the hall toward the bedroom. Nice ass, he thought to himself. He dearly loved his wife and still thought she was the most beautiful woman he had ever seen. His love for her was as strong as the day they met. Danny knew she felt the same way. Not only were they lovers but they were best friends. They finished dinner and Danny stretched out in a chair while his wife cleaned up the dishes. He was just about to doze off when she entered the room and plopped down in his lap. He reached up and stroked the back of her hair and she snuggled deeper into his lap and sighed. Danny loved to spend time with her just sitting and talking.

Danny stood at the end of the alley and squinted into the rifle's scope, trying to see the man's face. He could barely make out the slanted eyes and yellowish tint to his skin. He let his breath halfway out and held it, slowly taking up the slack of the trigger. He was startled by a beeping noise and turned just in time to dive out of the way of the garbage truck, its warning beeper getting louder as it backed up past him. The truck backed out of his line of sight but the beeping continued.

Danny jerked awake and grabbed for the pager, beeping in the dark. His wife moaned beside him and rolled over, turning her back to him. He rose quietly and shuffled to the kitchen, blinded momentarily by the light when he flipped it on. He squinted at the display on the pager and punched the numbers on the telephone, having to wait only two rings before a weary voice said, "Communications. Duty Officer."

"This is Sergeant Quinn," Danny croaked, trying to find his voice, "Did you page me?"

"Yessir. Sorry to wake you. We have a dead body on the Alley and the district Sergeant requested Homicide." The communications operator replied. "Female victim found burned in her car. Arson is enroute and so is Crime Scene. They're at mile marker forty."

"Okay. Call Detective Richards and tell him I'll meet him there." Danny quietly replaced the receiver. He moved silently into the bedroom and found his blue jeans and shirt in the darkness. He could tell what they were by the texture on his fingers, another trick he had learned in Vietnam. He sat at the kitchen table and pulled on his cowboy boots while waiting for his coffee water to heat in the microwave. He wrote his wife a note and silently slipped out into the dark. It was fairly cool out tonight, considering it was summer. Danny left the air conditioner off as he drove.

Danny flashed his badge to the weary toll booth attendant who waved him through without charging him. He accelerated around a slow moving car that pulled out of the toll booth ahead of him and settled in for the forty mile drive through the Everglades.

CHAPTER 8

Danny settled back and watched as dark shapes outside glided past. The Everglades at night could be as dark as a black hole. Behind the car the sky had a permanent glow from the city lights reflecting off the clouds. The farther west he drove, the deeper the gloom became. He could see the moon reflected off the canal running parallel to the road.

Occasionally, a dark shape would take wing from the canal bank like a ghostly specter in the dark. Danny remembered the times spent in the dark with his father hunting. He smiled at the thought.

Danny approached the scene and saw a few vehicles were already parked around the side of the road. He noticed the silhouette of an airboat nosed up onto the bank of the canal, the propeller cage rising high in the gray of morning. As Danny got out of his car, he noticed the eastern sky was turning pink. The world was turning from black to gray. Soon, it would turn blue, then the sun would cause the colors of the Everglades to turn green and brown. Danny loved the beginning of the day in the 'Glades. It reminded him of happier times. Danny walked past the row of marked police cars and plain looking detective cars lining the road. At the head of the line was the charred hulk of what Danny guessed was a Lincoln Continental. A group of uniformed officers clustered around the car and Danny noticed a gray and green uniform of the Florida Game and Fish Commission in the group. That explained the airboat.

Danny was met by the detective from the Arson unit.

"Hey Sarge, pretty early for this shit, huh?"

"Yeah, I've only had one cup of coffee. I'm not awake yet." Danny replied with a frown.

"Well, at least you've had one. I didn't even get that yet," the detective yawned.

"What's it look like?" Danny moved toward the burned out car. The passenger compartment was charred. The side of the car had the paint peeled off from the bottom of the door to the roof. The center of the roof glinted in the beam of Danny's flashlight where the metal was exposed.

"Well, we're not sure yet. Could be accidental or not. The victim is seated in the driver's seat, seat belt undone. She looks undisturbed, like she might have been asleep. The ground around the car is charred but not like you would expect from spontaneous combustion. I just got here a little while ago and haven't had time to do a thorough scene examination yet."

Danny knelt and looked under the car. His first thought was the car had been parked by the side of the road and the grass underneath had been ignited by the heat from the catalytic converter. Not that uncommon. In fact, the Highway Patrol had lost a few cars out here. One trooper had pulled over a car and while talking to the driver glanced back to discover his patrol car in flames. Another trooper had been parked by the road writing a report and barely escaped with his life when the flames from under his car began licking up next to his window. The Highway Patrol had been forced to issue orders to its troopers to minimize the amount of time they were stopped by the road during dry season. After all, the cars cost money. They never mentioned the potential loss of life to a trooper.

Danny straightened up and glanced at the Arson detective, his eyebrows raised in question. The detective nodded.

"I agree. The burn pattern is consistent with a fire starting in the vehicle, not in the grass. The tops of the grass are burned but not the bottom. That tells me the car was on fire first and the heat burned the grass from the top down." He pointed at the driver's window. "The amount of damage in the interior also tells me the fire started in the back seat."

Danny looked into the driver's window trying to ignore the sight of the burned body and the smell of charred flesh. The passenger side of the rear seat was only partially burned through. The rear of the driver's seat was burned. The seat back was almost completely gone. Only the metal framework and bits of the upholstery remained. The cushion the body was seated on was only partially burned and the passenger side of the front seat was still intact. Danny looked at the top of the car. The paint was burned off, down to bare metal, directly above the rear driver's side seat and driver's seat. The paint was bubbled and peeled above the passenger sides, both front and back, showing the area of highest heat to be above the driver's side. What Danny saw told him the fire had been extinguished before the car had been burned completely.

"How did we get this call?" Danny asked the Arson detective.

"Game Warden," he pointed with his chin. The Game Warden was standing by his airboat now, talking with a uniformed deputy. "He spotted the fire while on patrol. Came over to investigate and put out the fire the best he could with an extinguisher. Then he called for the Fire Department. Luckily, he was able to get the fire pretty much out. You know how long the Fire guys take to get way out here." Danny nodded. This far out in the 'Glades, the nearest Fire Station was either Naples or out of the east side. Thirty minutes minimum to get this far out from either direction.

Danny watched as Mike Richards parked his car at the front of the row of vehicles, in front of the fire truck. He glanced at the Arson detective.

"Here comes my partner. Coordinate with him while I talk to Game and Fish." He headed toward the airboat.

"Mornin," Danny nodded at the Game Warden as he approached him, holding out his hand. "Danny Quinn."

"Glen Busch." The Game Warden replied, shaking Danny's hand. Danny noticed the hand was rough and callused. The knuckles and fingers had numerous small cuts and scars, probably from the hours spent in the Sawgrass which could cut like a razor. Busch had an extremely strong grip.

"Nice rig," Danny said, admiring the airboat. The airboat was a flat aluminum skiff with an airplane engine and propeller on the back. The propeller was encased in a metal cage which prevented accidentally walking into the prop. Two padded seats, raised on pedestals, were mounted in front of the engine. The rear seat was higher than the front to allow the driver, who sat in the rear, to see over the passenger's head. The front of the airboat had a metal framework attached, extending almost six feet in front of the boat. This kept debris from hitting the occupants and pushed down the sawgrass in front of the boat as it raced over the grass.

"One of the fun perks of the job." Busch smiled.

Danny wistfully remembered how he had wanted to join Game and Fish when he returned from Vietnam but found the pay was near poverty level. The pay was better now and Danny almost wished he had taken the job.

"We appreciate you finding this and putting out the fire. Usually in these cases, we don't have much to work with by the time the Fire Department gets here."

"No problem. I just wish I had gotten here sooner. Might have saved that woman's life."

"Don't be too hard on yourself. Looks like she might have already been dead when the fire started. The fire looks like it was to cover something else."

"Shit. Homicide? Damn, it sure would have been nice to catch those sons of bitches." Busch had the look of the hunter in his eyes now. Danny knew the feeling.

"Hey, leave me something to do." Danny frowned at him. They both chuckled.

Danny trudged back up the canal bank and could feel the humidity cause sweat to trickle down his back. It was going to be another hot one. He met Richards at the victim's car. Richards was holding a brown and yellow striped cloth purse and frowning at something in his hand. Danny glanced over his shoulder and saw it was a Sheriff's Department business card. He recognized the gold star in the center.

"What's that?" he asked his partner who frowned up at him and handed him the card. Danny read it. He didn't recognize the name on the card. He turned it over and saw someone had printed **"In case of emergency, please call"** on the back of the card. He glanced up at Richards who shrugged.

"This come out of the purse?" Danny asked, glancing around to be sure none of the other detectives were within earshot. Richards nodded. Danny slipped the card in his pocket. He leaned towards Richards and quietly mumbled to him.

"Call communications and see if he still works for us. If so, get an address." Richards turned and headed towards his car.

Danny turned to watch as the attendants from the morgue began to attempt to remove the body from the car. The body was frozen in the seated position, making it difficult to maneuver out of the driver's door. The attendants pushed and pulled and strained until the body suddenly slipped from behind the steering wheel. Danny glanced at the rubberneckers driving past and wondered if they were getting their fill. Probably telling their kids to "look at the dead person." The body was lying on its back now, knees up in the air. Danny felt a sudden twinge of sympathy for her. No dignity left in death.

Danny noticed Richards waving at him from the open door of his car. He took one final look at the body as the attendants laid it on a black rubber body bag and zipped it closed. Poor kid, he thought.

"He still works for us. I've got his address. Dispatch doesn't have a clue why we want to know." Richards looked in his partner's eyes and wondered what he was thinking. Was the deputy whose name was on the card, a killer? A passing acquaintance. A lover. Richards knew his partner would want to handle this delicately.

"Okay. I'll meet you at the office and we'll go talk to him together," Danny said.

"Sounds like the best way to handle it. I would hate to fuck up the kid's career. We keep IA out as long as possible?" Richards asked.

"Completely, if possible." Danny replied, his brow furrowed, deep in thought. Richards nodded in agreement.

"Wonder who and what Gina Morelli was?" Richards asked as he watched the morgue attendants wheel past, the body covered with a blanket.

"Well, let's hope Deputy Spencer can tell us," Danny answered.

Danny entered the office and waited for Richards to join him. While he waited, he scanned the daily reports from the rest of the team. Nothing interesting. The trip to the Everglades had given him a sense of longing and regret. He wished his parents were still with him. He missed his mother's smiling face and his father's firm hand on his shoulder. They would never be there and the thought left an empty feeling inside him. He needed to make a trip to the reservation. That always seemed to cleanse his soul and make him feel whole again. Maybe Saturday he would go.

Richards pulled into the apartment complex and drove toward the back building. The buildings were faced with a fake brick and had tan walls. The complex was arranged in a square with a community pool in the center of the square. Each building had eight apartments, four upstairs and four downstairs. Danny and Richards saw the patrol car at the same time. It was parked in front of the last building, indicating a cop lived in that building. Richards parked at the end of the line of cars in the parking lot. He did not want to park right in front since they weren't sure how this man fit into the murder of Gina Morelli.

Deputy Spencer opened the door and squinted at them through half open eyes. The sunlight made him blink rapidly. His hair was scattered across his head and he was dressed in a pair of old cotton shorts he appeared to have just woken up.

"Who are you?" Spencer blinked at them.

"Deputy Spencer. Sergeant Quinn. Homicide. This is Detective Richards. May we come in ?" Danny watched his face for a reaction. He got none.

Spencer turned aside and allowed them to enter. He appeared to be half asleep and Danny guessed Spencer must work the graveyard shift. He glanced around the apartment and noticed a uniform shirt hanging over the back of a chair in the dining room, a gun belt coiled on the dining room table. Danny saw nothing to indicate a woman lived in the apartment. All the furnishings were decidedly masculine, a conglomeration of items picked up here and there and nothing appeared to match anything else.

"What's this all about?" Spencer asked dropping onto a worn-out couch and rubbing his eyes.

"Deputy Spencer, do you know a Gina Morelli?" Danny asked, carefully watching him. He could see the realization begin to rise up through the fog of sleep. Spencer was beginning to put the words Homicide and Gina Morelli together. Danny saw the words connect in Spencer's head and the connection made his eyes open wider. Danny also saw sudden dread appear in Spencer's eyes. He waited.

"Gina's dead." It came as a whisper. Danny thought he saw tears begin to form in Spencer's eyes. Spencer rubbed his face with both hands, took a deep breath and his composure returned. Cops were so used to controlling their emotions it became second nature.

"How did she die?" Spencer asked quietly.

Danny sat silently for a few seconds, mulling Ramondi's reaction. This man obviously cared for Gina Morelli so there must have been a romantic relationship between them. The surprise told Danny Spencer had not been the killer and did not know until this moment Gina was dead.

"She was found in her car in the Everglades. She was burned pretty badly. We found her driver's license and your card in her purse. That's how we found you." Danny felt being brutally honest was the only way to tell a cop bad news.

"We won't have a positive identification until we compare dental records."

"Burned." Spencer breathed. He turned away for a second and jumped to his feet. He stood motionless as if forgetting where he was going. Then he seemed to lose all control of his muscles and dropped back onto the couch and stared at the floor. "Burned." He whispered again.

Finally, he looked up at Danny with wet eyes and nodded.

"What can I do?" he asked.

"We need to know everything you can tell us about her. About your relationship. Her friends. Her job. Anything you know, we need to know."

"We've been dating for a while. Maybe eight months. I really thought she was the one, but one day she just broke it off. Said she couldn't see me anymore. Said she was friends with some people who wouldn't like her seeing a cop. I figured it was just some of her yuppie friends that didn't want her inviting a lowly cop to their fancy dinner parties, ya' know. Some of the people she hung around with were trying to live life in the fast lane. Ya know, fancy cars, fancy clothes, dish of nose candy at parties for party favors." Spencer stopped talking and stood up. He began to pace back and forth across the room, staring at the floor.

"Was Gina using cocaine?" Danny asked.

"I don't think so. She said she wouldn't ever get into that." Spencer looked up suddenly, a questioning look on his face. "Am I in trouble here, Sarge?"

"I don't know kid. How far did you go personally? Were you doing any drugs?" Danny watched his eyes for a lie.

"Fuck no. I've never even tried pot. The kids I grew up with did. The guys in the army did, but not me. I wanted to be a cop."

"You better be straight with me. I can have Internal Affairs here in twenty minutes and make you take a piss test," Danny growled at him.

"I swear to God," Spencer pleaded, "I've never done it. That would ruin my career."

"Tell me the rest of it then," Danny said soothingly. He waited while Spencer absorbed it all. The kid was wondering how much to tell. He was weighing how much damage he could do to his career by telling Danny what he wanted to know. Danny waited. You have to give them time to think and decide. It you push too hard, sometimes they shut down and you've lost them.

"Is Internal Affairs gonna get involved in this?" Spencer asked, still trying to reach a decision.

"That depends. You know I can't let you break the law. If you are involved in drugs, then you hang. If not, then we have to see."

Spencer nodded and sighed. Danny knew he was close. He waited patiently. Time to let it all sink in. Spencer would tell Danny as much as he thought he could trust him to know.

Finally, Spencer glanced around the room and Danny could sense the resignation in his eyes. He seemed to be looking around as if trying to memorize everything. Like he was afraid he would lose it all. Spencer dropped his eyes to the floor and took a breath.

"I never did drugs. I've never even tried them. Gina did pot on occasion. She swore to me she never did cocaine. Had friends who did. She didn't like what it did to them. She had a desire to make big money though. Or so she said. She once told me she had connections to some people who made big money in dope. She wanted to be a go-between, an entrepreneur as she called it. She said her friends were legitimate business men who wouldn't like it that she was seeing a cop. She came here once with a small duffel bag. She was very protective of it. I knew what was in it. Shit, you could smell the pot in it from two feet away. I told her never to bring that shit in my house. And she never did again. But I never turned her in." Spencer looked at Danny pleadingly. "I really thought I cared for her. But it was all a fraud. That's what split us up I guess. I couldn't accept her way of life. Am I gonna lose my job for this, Sarge?"

Danny sat back and thought about it. The kid was a good cop according to his file. He just made a few mistakes of the heart. But then, who hasn't.

"I don't think we have to go any further with this. As long as you didn't break the law. Like possessing or selling drugs." Danny made it a statement and a question.

"I swear I didn't. I wasn't brought up that way." Spencer shook his head vigorously. Danny believed him.

"Do you know who these people were that Gina was involved with?" Danny leaned forward toward Spencer.

"No. Gina was very secretive about who she knew. I don't know if she was protecting me or herself. I only know her best friend. And only just barely." Spencer rose and walked to the kitchen counter. He picked up a small blue address book. He flipped through the book to the back page. He wrote something on a piece of paper and handed it to Danny.

"That's her friend Karen's phone number." Spencer seemed to relax a little. Danny tucked the paper in his top shirt pocket. He walked toward the door to leave. He stopped and turned to face Spencer again.

"For what it's worth, I'm sorry about Gina. We'll keep the rest between us for now. Just keep your nose clean from now on."

Spencer nodded.

The Galt Ocean Mile area was a concrete canyon of tall condominiums towering above A1A. The buildings were erected twenty-five years ago and were allegedly able to withstand the hurricane winds that occasionally pounded the Florida coast. However, South Florida and the condos in particular had never faced the brutal winds of a killer hurricane. Danny wondered if they would still stand after a wind of 150 miles per hour. He doubted it. The buildings perched on the beach and one could occasionally catch a quick glimpse of the ocean in the spaces between the buildings. Both sides of A1A had condos. The ones on the west side sat along the Intracoastal waterway. The beach side cost twice as much as the ones along the Intracoastal. A good view cost big bucks. In the millions actually.

Danny finally found Majestik Towers wedged in among the other buildings and parked under the concrete overhang in front. He had bicycled past here an hundred times and never noticed the building. Majestik Towers was a twenty-story, green building, which, like all the rest along the street, was a monument to greed and wealth, except for the strange green color. Danny wondered if all residents were color blind. Danny approached two thick glass doors which opened, with a hiss, into a lobby with mirrored walls and a gray and blue cloth couch and chairs. Probably for the residents to rest before going up to their apartments. Carrying those fat checkbooks must be tiring. In a corner, near the elevator, sat a circular desk for the security guard. Danny could see a full head of white hair and the top of a newspaper over the top of the desk.

The security guard, who had to be pushing eighty years old, looked up at Danny as he stepped up to the desk. Every one of these buildings had a security guard and a steel gate across the entrance to the underground parking garage. Made the residents feel safe. But Danny knew better. He had worked burglaries a few years back and learned a lesson on condo security. Danny and his squad had been told of a professional burglar, working the county, by an informant. The informant, also a professional burglar and former business associate of the target, had given them specific information about his former partner's method of operation. The squad spent three weeks conducting surveillance on the burglar whom they quickly nicknamed the Ghost. The nickname came from the Ghost's ability to alter his appearance and also to enter supposedly secure homes and condos. The Ghost was balding on top and wore glasses. However, the Ghost sometimes wore contact lenses or a hairpiece. He even went so far as to grow beards or mustaches. The Ghost had fifteen or twenty descriptions by different victims.

Danny and company had tailed the Ghost to a condominium just like this and watched him enter the building. Ten minutes later he left and was followed to a pawn shop he used to dispose of his treasures. When the elderly condo residents returned home they found nothing amiss with the exception of one cloth work glove on the floor. They never determined how the Ghost got into the condo but he left with twenty-five thousand dollars worth of jewelry which was never recovered. Shortly thereafter, the Ghost apparently began to feel the heat and made a mistake and was caught. He was booked into the county jail and was almost immediately bonded out and disappeared, before it was discovered the Ghost was wanted in New Jersey for stabbing a cop.

Danny and his partners were able to secure a search warrant on the Ghost's townhouse and the treasure trove of recovered property filled a warehouse. Everything in the house was stolen, including the salt-and-pepper shakers on the dining room table. They were eventually able to secure warrants charging the Ghost with two hundred counts of burglary. But the Ghost had vanished. Weeks and weeks of searching turned up nothing. The detectives were frustrated. They wanted the Ghost badly. Then Danny got a phone call from NYPD. A rookie cop, first day out of the academy, had come face to face with Ghost in the hallway of the Waldorf Astoria hotel. The Ghost had a pocket full of pilfered jewelry and two hundred warrants. The rookie got a big attaboy from the mayor. So much for secure living.

"Can I help you?" the security guard asked, peering at Danny over his bifocals. He was wearing a burgundy-colored blazer with the emblem of Majestik Towers on the breast pocket.

"Sergeant Quinn. I'm here to see Karen Gould."

The guard squinted at Danny's I.D. for almost a full five minutes.

"She's expecting me," Danny finally said when his patience wore out. He had spent nearly an hour arguing with the phone company supervisor before finally getting the address at Majestik Towers. The phone company considered unlisted numbers as precious as gold. But any con man worth his salt could get any number any time.

The security guard finally picked up the phone on the desk and dialed. He spoke quietly into the receiver for a few seconds then hung up. He frowned at Danny and pointed at a pair of elevators in the lobby.

"Twelve ten. Take the elevator to the twelfth floor and turn right." The guard sat down in his chair and picked up his newspaper. Danny was officially dismissed.

Danny turned right and followed the arrows on a gold placard to the door of twelve ten. He glanced around at the plush carpeted hallway and the artificial plants interspersed in the hallway. Yeah, the Ghost would love this place. The door swung open at the first knock. She must have been standing inside the door with her hand on the knob, waiting for him. Karen Gould appeared to be about thirty-five years old with dark hair pulled back in a braid, secured by a gold lame knot. She was wearing subtle makeup, accenting very deep blue eyes. Colored contacts, Danny guessed. She wore a white silk blouse sheer enough to reveal the lace bra underneath. Danny suspected it was not by accident. Her black stretch pants were the kind with a stirrup around the bottom of her foot. Black high heels. She wore a diamond necklace that looked real and matching earrings. Subtle, but obvious there was a comfortable amount of money here.

"Officer Quinn?" she asked as she stood aside to let him into the apartment. Danny nodded as he eased past her, feeling her breasts rub his arm. Obviously intentional on her part. Danny began to wish Richards had come with him as a witness in case she claimed he had some something inappropriate. But he suspected Karen Gould was very accustomed to using her feminine gifts to get what she wanted.

"Mrs. Gould. I'm sorry to intrude but I need to ask you a few questions." Danny had discovered she was a Mrs. from the phone company listing. He looked around the apartment as she led him into a very large living room. The living room opened onto a balcony and Danny could see the ocean in the distance. The furniture appeared to be very expensive black leather, arranged around a glass-top table in the center of the room. One entire wall was mirrored and reflected the view through the sliding glass doors, giving the room the appearance of being monstrous.

Karen Gould folded herself into a leather armchair. There was a half empty cup of coffee on the glass end table next to the chair.

"Can I offer you something, Officer? Coffee, something stronger?" She smiled up at him. Her accent suggested Boston or at least Massachusetts somewhere. The soft Bostonian accent of the upper crust, not the harder accent of the working class that drew out the letter A.

"No ma'am, thank you. Is your husband around?" Danny glanced around the apartment.

"My husband does not live with me, officer. We have separate residences and separate lifestyles. Just the same money. Why do you ask?"

"Well, I'm afraid the reason I'm here is not a pleasant one and I thought it might help to have someone here." Danny eased into a chair across from her. She eyed him warily.

"My husband doesn't help much with anything except the checking account. What could possibly be so ominous?"

"Are you acquainted with Gina Morelli?" Danny asked.

"Yes, Gina is a very good friend of mine. Why?"

"I'm very sorry to have to tell you this, but Gina is dead," Danny said softly.

She let out a gasp and a look of disbelief leapt to her face. "Dead how?"

"She was found dead in her car this morning. She died in a fire. We believe it was murder but we'll know for sure later."

"Murder. My God. Who the fuck would kill Gina?" she whispered.

"I was hoping you could help us figure that out." Danny was surprised how her use of profanity made her seem less elegant. But then it always did with people who tried to act like royalty. "If you could help us with her friends and acquaintances. Sort of point us in the right direction as to who to talk to."

"I only know a few of her friends. She and I go out together quite a bit to clubs. You know, to meet people and have fun."

Danny wondered if the 'people' included men and how her husband would feel about it. She looked at him and he realized she must have read his mind.

"Officer, my husband and I have an understanding. I do what I wish and he stays up North and does what he wants. Which generally encompasses his work and any bimbos he can impress enough to sleep with him. My husband is a very well known corporate attorney. Maybe you know him? Edgar Jerome Gould?"

Danny knew Edgar Jerome Gould. Gould had been a practicing lawyer in South Florida earlier in his career. He began as a young Public Defender taking any and every case assigned to him. After a few drug cases Gould discovered he had a flair for winning those types of cases. He soon left the employ of the Public Defender's Office and opened a private practice with two partners. The firm specialized in defending high profile drug cases and became well known and very wealthy. Many an unsuspecting cop had been verbally abused on the stand by Edgar Jerome Gould who took great pride in belittling cops in front of juries. He had won most of his cases at the expense of the arresting officer and creatively redesigning the search and seizure laws to his clients' benefit. All the cops thought he was an asshole and scumbag. And all unscrupulous lawyers thought cops were a bunch of idiots and buffoons. Gould had finally left Florida to become a senior partner in a corporate firm in New England, to the collective relief of the cops who knew him. Danny figured Gould was probably still an asshole and scumbag.

"I knew your husband years ago," Danny replied. "But right now I'm interested in who Gina Morelli knew and who she spent time with."

"Gina spent time with lots of people." Karen Gould rose and stood by the door to the balcony. She held her arms folded across her chest and appeared to have regained her composure.

"Any one in particular?" Danny asked.

"We have some of the same friends. Gina wanted to be somebody. Somebody with money."

"Like you?" Danny asked, watching for a reaction.

"She was beginning to make the right connections in the right places." She apparently chose to ignore the question. "She was involved with one special person. Seemed to have a real feeling for him. But that's past history I guess. She recently broke it off, according to her. Besides, he's married."

"Do you know about Spencer?" Danny asked.

"The cop?" She chuckled. "He was a passing fancy. Too straight. She was looking for society and excitement. He was looking for a relationship. Gina wasn't interested in anything long lasting."

"Who was the married man?"

"Sorry. That is privileged information." She scowled at him. "Besides, she never really told me his name."

"What about work? Business contacts?"

"Gina was a personal assistant to a group of developers. She arranged their business meetings. Entertained clients, things like that. It's called Sawgrass Development Corporation, I think." She eased back into her chair and lit a cigarette with a pearl encrusted lighter.

"Was Gina involved in drugs?"

"You must have gotten that from that cop." She flared. "Gina was not a druggie. She smoked a little pot now and then, that's all. Besides, pot is socially acceptable these days or haven't you heard."

Danny carefully watched her eyes when he asked the next question. His experience told him people reacted unconsciously when cornered without realizing it. They tended to give a lot away without saying a word.

"Do you use cocaine?"

Her eyes darted to a silver container on the coffee table then flicked back to his face. The container had a top on it and Danny couldn't see what was inside. But he knew. Yeah, you snort dope and your stash is in that container, I'll bet.

"No, officer, I don't," she lied. He knew he had gone as far with the interview as he could for now. Besides, he had the answers he needed. He rose and she followed him to the door. He handed her his business card.

"If you think of anything, call me."

Danny parked in front of the Medical Examiner's office and steeled himself. He suddenly felt weary. He was tired of seeing the horror of death. Strange attitude for a Homicide cop. Death was his business and he knew it. He was always intrigued with a puzzle and how to solve it. That was what homicide work was like. A puzzle with bizarre-shaped pieces to be shuffled to fit a mold, only revealed when the pieces were shaped. Danny liked the challenge of Homicide but the day to day gore sometimes made him wish he could take his wife and move out into the Everglades and stay forever. He knew what he needed at times like this. He needed to go out into the Glades and recharge. When he got time, he would go and forget Gina Morelli and Gus Conrad and all of it for a while.

Irving Berkowitz had his back to Danny when he pushed through the double doors into the autopsy room. Berkowitz was bent over an examination table and Danny saw past him where two small delicate feet protruded. Danny smelled the sickening sweet smell of charred flesh and formaldehyde and other chemicals he didn't even want to know about. Berkowitz was softly singing to himself, some little tune about a prostitute in Tijuana. Danny cleared his throat and Berkowitz glanced over his shoulder at him. Small glasses perched at the end of his nose. A microphone hovered over his head.

"Ah, Daniel. How is my favorite cop?" Berkowitz had a scalpel poised in midair.

"Tolerable, Doc." Danny's nose wrinkled at the smell in the room.

"You look bummed out. What's wrong.?" Berkowitz turned to face him. Danny saw Gina Morelli's charred remains behind Berkowitz on the table.

"Just tired. Got called out too early this morning." Danny smiled wearily. Berkowitz nodded slightly. Danny moved closer to the table. He could see the chest of the corpse gaping open.

"Well, it seems our poor unfortunate here died a quiet death. But she was alive when the fire started. Official cause of death is smoke inhalation. Smoke in her lungs indicates she breathed in quite a bit. I just wonder if she was asleep or unconscious when she inhaled it." Berkowitz frowned at the body. "Unfortunately, it will be hard to prove either way."

Before Danny could reply, the doors swished open and Dana Fielding breezed in. Fielding was an ex-cop now employed as an investigator for the Medical Examiner. She wore a blue business suit, a file folder in her hands.

"Hey Dan. Haven't seen you in a while." She smiled a bright smile.

"Nice to see you too Dana." Danny replied. He and Dana were old friends. Fielding handed the folder to Berkowitz.

"I tracked down Gina Morelli's parents in Jersey. They Federal Expressed her dental records. I think they are really hoping we're wrong and that Gina is off with some boyfriend somewhere." She said. She spun on her heels and headed for the door. "I'd love to stay and visit but I'm swamped right now. See ya' Dan." Then she was gone.

Berkowitz opened the folder and turned back to the body on the table.

"Alrighty. Let's see if this poor unfortunate soul is really Gina Morelli. Call me in about two hours and I'll let you know." Danny realized he was being dismissed and headed for the door.

CHAPTER 9

Moses Hammond scratched his chest for the thousandth time. The tape holding the tiny microphone to his chest burned. There had to be an easier, or better, way to hold the body bug to the skin. Maybe I'll invent a new tape that doesn't burn and get rich, he thought. He knew he couldn't scratch it anymore. He would have to live with it. If he scratched it at the wrong time it could be fatal. He drove slowly down the residential street, looking for the surveillance van. He spotted it on the corner, ten houses down from the target. He took a deep breath to slow his heart because it was beating like a bass drum. Happened every time he made a buy. He knew what the stakes were. He would have to be calm and act normally. He took another deep breath and spoke quietly. "Testing, one two." The headlights on the surveillance van blinked quickly. They were receiving him.

Moses found the house. It looked like all the rest of the houses on the block. A child's bicycle lay on its side in the front yard. A garden hose snaked across the front lawn to a sprinkler watering a bed of flowers. Nice touch, Moses thought. He wondered if they brought in a woman and kids to make the house look normal. Stash houses were like this sometimes. The professionals took great pains to blend in. The less professional ones just put blankets over the windows to keep the curious neighbors from peeking in. The less professional ones were the easy ones to catch.

Moses backed the rental car into the driveway. He had rented it that morning and it smelled sweetly of air freshener which barely masked the faint smell of vomit. Probably some college kids had rented it before Moses and had partied all weekend. Apparently, one of them couldn't party as well as the rest. The smell was making his stomach queasy. Thank God he would only use the car for one day. It was just a prop. Drug transporters liked to use rental cars so if they were caught, the cops couldn't confiscate their cars. It would have to be returned to the rental company to be rented again, probably to another drug runner. Moses had put two large boxes of laundry detergent on the back seat. Another prop. It would be sprinkled over the drugs to try and hide the smell from drug sniffing dogs. Moses had studied drug runners and copied their methods so he would appear to be just another doper.

He backed the car up to the garage door and beeped the horn. The garage door slid open and he backed all the way into the garage. The door slid down, closing him in. Andre Baptiste waited for him at the rear of the car. The slamming of the car door echoed hollow in the empty garage as Moses got out.

"Hey mon. How it's goin?" Andre shook his hand.

"Everything's good Andre. Are we set.?" Moses returned the handshake. Andre nodded and smiled widely.

The door leading into the house opened and Alejandro Castellanos stepped into the garage. He was followed by a short dark Latin in a gray t-shirt. The Latin had a small, deadly looking, black submachine gun slung over his shoulder. Andre introduced them and Castellanos shook Moses' hand. He studied Moses' face silently, his eyes boring into him. Moses held Castellanos' gaze, trying hard not to show any nervousness. He studied the ugly red scar running from Alejandro's ear down to his chin.

"Dinero?" Castellanos asked, glancing at Andre.

"Himself want to see the money, Mon." Andre translated. Moses opened the trunk of the car and retrieved a small black duffel bag. He held it out to Castellanos. Castellanos gestured to his companion who took the bag and set it on the floor. Another Latin male came into the garage from the house. He moved to the side and watched Moses carefully. He had a Beretta 9mm automatic tucked in the front of his waistband. His hand rested on the gun. The first Latin zipped open the bag and began to count the money stacked inside. Finally, he stood and nodded to Alejandro. Alejandro smiled and the tension dropped from the room. He headed into the house. Moses and Andre followed him with the two guards bringing up the rear.

The house was void of furniture except for a table and chairs standing in the middle of the dining room. There was a small portable color television on the table being watched by another Latin male. On the table, near his hand, lay another submachine gun. He wore a large revolver in a shoulder holster. Moses glanced around, making a mental map of the layout of the house. He would have to remember it later for the search warrant and to diagram it for the Raid Team. He silently counted the number of occupants and their weaponry. He couldn't see into the other rooms and wondered if there were any more. One way to find out.

"Bano?" Moses asked Castellanos, requesting the bathroom. Castellanos frowned but jerked his head toward the hallway leading to the bedrooms. Moses walked slowly toward the hallway, his footsteps echoing on the concrete floors and empty walls. He glanced into the bedrooms as he passed them, noting there were no other suspects in the rooms. There was something else in the rooms, however. Along the walls were stacks of square packages, each about eight inches square. They appeared to be covered with plastic and wrapped at the ends with gray tape. Each stack was approximately waist high. Moses tried not to stare. Jesus, that was a lot of dope. There had to be five hundred kilos. Moses wondered if it was one shipment or if they were stockpiling the drugs. Had to be stockpiling. Nobody brought that much dope in at one time. Moses used the bathroom and hurried back to the dining room.

When Moses returned Castellanos eyed him carefully. Apparently satisfied he nodded to the Latin in the gray t-shirt who disappeared into one of the bedrooms. He returned shortly with fifteen of the packages Moses had seen stacked in the bedrooms. The packages were placed into a small duffel bag and into the trunk of Moses' rental car. Moses opened one of the boxes of laundry detergent and sprinkled it around inside the trunk. Opening the other box, he placed it between the packages. He closed the trunk and turned to Castellanos and Baptiste.

"Thank you gentlemen" Moses said and turned to the driver's door of the car. He knew he was almost home free. If they were going to rip him off it would have happened when he showed the money. Moses opened the car door and slid in. Inserting the key in the ignition, he started the engine. He turned toward Baptiste and smiled. "I'll be talking to you later."

Baptiste nodded. The garage door opened and Moses drove out into the sunlight. He breathed a sigh of relief. Well, that was easy. As he passed the surveillance van he noticed the roof vent was open. He hoped they got it all on video. While they couldn't videotape the actual transaction, they could capture his arrival and exit on tape. That, coupled with the audio tape and the pictures of the empty trunk before and the dope in the trunk afterwards should be enough. Moses smiled to himself. They had even been nice enough to write the initials MH on each package for him.

The surveillance van fell in behind him and Moses knew they would videotape the entire drive back to the office and the opening of the trunk. That way, when some smart college boy attorney tried to say Moses stopped somewhere along the way and placed the drugs in the trunk after leaving the house, the video would prove him wrong. Moses drove carefully so the surveillance van could keep up.

They arrived at the DEA office in tandem. Moses parked inside the garage. Diaz was waiting for them. Normally, the SAC wouldn't be interested in one of his agents' cases, but Diaz had a feeling this one was different. He believed this deal would lead to something big. Moses joined him and together they watched the trunk being opened and videotaped. Diaz whistled when he saw the fifteen packages. He glanced at Moses.

"Any problems.?" He asked, glancing at Moses.

"Nope. Went nice and smooth. Lots of guns around though. I counted three along with the boss, Castellanos. When and if we take them the entry team better be real ready to party," Moses answered.

"No big surprise really," Diaz replied.

They watched together as an evidence technician removed the packages one by one from the duffel bag. The technician marked each one with a number, working backward from fifteen to one, as each was removed from the bag. Moses marked each one with his initials and ID number. The evidence technician then used a small pen knife and inserted it into each package in turn, and removing a small sliver of white powder. The powder was dropped into a glass vial to which was added a few drops of chemical. The contents of each vial turned an electric blue color, positive test for cocaine. Each package was sealed with a strip of gray duct tape. Moses and the evidence tech then each signed their initials to the duct tape. Each package was encircled with a strip of red tape proclaiming it EVIDENCE. The packages were replaced in the duffel bag which was also marked with red EVIDENCE tape. The entire process was videotaped. The evidence technician carried the bag away.

"C'mon up to the office. INS is waiting for us." Diaz motioned for Moses to follow him.

"Clancy Grainger. Moses Hammond." Diaz made the introductions. Grainger was a tall, powerfully built man in his mid-forties. Moses guessed he was a weightlifter. He had gray hair and a neatly trimmed gray beard. He was dressed in a blue work shirt and faded blue jeans. A large revolver rested in a holster on his hip and he had a gold federal agent badge, proclaiming Immigration and Naturalization Service, clipped to his belt.

"Sorry it took so long to get this," Grainger said, settling into a chair and opening a tan file folder. "But you know how it goes with Federal bureaucracies and case loads." Moses knew.

"Let's see. Andre Baptiste. Born in Haiti. Parents fled with him to Jamaica to escape the Papa Doc Duvalier government. Daddy was a doctor, Mother dear was a witch." Grainger glanced at them. "Actually she was a faith healer, but in the Islands they are considered witches. All that Voodoo shit. Lived in Jamaica for the rest of their lives. Never obtained Jamaican citizenship so they were illegal there too. Andre snuck into the U.S. in 1989. Illegally, of course. Still living here illegally." Grainger handed Moses a birth certificate and other papers on Andre.

"If we need to squeeze him we have some different routes to go here. First, under immigration law he can be deported as an undesirable alien. But, we send him back to Haiti, not Jamaica. That may scare him into cooperating. Nobody wants to go to Haiti as unstable as it is. The Aristide government would probably put him in prison when he got there anyway if we asked them to. Political favors and all that. Second, we prosecute him under federal law as a drug trafficker. Which, as you know, a conviction gets him life in an American prison. American prisons are a lot better than Haitian prisons. And if he ever gets out of our jail, he goes back to Haiti anyway. Or we offer him a deal. For his 'substantial assistance' we send him to Jamaica where he can lie on the white sandy beaches and sip rum or whatever, as long as he never sets foot on U.S. soil. If he does, he spends life in prison as a drug trafficker." Grainger closed his folder and glanced at Diaz and Moses.

"Sounds like we got him where we need him." Diaz smiled. "What do you think Moses?"

"I don't know if we have any choice. I thought we might be able to finesse him into working me higher into the organization. We may still be able to do it. But he may want to protect his own interests. He does have his own street level operation to protect. Our plan was to persuade him to act as go-between and get me more and more dope. He may decide to increase his operation and also act as supplier. I need to get into the group on my own terms. Convince them I can make them more money by dealing directly with me. It's risky though. What if he decides to burn me with the group and we lose it all? That's a lot of time and effort to end up with Andre. Sure, we can shut down his operation but I have a feeling that there is more to this group than we realize." Moses stopped then, feeling he made his point.

"Well, there's always that risk. But, I think we have to go with bringing Andre in and see where it takes us," Diaz answered. Moses and Grainger nodded.

"It's your ballgame, guys. We'll play it anyway you want. My function in this is as the big bat to hit him over the head with," Grainger said.

"Okay. Let's give Andre a few days. We'll keep the surveillance team on the stash house. Let them make a few more deliveries. That way when we hit them they won't put it together that Moses is the cause of them getting hit. Maybe, if we get enough of their dope and money they will need Moses to take up the slack. Make them hungry. Then, we'll get Andre to take you to the big boys. We'll convince them Moses' operation is expanding and can sell lots of their product throughout Florida and Georgia. Show them by taking Moses into the organization, they can increase their profit margin." Diaz looked at Moses with a quizzical look.

"Sounds like a plan." Moses wasn't as confident as he sounded.

He wondered if he were stepping out on a very thin limb that could break under him at any second. He suspected they had stumbled on a large organization. The only thing they had going for them was greed. Drug dealers were greedy. Judging by the large amount of dope he saw in the stash house these guys were greedy. And probably well organized.

Moses left the office late. He stayed to catch up on the investigative reports on the buy with Andre. He felt good about the events of the day. Fifteen kilos was a sizable seizure. He felt like he was getting somewhere with the Task Force. He had made large buys with the sheriffs office drug unit, but this was different. Since being assigned to the Task Force, he had learned a lot about the drug trade. He learned how the money was laundered, how the dope came into the country. He discovered a larger perspective on the drug trade since he started playing with the Feds. Working street level drugs, he spent most of his time making small buys then chasing some little street dealer through back yards and alleys on foot until he felt as if his lungs would burst. He loved doing it but now he felt as if he could make a dent in the business. Kick some serious ass for his brother.

Moses unlocked the front door and threw his keys on the television in the living room. He pushed the front door to his townhouse with his foot. He held the stack of mail in his right hand, his cell phone in his left. He felt as if the cell phone was attached to him, like an extra limb. Sometimes Moses believed the cell phone had caused Theresa to leave.

Moses and Theresa had first met in a Sociology class at the local Community College where they were both taking classes. Moses had been a uniformed deputy working patrol at the time. Theresa's father had retired from the Washington D.C. police department. Theresa liked what she saw in Moses after they had spent hours debating the social status of women in the workplace. Moses finally worked up the nerve to invite her to dinner and she accepted. After that, they were inseparable. They married a year later and dreamed of having a big family with lots of kids. Then Moses accepted the transfer to Narcotics. The job had ended the stability of their lives.

The hours were erratic and uncertain. Working patrol Moses had the same days off all the time and worked the same time every day, except when he had to go to court. Working dope, it seemed Moses was never home. Theresa's father had always worked patrol and she saw police work as a stable home life. Why couldn't Moses be like that? And that damn cell phone and pager. Theresa could never understand the need Moses had to do what he did. It led to lots of fights. Suddenly, after two years Moses dragged in the door after a long two straight days of being on surveillance to find her gone, along with everything she owned. A note on the kitchen counter told him she had gone home to D.C. Moses tried numerous times to call her, but her mother informed him in no uncertain terms that Theresa didn't want to talk to him. Three weeks later the divorce papers arrived and he signed them. And that was that. Moses still loved her and wanted her back but the feeling dulled over time. He still missed her though. Well, at least she hadn't tried to screw him in the divorce by taking the house and car and everything he owned. He supposed he could be thankful for that.

Moses poured himself a glass of iced tea, kicked off his shoes and stretched out on the couch. He didn't drink alcohol much, only when an undercover assignment required it and then just barely. He supposed he learned that from his father, the preacher. At least he hadn't become a drunk like most divorced cops. Divorce and booze. The two most common cop diseases. Well, one out of two wasn't bad. He snuggled into the cushions of the couch. He and the couch had become good friends after the divorce. He had not been able to sleep in their bed at first. It had seemed too empty. He was instantly asleep.

CHAPTER 10

Danny sat at his desk, making a list of things to do. He needed to get into Gina Morelli's house and check the environment. They needed to find out who her friends were and interview them. Gina's parents were due in today from New Jersey. When her parents arrived they would have to give permission to search Gina's belongings or Danny would have to get a search warrant and that was a pain in the ass. They would have to spend a lot of time dealing with an overworked and harried prosecutor and mounds of paperwork. The judge would have to sign the warrant. It was just easier, in these cases, if the family would allow the search so they could get to the business of finding Gina's killer or killers.

Danny called the Bomb and Arson office and learned Detective Fagin was due in the office in about an hour. He was out on a house fire and should return shortly. Danny always wondered how Fagin felt about his name. He always reminded Danny of the Fagin from Dickens story would look. Heavy, tousled hair and thick eyebrows that met in the middle.

The second team homicide sergeant wandered into the cubicle, dropping into a chair. He had the drained look of a man who had been up all night. Danny was surprised to see him. His usual M.O. was to let his squad handle things he would read about it in the morning when the reports were turned in. Danny nodded at him.

"Rough night?" Danny asked. The other sergeant nodded and rubbed his eyes.

"It never ceases to amaze me what scum people are," he replied. Danny wondered what people he was referring to.

"We got called out last night on a family dispute turned shitty. Road deputies arrived and the wife tells them her husband and her brother got into a fight and the brother stabbed the husband who ran off into the neighborhood. Because of the amount of blood on the porch, Patrol figured the husband was cut pretty bad. They started canvassing the neighborhood. A patrol deputy was flagged down by a guy three blocks over who told the deputy that there was a dead man in his yard. The husband had bled out. Anyway, we get called and as we are waiting for Crime Scene to show up, the wife comes wandering down the street. She stands there looking over the crime scene tape, at the poor old shit lying under the blanket and finally she looks at me and says, 'Is he dead?' No shit lady, he's lying under the blanket taking a snooze. Dumb ass! So she looks at him for a few minutes and then she says to me, 'Well, befo' ya'll takes him can I have the rent money out his pocket?' Fucking compassionate right? Fucking people are animals. Another beautiful morning in the Danger Zone." The sergeant laid his head back and closed his eyes.

The Danger Zone was the name given to the neighborhood by the cops who patrolled it. It was a typical ghetto area which could have been anywhere, a neighborhood of run down houses with junk and old broken down cars littering the yards. Crack cocaine dealers, ranging from age ten to thirty, hung out on nearly every corner after dark, plying their trade. Robberies and assaults were the rule rather than the exception.

Stabbings were commonplace and shootings occurred nearly every day. It was, to Danny, a place of despair, without hope. The only dreams the kids living there had was a quick buck to buy one day worth of imagined happiness. There were good people there too. The ones who worked long hours at low paying jobs just to put a meal on the table. Those were the ones the police rarely saw. They locked themselves in their houses at sundown, when street predators came out, to keep from becoming victims themselves. Danny felt for them. They reminded him of many people on the Reservation, where money was scarce and living was a day-to-day struggle.

The second squad sergeant rose and stretched. "Well, time to go make sure my people don't screw up this case."

As he left the room, Danny wondered how you could think that about your team. You had to have faith your team would do their jobs right every time. Danny had faith in his people. He hoped his team didn't feel about him the way the second squad felt about their sergeant. He tried hard to let the team function as a unit. He learned that in the service. Have faith and your team would show you brilliance. Treat them like idiots and they would prove you right, just because of your attitude. Danny wondered why so many police supervisors never learned that. Promotion didn't make you all knowing, even though some supervisors thought it did.

Danny tried Bomb and Arson again and learned Fagin had just arrived. Fagin picked up the phone.

"Morning, Sarge. How goes the battle?" Fagin asked.

"Same shit, different day," Danny chuckled. "Are you available to me for a few minutes?"

"Sure, come on down. I'm making coffee," Fagin answered.

"Be there shortly," Danny replied.

Telling the secretary where he was going, Danny walked through the lobby of headquarters, passing the large glass window of the executive staff conference room. He glanced in. The sheriff was gesturing wildly. Captain Barton was seated near the window and glanced at Danny as he passed. Barton rolled his eyes at him.

The office of the Bomb and Arson unit was on the bottom floor and had been assigned as an afterthought. When the building was erected, no one thought about the needs of certain special units like Bomb and Arson. Those special needs included the fact the Bomb and Arson unit stored explosive materials and needed things like extra thick walls and an explosion proof storage room. The Bomb and Arson detectives took great pleasure in pointing out their office was on the bottom floor and right next to the main support column. One small accident could level the building. They also laughed about the fact the personal office of the sheriff was right above them on the next floor. The Administration was currently scrambling to find an office for the unit as far away from the building as they could.

Fagin was stirring a steaming cup of coffee when Danny arrived at his cubicle. Fagin was wearing blue jeans and a black t-shirt with the Bomb Squad logo over the left breast pocket. There were black soot smudges on his pants leg and one over his right eye. He motioned Danny to a chair in the corner.

"Sorry about my dirt. Been a long night. House fires are a pain in the ass. Coffee?" Fagin said it all at once.

"No thanks. I came to find out about the Gina Morelli thing." Danny answered, thinking it had been a busy night for lots of detectives. The brass would be bitching about overtime again.

Fagin nodded, opening a drawer of his desk. He dropped a file folder in front of Danny. Danny opened it and saw the pictures had been developed. He glanced through them.

" As I told you at the scene, the fire started in the interior of the vehicle. The grass under the vehicle was burned only on the top, indicating the heat source was above ground level. If it had been a catalytic converter fire, the grass would have been burned all the way to the ground. Spontaneous ignition. The burn pattern in the interior shows the fire originated on the interior, rear drivers side floor. I took carpet samples to the lab and they show what I suspected. Looks like common gasoline was used as a propellant." Fagin put his feet up on the desk. Danny flipped through the photographs, stopping at the one of Gina Morelli's charred corpse. Poor kid. Nobody should die that way.

"The M.E. says she was alive when the fire started. Smoke in the lungs. "Danny handed the folder back.

"Shit," Fagin cursed, dropping his feet to the floor. "That sucks! What kind of asshole would kill a beautiful woman like that? She been positively I.D.'d yet?" Danny shook his head.

"Berkowitz has the dental records for comparison. Should know today sometime. Her parents are due in later today. We'll see."

"I hate that part," Fagin shook his head sadly. "Better you than me. What about the deputy boyfriend?"

Danny looked up sharply. Fagin had a sly look on his face. Wonder how he knew, Danny thought. Fagin answered the question for him.

"I overheard Richards call communications," he said. "Don't worry. I can keep it to myself. I would just hate to think it was one of us."

"We talked to him already. I don't think he was involved and I would appreciate it being kept under wraps. Hate to fuck the kid's career if he's clean." Danny watched Fagin's face for agreement.

"I don't talk to those I.A. assholes without a subpoena and a PBA attorney. A few years ago I spent so much time in there I had my own chair and coffee cup." Fagin grinned. "They tried to screw me too many times for me to run to them with anything but a pound of C-4."

"Thanks, Fagin." Danny rose to leave.

"My reports will be up to you by the end of the day," Fagin held out his hand.

"Whenever. No rush," Danny shook his hand. Fagin decided if he ever left The Bang Squad he would go to homicide and work for Quinn.

When Danny arrived at the office there was a message to call Dr. Berkowitz. He waited while the phone rang for an interminable time. Danny glanced again through the photographs Fagin gave him. He felt deep sadness for Gina Morelli and her family, the same sadness he felt in Vietnam when he learned that another G.I. was killed, even if he did not know the deceased. He remembered how he felt when he was told his parents had been killed. The sadness stayed with him for years. He knew what the Morelli family would go through. It was the reason his job was so important to him. He knew arresting the killer would never make up for the loss but believed it gave the family some closure. It also gave them some justice. He thought of Mrs. Conrad and what she must be going through too. The emptiness, the gap in your life, seemed to never close. The hope the dead would walk through the door at any minute and you would wake up from a bad dream. But it didn't happen and the emptiness grew worse. Those left behind would live in a void for a long time. They said time heals all wounds but they were wrong. The ache just eased but never really went away. It was a part of you forever. Danny sometimes thought of what would happen if he lost his wife. He dreaded the thought of being without her. He loved her so much, he feared ever being alone and without her. He decided to call her later.

There was a pink phone message slip from Berkowitz on Danny's desk when he returned to the office. Gina Morelli had been positively identified. Gina's parents were on a plane from New Jersey, Richards was waiting at the airport. Danny would now have to make the notification.

Danny closed his eyes. He thought better with his eyes closed. He thought about Gina Morelli and what Karen Gould had said. Gina wanted to be somebody, somebody with money. Karen Gould was somebody with money. Karen Gould was also somebody who used cocaine. Danny knew cocaine was a common party favor with the nouveau riche. It was often used at social gatherings, oftentimes laid out on the table like an hor d' eouvre for guests to partake at their whim. It was also very common at the bars and clubs frequented by the rich or wanna-be rich.

Gina Morelli was a wanna-be rich. Danny wondered what Gina Morelli did at Sawgrass Development Corporation. Arranged business meetings, entertained clients, Karen Gould said. Danny wondered what 'entertained' meant. Was Gina Morelli sleeping with the clients to keep them happy or giving them nose candy to make the deal go through? Danny had an idea and it was time to see where it went. Sometimes hunches paid off.

Danny sat in front of the desk and surveyed the plaques on the walls. There were commendations from three different sheriffs, numerous official letters with various government seals on them. DEA, FBI U.S. State Department. It was an impressive collection, what Danny called the Ego wall. Everybody had one.

The owner of the office was a cop legend for his ability to work drugs and get into places no one else could. He was given the name of 'the Ferret' for his uncanny ability to burrow into drug organizations and ferret out drug dealers. But that was years ago. Now he was the Deputy Director of the Organized Crime Bureau. Walt Arens held the official rank of Lieutenant but Danny had known him long enough to call him by his nickname. The Ferret bustled into the office and launched himself into his chair behind the desk.

" Danny. How the fuck are ya?" The Ferret asked, rocking back and forth in his chair.

The Ferret was what the troops referred to as a 'Cop's Cop.' He never forgot where he came from and still went on raids with the squads. He loved being a cop. The action was like a drug to him. He was profane and down to earth with the cops but Danny knew he could play politics with the best of them. That was how he survived so long at his present rank. The Ferret wore his light, straw color hair just long enough not to piss off the empty suits running the organization but be accepted by the dope cops working for him. His Fu Manchu mustache caused more than one empty suit to wonder if he was Director material but when the Ferret went into his administrator act, all doubt vanished. The Ferret had learned long ago how to play a part. The Ferret wore sharply pressed jeans and cowboy boots, Danny's kind of cop.

"Hey Ferret, how are ya?" Danny shook Ferret's outstretched hand.

" hat brings the best homicide cop in the county up to Fantasyland?" The Ferret asked.

"I need to run something by you. I know you guys do only Secret Squirrel stuff and it's top secret but I've got a puzzler homicide and it may have a dope connection." Danny watched Ferret's face for a reaction.

"Do what I can. Lay it on me." Ferret smiled.

"Have you ever heard of Sawgrass Development Corporation?" Danny asked. The Ferret thought for a second and shook his head.

" Doesn't ring any bells, Why?"

"I'm playing hunches here. I've got a dead woman who was working for the group. She died in her car under suspicious circumstances. Fire. According to her friend, Karen Gould, she set up business meetings and entertained clients for them. There are some rich people involved and Karen Gould uses coke. I really am fishing here."

"Gould? As in Edgar Jerome Gould the scumbag attorney?" Ferret interrupted.

"Wife of same. They have what they call an arrangement. He's in New England, she's playing in South Florida," Danny answered.

"Well, at least the asshole is out of our hair." Ferret laughed. "I tried to bag the fuck once for his drug connections. Never got lucky though."

"Anything you can do for me?" Danny asked hopefully.

"Well let's go ask the NERD." Ferret rose. Danny followed, wondering who the Nerd was. Ferret led the way to the next floor up and into a computer room.

"This is the NERD." Ferret said pointing to a computer terminal in the corner of the room. "Stands for Narcotics Enforcement Reference Database. All narcotics units operating locally enter their cases into it. That way we share information so nobody is investigating another undercover cop by mistake. Remember a few years ago when the city narc from one department was unknowingly investigating another cop from another department?"

Danny remembered the case had ended in a shoot-out between two narcs from different agencies. Luckily, they were both lousy shots and nobody got hit.

"NERD was created to keep that from happening again." Ferret said, sitting down at the terminal. He entered his password and typed in a query about Sawgrass Development Corporation. The terminal informed him that no reference was found. He entered a request for any agency with information to contact him.

"That's it for now. If I get any replies, I'll call you. Might take some time." Ferret offered his hand and Danny shook it.

"Thanks, Ferret. " Danny said and left.

Danny arrived back at his office to find Mike Richards had returned with Gina Morelli's parents. Richards introduced them and Danny told them how sorry he was for their loss. Her father nodded stonily. Guisseppe Morelli was a small, stout man with hair that had once been jet black but now was a dark gray with dark roots. Danny guessed his age at sixty or thereabouts. Guisseppe Morelli wore very thick glasses. His suit was worn and showed signs of being threadbare at the ends of the sleeves. Danny could tell he was a man used to hard work and had probably worked every day of his life, toiling long hours to provide for his family. Mrs. Morelli, whose first name was also Gina, was also short and squat. Her hair had long ago turned silver white. Her face showed the lines of worry that a mother who lived for her children would show. Her dress was faded and Danny surmised it was probably her only good outfit. Danny could see the sorrow in her eyes.

"Mr. and Mrs. Morelli, I'm very sorry to have to meet you under these circumstances," Danny began gently, "I know how this must hurt you and again I apologize. We have positively identified your daughter's body." Mrs. Morelli caught her breath and turned away quickly. Her husband stared at Danny.

"Sergeant Quinn. Why would anyone hurt my little Gina?" Mr. Morrelli asked, his voice breaking.

"I don't know sir, but I intend to find out and put them away," Danny replied, waiting for them to compose themselves.

"What can we do to help?" Guisseppe Morrelli asked finally.

"In order to continue the investigation I have some procedures I need to follow. First, I need to ask you some questions. Questions about Gina and her life here in Florida. Friends, acquaintances, work, anything you can tell me."

"We do not know very much about Gina's life here, Sergeant. We only know what little she has told us," Mr. Morrelli said.

"Can you tell me about her friends here? Did she ever tell you about them?" Danny asked.

"She never told us about her friends. She came home last Christmas and stayed for two weeks. We didn't discuss her friends."

"Mr. Morrelli, do you have any acquaintances or enemies who would want to hurt you through Gina? Anyone you owe money to, anything of that nature?" He hated to even have to ask the question.

"Sergeant," Guisseppe answered, an angry edge to his voice, "I have owned my store for forty years. I am a baker. I work hard every day of those forty years. I don't owe nobody nothing. I know what you're thinking. You think I'm Italian and from New Jersey so I must be mixed up with the mob. Well, I tell you here and now, you're wrong."

"That isn't what I meant sir. I'm sorry if you misunderstood my question. I just meant everybody has enemies. Did Gina ever tell you about any trouble with anyone here? Boyfriends maybe?"

"Gina was a good girl. She sent money home to us every month. Not that we needed anything from her. We are very comfortable in our lives. But Gina said it was the least she could do for us."

"Did Gina say where she got the money?" Danny asked.

"She worked. She was working for a big bank she said. That's all." Morrelli was becoming red-faced, trying to control his anger.

"Okay. The other thing we need to do is get your permission to go through Gina's things and her apartment. This will help us discover more about her life and what may have caused this situation. As Gina's only living relatives, that will require your signing a consent form to allow us to conduct a search without a warrant. If you don't mind."

Guisseppe Morelli signed the form with a grim face.

"Okay Sir. I think we're finished for now. Detective Richards will help you make the arrangements for taking Gina home."

After the Morrelli's left, Danny thought about what Guisseppe had told him. Not much. Gina sent money home. That was interesting. Danny thought about the parents. He could imagine them living in the same neighborhood all their lives, knowing all their neighbors. He could imagine the smell of fresh baked bread wafting through the open doors of Morrelli's bakery, causing the mouths of every kid in the area to water. Danny loved the smell of fresh baked bread.

Danny called the Crime Scene Unit offices and requested a team meet him at Gina Morelli's apartment in an hour.

Danny parked behind the green and white Crime Scene unit's van in front of the apartment building. The building was a renovated two story hotel facing the ocean. Many of the apartment buildings on this street had been built in the fifties, when structures were built solidly to withstand the winds of a major hurricane. Danny figured those newer ones would be scattered all the way to Naples in a big blow. The building was painted white and each apartment had a small balcony with an aqua blue railing. Danny looked across the street. He could see the ocean between the buildings on the other side.

Bicyclists and joggers passed on the sidewalk. A very tan, very shapely brunette wearing a fluorescent thong bikini skated past on rollerblades. Danny and the Crime Scene detectives turned to watch her progress. From the rear she appeared to be wearing nothing at all from the waist down. Danny could feel the strong, warm ocean breeze blowing from across the street.

Danny and the Crime Scene detectives passed under an aqua colored canopy and through an alcove into a main courtyard. The courtyard was lush with tropical plants and a small waterfall. The apartments lined the courtyard. White concrete stairways led up to the apartments on the second floor. In the alcove passageway were mailboxes mounted into the wall. Danny checked them for the name Morrelli to verify they were at the right place. He located the name and the apartment number 1J. He checked for a manager's apartment and was not surprised to find it listed as 1A.

The windows to the manager's apartment were open. Danny could hear a television playing from somewhere within. The door opened at the third knock. The manager was a woman in her mid fifties who appeared lost in the 1960's. She wore a shapeless, tie –dyed, garishly colored dress once popular with the Woodstock generation. Her bleached blond hair needed to be redone as some gray was sneaking through the dye job. She wore sandals on her feet and a long strand of love beads around her neck. Her skin was brown and leathery from too many hours in the Florida sun.

"Sheriffs Department," Danny said, holding up his badge. The woman looked at the badge with disdain, probably thinking he was a narc looking for her marijuana stash. "I'm Sergeant Quinn. Homicide. I'm investigating the death of Gina Morelli."

The woman's expression softened when she realized he wasn't here to confiscate her smoke. She glanced at the Crime Scene detectives suspiciously, probably now wondering if they were going to take her stash.

"Terrible thing that poor girl dying like that. She was really a groovy chick for a kid," The woman said finally. Lost WAY back in the sixties, Danny thought.

"Are you the manager?" Danny asked. "We need access to Miss Morrelli's apartment."

"Don't you need a warrant for that?"

"No. We have a consent from the parents." Danny held it up for her inspection. "Do you have a key?" The woman disappeared inside and returned with a key to Gina's apartment.

"Thanks."

Danny led the way to the apartment. He unlocked the apartment door, moving aside to let the Crime Scene Team enter first. One of the detectives opened a large black case and removed a laser scanner. He began to set it up in the hallway. Danny watched with fascination. The scanner could detect blood and fingerprints even if they had been painted over. The idea was to locate any evidence indicating Gina was killed in her apartment. If no evidence was found, it would corroborate the M.E.'s findings in court.

Danny walked around the apartment, realizing it was much larger than it appeared from the outside. The entry hall opened into a large living room. Two sliding glass doors led to the balcony. Off the hallway to the right was a large kitchen of sufficient size for the dinner table occupying it. The apartment was neat, indicating Gina Morrelli was a careful housekeeper. The apartment and its two bedrooms were furnished with fairly expensive furniture. Danny left the technicians to their work and went to question the manager.

Danny asked the manager if she had ever seen Gina with anyone at her apartment and she described two men, one of whom she had not seen in awhile. The description fit Deputy Spencer. The other was described as "A really cool cat. Very well dressed in expensive suits." The manager once heard Gina call him "Trevor". There was a knock on the door and Danny was summoned outside by a Crime Scene detective.

"Sarge. You better come see this." The detective said, leading the way back to Gina's apartment. In the bedroom, he opened a cabinet and slid open a hidden compartment. Money was stacked in the compartment. Lying on top was a sandwich bag of white powder. The money was stacked in hundred dollar bills. "Looks like about fifty, sixty grand."

Danny felt his heart sink. He was glad Gina's parents weren't there. He decided not to tell them. He nodded to the detective and watched him place the money and cocaine in an evidence bag. The Crime Scene was almost finished and one of the detectives handed him an evidence bag containing Gina's address book and personal papers. It also contained her checkbook, bankbook, and everything else that would give Danny an insight into Gina Morrelli's life. Danny left the apartment and on his way to his car he thanked the manager for her help.

Danny sat at his computer terminal and punched up the DATA TRACK system. He entered the State Department of Commerce area, entering the name, Sawgrass Development Corporation. When the computer listed the corporation history, Danny requested the Corporate officer's list. He never ceased to be amazed how easy it was to snoop into people's lives with the computer. With basic information, one could find credit card account numbers, credit histories, and almost any other personal information. The computer enhanced the abilities of an investigator a million fold. In the old days, it would take weeks of investigating to find the same information that took seconds on a computer terminal. Danny wasn't sure he liked the fact all that information was there.

The computer listed the corporate officers of Sawgrass Development Corporation and the first name to appear was one Trevor Daniels, the same name the landlord heard Gina Morelli call her unknown visitor.

Karen Gould said Gina worked for Sawgrass. Maybe this guy Trevor was a casual acquaintance from the office. Or maybe he was something more. Danny punched up the search mode and entered Daniel's name. Trevor Daniels was also President of First Bank of South Florida. Danny realized he had heard the bank's name recently. He pulled out the file on Officer Gus Conrad's murder. The same bank. The same Goddamn bank the phony account in Conrad's name belonged to! They had to be connected. Two dead bodies, both connected to the same bank?

Okay, take a breath. Don't jump to conclusions. The bank was remotely connected. First Bank was one of the largest in the area. It might be a coincidence. There were probably thousands of people in South Florida connected to First Bank. Danny's gut told him otherwise. Conrad's son is busted with drugs. Gina Morelli is hooked into the drug trade somehow and both are connected to First Bank? Worth digging further though. Might be worth another visit to Gus Junior. A less friendly visit.

Danny picked up Gina Morelli's address book and thumbed through it. Karen Gould was in there. Spencer too. He flipped to the D's. Trevor Daniels was there and numerous other names.

CHAPTER 11

The U.S. Customs service headquarters in Miami had the most sophisticated radar system in the southern United States. The radar system constantly monitored the coast of South America and the area of Colombia. The second radar kept a watchful eye on the Caribbean including Cuba, Haiti, and the Dominican Republic. The operator could switch from any area by the punch of a button. The radar screens were computer-controlled and the operator could also zoom into any specific area.

Glenn Mendoza had been monitoring the radar for three hours and his eyes were tired. He leaned back in his chair and sipped his coffee. The novel he was reading was getting very boring. It started well but the author was getting into the technical aspects of forensic investigation and it was tedious, although it wasn't bad for the first novel written by a former cop. Mendoza had the radar on automatic and the coast of South America was being scanned continuously. Suddenly, the warning tone beeped and jolted Mendoza out of his book. He checked the radar monitor and saw a blip crossing the coast headed into the Caribbean, the usual route for drug planes. This one needed to be checked visually. The computer told him the plane was a slow mover, probably prop driven. The size told him it was probably a DC-3. It fit the profile of a drug plane, large enough to carry a sizable load of drugs and the same configuration of many transport planes used by companies flying freight to Miami and the other Caribbean countries. The dope runners used these planes in hopes that Customs would discount them, thinking they were a legitimate transport.

Mendoza picked up the phone and called his on duty supervisor. The supervisor would determine if the radar contact justified sending an intercept and identify the transport. The system seemed stupid to Mendoza but since it cost almost three hundred dollars per hour to fly the intercept, the government wanted to make sure the money was being well spent. Only about ten percent of radar contacts justified sending an intercept. Mendoza figured a whole lot of drugs made it through, due to cost effective management.

The supervisor listened carefully as Mendoza described the plane's flight configuration. The altitude was a little low for a legitimate transport and not many transports flew at three in the morning. The supervisor agreed it was worth checking out and authorized the intercept. I already knew that, Mendoza thought.

Mendoza dialed the crew quarters and Agent Mike Shotworth answered the phone with a sleep laden voice. Mendoza explained the situation and Shotworth said he would be right there. The U.S. Customs Air Wing kept an intercept crew on site and on standby twenty-four hours a day. Shotworth was Pilot In Charge of the intercept crew tonight. Shotworth entered the radar room five minutes later, dressed in a rumpled flight suit that looked as if it had been slept in. Shotworth slept in his flight suit to be ready if needed.

"What's it look like?" Shotworth asked, peering at the radar screen.

"Slow mover. DC-3 most likely. Popped up as he crossed the coastline. Should be turning eastbound soon. Headed toward Haiti or the Dominican Republic," the operator replied, looking at Shotworth over his shoulder. Shotworth nodded and headed out the door toward the tarmac.

The U.S. Customs Citation jet was already warmed up on the tarmac. The co-pilot, Pat Garvey, had already done the preflight check and warmed up the engines. The ground crew chief waited for Shotworth to climb in and then shut and locked the door. Shotworth eased into the pilot's seat and grinned at Garvey.

"Ready to go for a ride?" Shotworth asked, slipping the headset over his ears.

"Oh, do we have to?" Garvey pretended to whine. Both pilots laughed. They loved this job.

Shotworth flew jets in Vietnam, starting in the A6 Intruder flying bombing missions from an air craft carrier off the coast. He transferred to fighters when the Navy needed pilots to fly missions when too many pilots had been shot out of the sky. Actually, Shotworth had volunteered because he loved the action and had become bored with flying into the night and dropping bombs then going home, never knowing if he was successful. He had been successful in air-to-air combat even after being shot down twice and surviving, being wounded both times. His right thigh still contained a metal plate which caused him to walk with a slight limp.

Shotworth taxied the Citation toward the runway and advised the control tower of their request for takeoff. The tower acknowledged their permission. U. S. Customs missions had first priority and other flights would be forced to wait, if there had been any other flights at this time of the morning. Shotworth pushed the throttles forward and the jet raced toward the sky, lifting smoothly into the night. Shotworth climbed the aircraft quickly and leveled off at forty thousand feet, turning southwest. Garvey called the Customs controller for an uplink to the main radar. The Customs radar was linked to a military satellite orbiting high above the earth. Called the Downward Looking Tracking Satellite, the satellite watched the northern areas of South America looking for potential narcotics flights. The satellite could be slaved to the onboard radar on the Citation to direct the intercepting jet right to the target. Garvey slaved the radar to the satellite and watched as the target aircraft continued its easterly trek. He gave Shotworth the current location. Shotworth nodded and continued to fly southwest. He had to fly southwest around the western tip of Cuba, since Castro's government would not allow flights to violate Cuban airspace. Castro had even sent his MIG's when a Customs flight wandered too far east into Cuba's territorial boundaries. Garvey plotted a course that would take them around the western tip of Cuba, outside the no-fly zone and then east to intercept the target from behind. Customs procedures dictated they ease up behind the target and get as close as possible, to identify the plane and follow it to it's destination. They would then call in the BAT teams. The BAT teams would attempt to intercept the flight as it landed and leap from their Blackhawk helicopters to make the arrest. Hopefully. Shotworth and Garvey settled down for the flight that would take them approximately an hour. At over 300 miles an hour, the Citation would have no problem overtaking the slow mover.

Fifty miles behind the slow mover, Shotworth began his descent. He eased the citation onto the same heading as the target and allowed the jet to descend to the same altitude. Garvey counted out the distance between the two planes as they crept in behind. Three miles behind the target, Shotworth slipped his night vision goggles over his eyes. He squinted into the dark, trying to make out the outline of the DC-3. The target was running without lights and Shotworth shut down their safety beacons and blacked out the jet.

They were in what the Customs pilots called the SLOT, the area between Haiti and Cuba gave them a direct route into the Bahamas. The Bahamas were a common destination for drug planes which landed in the remote out Islands and off loaded the drugs onto boats for the trip into

South Florida. Sometimes, the drug planes landed on the main Islands where the local law had been paid to protect drug shipments.

"Three miles and closing," Garvey informed Shotworth. Shotworth eased back the throttles to keep from overshooting the target. He squinted into the night and finally could make out the shape of a DC-3 looming ahead. Shotworth eased closer and just below. He was sure they had not been spotted yet. He eased closer to allow them to read the numbers on the other plane. Shotworth and Garvey strained to make out the numbers on the target. Not yet. Shit! Not yet. Just a little closer. The DC-3 was so close it seemed to fill the windshield. Shotworth struggled to control the Citation, which was not designed to fly this slow. He eased back a little more on the throttles, courting disaster should the jet lose too much airspeed and begin to stall. It was a long swim home.

Suddenly, the DC-3 banked sharply to the west and picked up speed. Shotworth cursed as he fought to veer to the right to avoid a midair collision. He punched the throttle forward to pick up airspeed to avoid a stall. The airspeed indicator screamed at them until the jet leveled off at a speed sufficient to stay in the air. Garvey watched the DLTS radar and muttered under his breath.

"He's running toward Cuban airspace. Get on him." Garvey hissed. Shotworth banked in a long left turn to swing back around and pursue the target. The planes would be in Cuban airspace in ten minutes. Shotworth leveled off and raced after it. This bastard almost knocked them out of the air. He wasn't going to get away.

Garvey called the Customs air controller and informed him of the near miss. The controller replied he was glad to hear from them. On his radar it looked like they had collided.

"Godammit!" Shotworth cursed. The DC-3 had entered Cuban airspace and was safe for now. He informed the Customs air controller they were going to orbit north of Cuba and see if it came out on the other side.

"Negative. Come on home. Our screen shows the target is on the ground or too low to read on DLTS. Better luck next time guys. Did you happen to get any numbers?"

"Negative," Shotworth answered. "We're heading home." Shotworth looked at Garvey who gave him a grim smile.

"I'd give my left arm to have just one missile for assholes like that," Garvey muttered. Shotworth nodded and turned the Citation towards Miami. Shotworth wished he was still flying his fighter. He would have loved to shoot a Sidewinder missile up the slow mover's ass. Well, maybe the Cuban Air Force would flame the son of a bitch and send him to the ocean in a ball of fire. Shotworth doubted it. Some fuck in Cuba was probably getting paid big bucks to let the doper land there.

Ricky Madeira paced around the motel room. He glanced at the phone every few minutes. Jose knew better than to disturb Ricky when he was like this. He could explode any second. Jose sat quietly.

"Why haven't they called yet?" Ricky snarled at the room. "If they were banged by Customs, they should have called by now. Right?" Jose nodded and was silent. Ricky continued to pace angrily. Suddenly, the phone rang and Ricky grabbed it up.

"Yes?" He snapped. He listened for a few seconds and Jose could see his expression turn from anger to aggravation. "Okay. First thing in the morning then?" Ricky nodded and slammed down the phone. He turned to face Jose. "Customs picked them up en-route. They were able to lose the Citation and landed at the emergency point. Colonel Del Fuego was waiting and is taking care of them. The pilot doesn't think the Citation got their numbers. They will leave before first light. Tell the boat captains of the delay and tell them to be ready tomorrow night. Dammit! This will make a day behind. Well, it can't be helped." Spent, Ricky dropped into a chair as Jose rose to leave.

" You will tell Trevor?" Jose asked. Ricky nodded in disgust.

Jose walked quickly along the docks. The air was warm and damp but a mild breeze blew off the water. The water lapped against the hulls of fishing boats tied at the docks. The lights at the ends of each dock glittered on the water and Jose took a deep breath of salt air, tainted with a faint fish smell. Jose loved the docks and he loved the Islands. He sometimes wished Ricky would put him in charge at the Island so he could be near the boats all the time. It gave him a feeling of freedom and contentment. A burst of laughter, from a yacht docked at the end of a long pier, drifted across the water. He could hear music from the yacht and decided the tourists on the yacht were having a party. He wished for a moment that he could be part of that party, with beautiful, slinky women that took his breath away with their graceful bodies, moving under snug-fitting, expensive dresses. Someday, Jose would be done with this business and he would live in these Caribbean Islands forever on a big boat and fish and cavort with beautiful women too. Someday.

Jose turned at the end of the dock, away from the fancy yachts and fishing boats. He walked toward a pier cloaked in darkness, the only lights the ones that glowed from the windows of the four fishing boats docked there. Jose nodded at the Bahamian police officer standing guard at the end of the pier. The cop nodded back. Jose pushed open a gate at the base of the pier and unconsciously shifted the gun on his hip under his coat. A sign on the gate read BAHAMIAN CUSTOMS AUTHORIZED ADMITTANCE ONLY.

Jose's footsteps echoed on the wooden planks of the dock as he approached the first fishing boat. A shadow materialized in the stern of the boat and Jose could see the small, deadly looking submachine gun hanging from the man's shoulder. Jose raised his hand in greeting and called out to the guard.

"Es Me. Jose.!" The guard disappeared back into the shadows. Jose stepped down onto the deck of the boat and opened the cabin door. He could smell fresh paint and knew the name on the stern of the boat had been repainted.

"Buenos noches mi Capitan," Jose nodded at the man who sat in the boat's cabin, sipping from a long-necked beer bottle. The man was small and dark with a gray beard. He wore a t-shirt with a leaping Marlin on the front, a baseball cap perched on his head, tilted to the rear. The captain nodded at Jose and handed him a beer. Jose sat on a folding deck chair and took a long drink from the beer bottle. The cold, slightly bitter liquid slithered down his throat.

"Problems?" The boat captain asked.

"Customs chased the plane and they were forced to land at our emergency location in Cuba. Colonel Del Fuego is assisting them. They will leave before first light. We will let them land and leave the plane sit at the airport as usual for the day, in case there are curious eyes. The transfer will be tomorrow night, you can leave the next morning. I am sorry for the delay but it can't be helped. Ricky also sends his apologies."

The boat captain shrugged. "Whatever is necessary. The moon will remain full for three more days and we will have enough light to cross. The weather should not be a problem."

"Bueno. Gracias Para la Cerveza." Jose stepped out of the cabin and nearly fell into the large hole cut in the deck of the boat. He caught himself on the side rail and heard the guard chuckle softly in the dark. "Maricon," Jose snarled and the guard was silent again. He walked gingerly around the hole and found his way to the dock. Tomorrow night the hole in the deck would be packed with enough cocaine to keep them rich for awhile. Even the Pendejo guard who had laughed.

Ricky tied his hair into a ponytail and admired himself in the mirror. Bueno, he thought. He straightened the silk shirt and turned his back to the mirror. He checked to be sure the knife in the small of his back was invisible. Ricky had once tried to go without the knife and felt so naked he returned to retrieve it. He locked the door to the motel room and headed toward the lounge. He could hear the music as he opened the door and a wave of cigarette smoke mixed with the smell of stale beer hit him in the face.

Ricky picked his way among the men and women who clustered around the bar and headed to the patio where he could see Trevor and his group seated at round tables. Three women hovered around the men and one was stroking Trevor's hair. Ricky pushed open the glass doors to the patio and Trevor waved. Ricky beckoned to Trevor and stepped off of the patio to the beach. Trevor followed.

"There is a slight problem," Ricky said as Trevor sipped a brightly colored drink. Trevor frowned and lowered the glass.

"What kind of problem?" Trevor frowned at him. Ricky explained about the Customs incident and that the plane had been forced to land in Cuba. He continued that it would put them a day behind schedule but the boat captains assured him it was not a major obstacle.

"Shit. That means Del Fuego will want a bonus. That bastard always wants more money when this kind of thing happens. Well, I guess that's why we pay him. Better than losing the whole load. The boat captains don't have a problem with the delay?" Ricky shook his head.

"Okay. Listen, something else I want to discuss with you. We have been talking and have decided the profit margin needs to be increased." Ricky opened his mouth to protest and Trevor held up his hand. "I know what you said about the risks. Running the product into Florida is risky enough. Andre's people are very useful, but shit Ricky, if we had some of the profit from the crack on the street we would have ten times what we have now. Andre has the connections with the people we need. Do you realize one pound of coke makes about one thousand rocks? The rocks sell for twenty to fifty bucks on the street. That would increase our profits that much. Selling the powder is fine but we could make so much more. Even if we provided the powder and took just a percentage of the street profits we would be much better off." Trevor waited for an answer.

"You sound like a typical banker. We make more than enough. More than you or your friends could ever imagine. I don't think this is a good idea." Ricky looked Trevor in the eye when he said it.

"Look. It gets more expensive every day to run this deal. Between the cost of the boats, paying those Cuban assholes to provide safe haven, the plane and the production costs, we need to increase the profits. The overhead is killing us. We've discussed it at length. This guy Hammond Andre's been dealing with. He seems to have a good network, Hell, he just bought fifteen keys. We need to bring him in. He could increase his profits and we could make a lot off of the top. Talk to Andre and see if he thinks Hammond can be trusted. We'll make him an offer he can't pass up. Okay?"

"Whatever you think is best." Ricky shrugged. He didn't like it. Ricky didn't trust new faces. He trusted Andre Baptiste. He didn't know about this guy Hammond. He would make sure Andre had checked him out.

"Good." Trevor patted him on the shoulder, "C'mon let's have some fun. This blond wants to play." He steered Ricky back towards the tables.

Ricky returned to the bar and ordered a beer. He had a lot on his mind. He was always nervous in the middle of a shipment. He imagined everyone was looking at him and knew what he was up to. He looked for anyone who seemed to be watching him or appeared to have too much interest in him or his group. The others could party and have a good time but it was his responsibility to protect the product. Ricky noticed a large blond man sitting at the bar looking at Trevor and his friends. The man seemed to be soaking up every move they made. He sipped a beer and turned every few minutes to watch the group at Trevor's table. Ricky caught Jose's eye across the bar and pointed at the blond man with his chin. The move was imperceptible to anyone else but Jose knew exactly what it meant.

The blond man left the bar stool and walked away from the bar, headed toward the row of rooms. Jose pushed away from the pole he was leaning on and followed at a safe distance. He scanned the route ahead and picked his spot. They were headed for a dark area between the hotel rooms and the beach. Jose's pulse quickened and he closed the distance behind the blond man. Jose could feel the adrenaline pumping through his body . His breath quickened. He could feel his muscles tense. He moved closer as they continued toward the dark. The blond man staggered slightly and Jose smiled to himself. An easy mark. Jose focused on the area at the base of the man's skull as he closed the gap. He caught up with the blond as they reached the dark area. Jose moved silently and struck the man quickly with the edge of his hand at the base of the skull. He caught the blond as he sagged toward the ground. Jose laid him down near the bushes and quickly but expertly searched the man's pockets and waistband. Jose slipped a wallet from the man's pocket and rifled through it. He found a driver's license from Wisconsin and a picture of the blond man with a woman and three smiling children. They were standing in front of a motorboat, a lake in the background. Jose checked the credit cards and money, pocketing both to make the attack look like a mugging. Jose found a pack of business cards with the same name as the driver's license. The cards were for a real estate office. Jose rose quickly and tossed the wallet into the bushes. When the man awoke, if he bothered to call the police, he would be discounted as just another tourist who should have used travelers cheques. Jose slipped the credit cards in a trash can as he passed. The money would buy him a few cervezas at the bar. Jose slipped back to his place by the pole. Ricky glanced at Jose and Jose shook his head. Not a cop the look said. Ricky nodded back and turned back to Trevor, who was telling a sexual joke and snuggling a blond woman.

Ricky was just finishing his breakfast when Jose slid into a chair beside him. Jose smiled at his boss who looked like he had drunk a little too much last night. Jose informed him the plane had arrived. Ricky pushed his plate away and they left the restaurant together. Once outside, Ricky slipped on a pair of sunglasses as the sunlight hit him full in the face. The sun made his headache worse.

The plane rested at the end of a row of warehouses and was being unloaded as they arrived. Ricky approached the Bahamian Customs officer who stood in the shade of the warehouse and watched the unloading. Ricky slipped him a pack of currency and the Customs officer tucked it expertly into his pocket with a practiced move. The Customs officer smiled at Ricky, his white teeth contrasting with the darkness of his skin. The man was so dark he appeared to be a deep indigo blue color. His starched and pressed uniform was stuck to his back with sweat. Ricky stood beside him in the shade and felt his headache get worse. His head pounded.

"Nice morning, don't you agree, Inspector?" Ricky said offhandedly to the Customs officer.

"Ya, Mon. And getting better all the time," The Customs officer replied, patting the money in his pocket. Ricky chuckled.

"Looks like a bit of coffee," The Customs officer smiled, nodding at the boxes being unloaded from the plane.

"Business is very good in the plantations," Ricky laughed. Two men carefully unloaded the boxes from the rear of the plane. One was shirtless, his skin glistening with sweat. Each box was stamped with CAFE DE COLOMBIA. The boxes were loaded into the back of a large container truck. When the truck was loaded the men shut the doors and climbed into the front. The Customs officer leaped into his open jeep and started the engine. Ricky and Jose joined him in the jeep and the convoy wound toward the boat docks.

When they arrived at the docks, Ricky slipped the Bahamian officer guarding the gate another pack of money. It also disappeared into the guard's pocket. The boxes were quickly unloaded onto the docks near the four fishing boats. They would remain there until darkness.

"Ride back to the hotel Mon?" The Customs officer asked Ricky. He shook his head. He would walk back to the hotel with Jose. They needed to discuss some more arrangements.

Trevor Daniels settled his duffel bag in the cabin of the fishing boat and popped open a beer. The cold liquid slid down his throat and cooled his stomach. He glanced at the other members of The Sawgrass Development Corporation as they settled their gear on the other boats. The sun was already warm in the early morning. A soft balmy breeze drifted across the bay and cooled him momentarily. It was a good day for fishing. He had taken his seasickness pills early this time. The last trip he had chummed over the side of the boat for three hours until his empty stomach retched. Afterwards, he had fallen into a deep exhausted sleep in the cabin and awakened to a foul taste in his mouth and sore stomach muscles. He assumed it was similar to childbirth, only less severe.

The blond woman bounced down the pier and hopped onto the deck of the boat, her breasts jiggling when she landed. She flashed him a bright white smile that contrasted with her tan. The fluorescent thong bikini seemed to glow against her skin. Trevor thought it was going to be a great trip. If they didn't catch any fish it wouldn't really matter. The cocaine concealed under the deck would make it a good trip no matter what.

The captain and the mate busied themselves arranging fishing poles in the rod holders along the edge of the deck. Large coolers of bait were stowed along the edges of the gunwales to help conceal the new seams along the deck. A faint smell of fresh fiberglass drifted into Trevor's nostrils. If anyone stopped them on the trip, a patch had been painted on the bow to explain the smell. If Customs decided to check out the boats they would seem like another rich fishing charter returning from the Islands. Fillets of fresh fish were stored in the refrigerator in the cabin as proof they had been successful on the trip. The boats would leave at two hour intervals to avoid suspicion. Each member of the group would identify themselves by their respective professions so if more than one boat were stopped there would seem to be no connection between them. Three hundred kilos of cocaine was worth the precaution.

CHAPTER 12

The blond man lay on his back and stroked the wispy blond mustache. He carefully watched the brunette through the open bathroom door. She slid the bra straps off her shoulders and smiled at him. He crooked one finger at her and she strode toward him with conspiratorial look. She knelt at his knees and looked up at him. She grinned evilly. She took him in her hand and began to stroke him erect. He sighed and arched his back. She stroked him until he was hard and then slid her mouth over him. He gritted his teeth and moaned. She moved up and down, causing his breath to quicken. He felt himself start to sweat. He began to writhe on the bed but she kept him in place with her ministrations. He felt as if his head would explode. She slid her body upwards on him until they were face to face. Suddenly, she thrust herself on him. She began to rock herself up and down upon him. He arched his back farther and began to pant, matching her thrusts. The pace began to quicken and he could feel a drop of sweat tumble across his forehead and slip into his ear. They continued to rock together, faster and faster. She gritted her teeth and began to moan in rhythm with their movements. He felt himself begin to climax and grabbed her hips, pulling her down on him harder and harder. She gave a little whimper as he climaxed with her. He held her tight against him until both their spasms stopped. She suddenly collapsed on his chest with a sigh and he wrapped his arms around her and held her close to him. He could feel her heart pounding in her chest in unison with his. He stroked her hair. She raised up and looked into his eyes.

"Dammit you're too good. I can't get enough," She smiled at him. He shrugged his shoulders.

"Just happy to please, baby," he replied. She rolled off of him and stretched out beside him. She wiped the sweat from her brow. He rolled over to face her and stroked her stomach.

"What time do you have to be back?" He asked.

"In about forty minutes." She replied, raising her watch in front of her face. "I better hurry. You know how the city is about taking too much time for lunch." Mrs. Richard "Dick" Stephens rose and headed for the bathroom to fix her makeup. As Supervisor of Human Resources for the city, she could be a little late returning from lunch. But the City Manager had been on her ass lately for spending too much time away from the office. These lunch time rendezvous were affecting her job and she had to be careful. Although she liked the game, she didn't want to lose her secure life with her husband. She knew he was screwing around on her but she had been able to keep him from discovering her secret. She didn't want to have to survive on a city supervisor's salary. The city pension her husband was collecting on top of the salary from the new position with the Sheriff's Office was very handy. She knew she could keep the affair secret if she was careful. She finished dressing and opened the bathroom door. He was sitting on the bed, wearing only a pair of blue jeans, smoking a cigarette. He blew smoke at her and she laughed. She bent down and kissed him. She turned and let herself out the front door.

After she left, Sergeant Glen Johannsen finished dressing and made a few phone calls. So far he had found nothing to indicate Moses Hammond was anything but a dope dealer. He dialed the cell phone number. Ricky Madeira answered on the second ring.

"Yes." Ricky waited.

"It's me. That guy Hammond appears legit. No one seems to know anything about him, at least nothing to indicate he's a narc. Of course, I can't possibly know every narc from every agency," Johannsen said.

"Good. We will be doing business with him in the future. Thank you for the assistance. The boats will begin arriving around dark. Make sure there are no problems," Ricky replied.

"I'll take care of it." Johannsen hung up.

Johannsen left the house and got into his city issued Corvette. It had been confiscated from a dope dealer in Naples and swapped with the city in exchange for a similar vehicle. The Corvette had become known as an undercover car and the police in Naples had needed a new vehicle. Johannsen had been only too happy to oblige. He loved Corvettes and had one of his own in the garage. He preferred to use the city car because the city paid for the gas.

He decided to cruise the beach and check out the bikini's for awhile. Maybe he could find a new friend to play with. After a year, Mrs. Stephens was getting boring even though he had three other women he was seeing. Johannsen knew he had a voracious appetite and he liked it that way. Even in high school he had dropped off his date from the prom and gone to a local hangout, found a willing partner and spent the rest of the night in a motel room with her. Besides, it was his day off and he had some time to kill before he had to meet the boats.

The buildings of downtown loomed over the marina as dusk began to fall. The lights in the high rises on the beach to the east were coming on as the residents settled in for the night. Johannsen sat in the Corvette and smoked another Marlboro. The ground on the driver's side of the Corvette was littered with cigarette butts. He had been waiting for almost two hours. Four trips around the parking lot had satisfied him there were no cops or Customs agents trolling for likely-looking dope boats arriving at the marina. Johannsen could hear the hum of traffic passing over the bridge on the south side of the marina.

The cell phone on the console rang and he pushed the talk button. Ricky Madeira's voice came in clear and Johannsen nodded. Fifteen minutes and the boats would be in. They would sit for two days at the marina, being watched for any sign of interest. If nothing happened, they would be moved one by one to another location and the false decks removed, allowing access to the cargo underneath. Piece of cake. Johannsen added his cigarette butt to the pile beside the car. Soon he could go home and sleep. She had worn him out today.

CHAPTER 13

D anny parked in front of the two story apartment building and surveyed the parking lot. The cars in the lot were what one would expect in this place. It was a typical, old motel, one block from the beach that had been converted into apartments. There were a few Camaros, one open Jeep, an older model van and two older sports cars. The tenants couldn't be more than thirty. There were probably two or three strippers living here, one or two bartenders and assorted other night shift workers, unmarried and living from day- to-day. They wanted to live near the beach and the condos but this was all they could afford. Danny figured most of the apartments were one bedroom or studio type. Most of these old motels were.

Danny knocked on apartment three and waited. A voice inside said to wait a minute. Seconds later the door was opened by a redhead who held her robe closed at the neck. Her hair was tousled and she still had the look of sleep in her eyes. Danny held up his badge and identified himself. Seemed like he was always holding up his badge to somebody. He thought maybe a big sign hung around his neck would be easier.

"Chrissy Mitchell?" Danny asked and the redhead nodded. "Sergeant Quinn, Homicide. I need to ask you a few questions about Gina Morelli." Danny realized he had said that phrase so many times it was starting to sound like his name was Quinn-homicide.

The redhead nodded and opened the door to let him in. She tied the robe around her waist. He entered and she led him to a small living room which looked like it was furnished from swap meets and second hand stores. He noticed a door to a bedroom and figured she could afford the one bedroom instead of the studio but not much was left to buy furniture. There were a number of ashtrays overflowing on tables and the room had a faint smell of stale beer and cigarette smoke. The trash can in the kitchen was piled with empty bottles. Chrissy Mitchell pointed Danny to a chair at the small dining room table and she sat across from him. The bedroom door opened and a long-haired male appeared, trying to rub sleep from his eyes. He had tattoos on both sides of his chest and one on his forearm. A long scar ran from his right shoulder to his left hip.

"What's the matter, babe?" The tattooed man yawned.

"Nothin'. Go back to bed," she snapped at him. He nodded and disappeared behind the bedroom door.

"So how did you find me and what about Gina?" Chrissy asked, resting her chin in her palm and looking Danny squarely in the eye. It was almost a challenge.

"Gina's dead." Danny watched for the surprise to settle in her eyes. The challenge was gone now.

"Fuck! How did she die?" Chrissy asked.

"She was found dead in her car out in the Everglades. We don't know if it was an accident or not yet," Danny lied. He knew it was no accident. "I found your name and number in Gina's address book. How did you know Gina?"

"I'm an entertainer, and I knew some of Gina's business associates. We partied together sometimes." Danny knew that meant Chrissy Mitchell was a stripper in one of the local clubs and she slept with men for money. Strippers never said they were strippers, they always referred to themselves as "entertainers" and Danny knew many of them prostituted themselves on the side. At least the ones in the lower class clubs did. The girls in higher class clubs made somewhere around four or five hundred dollars a night and didn't need to sleep around. Although some of them did because they liked to. Chrissy had the look of a dancer in a lower class club. The women in the higher class clubs had bodies which were more the result of modern technology than the result of nature. They could afford it and the improvements helped them earn more. Chrissy didn't look like technology had found her yet.

"Tell me about Gina and her associates." Danny pushed.

"Look, dude, she came into the club a few times with some guys with substantial cash. They threw lots of money around at the girls. Gina would set up some parties with them for us. These guys liked some kinky shit, Ya' know. They could have had some of the higher class girls with all those bucks but they liked to play some strange games. I guess the girls in my club were more agreeable. So was I." She tucked her feet under her.

"What kinds of games?" Danny approached the question carefully.

"Fuck you man. I tell you and we all get busted for hookin.'"

"Look Chrissy. We're not talking about your sex fun. I am investigating a possible homicide here. I could give a damn less about your side jobs. You are hindering a murder investigation here. And that I will bust your ass for. Now, talk to me," Danny said coldly.

"You sure you won't set vice on us?" she asked. Danny nodded patiently.

"Okay. We would go with them out to a place on the alley. Some kind of hunting camp and we would do things. Ya' know like bondage, threesomes, Anywhere in any way. That kind of thing."

"And Gina would set this up?"

"Well, she would call me and say the boys wanted to party and when to be there and we would go. Gina wasn't like pimping us or anything. I kind of got the feeling she had to do this stuff for these guys. Kind of like they were her bosses or something. Gina was nice too. She had class. I got the feeling she was getting ready to make a break from these guys. "

"What about drugs. Cocaine?" Danny asked.

"Oh yeah. These guys had some major blow. I don't do blow much, but some of the other girls did."

"Was Gina doing blow?" Danny switched his speech patterns and terminology to match hers, an old interrogation trick.

"Naw. Gina didn't do blow much. Only one time I saw her do it."

"I thought you said Gina wasn't involved in these parties," Danny replied.

"No. She wasn't involved in these parties. See, me and her became friends sort of. We hung out a few times and she was never interested in doing blow. She kind of like set up the get-togethers and we got to know each other. She was cool."

"Were these always the same guys?"

"No, some of them were from out of town. Kind of like visiting clients that wanted a good time while they were away from the wife and kiddies."

"What about the regulars?"

"Well, let's see. There was a blond guy named Trevor. Rich dude. Lots of big bills. And Rich something. And a dude named Jeff. They were the main ones. Like I said, the rest were like out of town guests. "

"Do you know where this place is you went?" Danny hoped she did.

"I dunno. Out on the Alley. In The Everglades someplace. It was dark as hell driving back at night. We would just drive west until we saw the sign."

"What sign?"

" The sign on the gate. Sawgrass Camp."

Danny drove past the sign and glanced into the property. The yard was empty. He parked about one hundred yards from the gate and strolled back slowly, listening to the birds. He strained his ears to hear any sounds from the area of the camp. Nothing. He didn't know if there was a caretaker on the property or not. He stopped at the gate and leaned on the top rail. He scanned the area and saw no sign of life. The house stood mute in the hot sun. He glanced up and watched a large blue heron soar overhead, its long neck and beak stretched out in front. He watched it soar over the road and land next to the canal across the road. The sawgrass swayed in a gentle breeze. An alligator was stretched out on the bank of the canal sunning itself. Danny felt a calm wash over him. He loved it out here, but forced himself to focus. He didn't know what he would find on the other side of that gate.

Danny hoisted himself over the gate and circled to the right along the tree line. He watched the windows for any movement. He followed the tree line to the back of the clearing where it met a muddy track leading into the heavy growth. He kept to the side of the track to keep from stepping into the worn ruts caused by the tires of four wheel drive vehicle and swamp buggies. The ruts were filled with water. He scanned the ground for snakes.

Three hundred yards further, the track opened into a large clearing. To the right was a pond, filled with sawgrass. In the center of the clearing was a gravel strip similar to a road. An airstrip, Danny guessed. Somebody went to a lot of trouble to build an airstrip back here. Danny estimated the airstrip to be three to four thousand feet long. Long enough for a small twin engine plane to land comfortably. The Everglades were dotted with old airstrips that had been used to run drugs during the seventies by the so-called cocaine cowboys. But most of them were abandoned and in disrepair. This one was carefully maintained.

Danny retraced his steps to the house. He stood in the tree line at the mouth of the clearing and scrutinized the house once more. Satisfied there was no one home, he took a circuitous route to the back of the house. He tried the back door. Locked. Behind the house were two wooden crosses with hooks at each end used for hanging game for cleaning. Fifty yards from the house were four hay bales propped against wooden supports. One of the bales had a worn piece of paper tacked to the front. Most of the paper was missing but what remained displayed half of a black human silhouette. The bales were used for target practice. Obviously target practice on people, not wild game. Danny tried to peek in the windows of the house but curtains blocked his view. He hoisted himself over the fence and hiked back to his car.

Danny's pager hummed as he drove back into town. He dialed the number and 'The Ferret' answered on the second ring.

"Hey, what's up?" Danny asked.

"Need to see you. Where are you now?" Ferret asked.

"Twenty miles out on the Alley. Should be back at the office in forty-five minutes or so." Danny replied.

"Make it thirty and come directly to my cave. "

"Sounds important ?" Danny answered.

"You got visitors. Important Visitors." Ferret hung up.

Danny arrived at Ferret's office in forty minutes. He had been forced to show his badge to a highway patrolman to get past an accident on the Alley. Ferret looked at his watch and frowned. Two men sat in Ferret's office. One was a distinguished-looking Latin with a long scar on his throat. The other was a slightly built black man whom Danny recognized immediately.

"Moses Hammond," Danny held out his hand, "Haven't seen you for years, where you been hiding?"

"DEA task force." Moses shook Danny's hand. "Good to see you Dan."

"I thought all of our people working for the Feds had been recalled by the new sheriff."

"Luckily, they forgot where I was." Moses smiled.

"Luck nothing. I made sure they didn't know where you were, "Ferret interrupted, "Danny, I want you to meet this other gentleman. Arturo Diaz, Special Agent in Charge of the local DEA office."

Diaz rose and shook Danny's hand.

"What's this all about?" Danny asked.

"You made an inquiry in NERD. We would like to know why," Diaz said quietly. Danny sat down, wondering what to tell him. The Feds weren't known for their discretion. More than once the Feds had used information gathered by local cops and turned it around to make a case and then take credit for it. They were also known for being tight-lipped with their own information and not helping local law in return. Local cops joked DEA stood for Don't Even Ask.

"It involves a case I'm working on."

"A homicide I assume, since that is your assignment," Diaz looked Danny straight in the eye. Danny glanced at Ferret for guidance.

"Look, Dan. These men can be trusted. There is no interagency rival bullshit with Arturo. I've known him for years and worked more than one case with him. Let's lay it out on the table and maybe we can help each other here," Ferret said.

Danny still wasn't sure but he agreed with Ferret's judgment. He explained the case so far. He intimated the Conrad murder might be connected and he told them about the drugs found in Gina Morrelli's apartment. He did not, however, reveal any names of anyone he had interviewed so far. He also didn't tell them about Sawgrass Camp. Not yet.

"Okay, your turn," Danny said when he was finished.

"Moses is involved in a deep cover investigation. He has made some controlled buys of large amounts of cocaine. The stash house is owned by the Sawgrass Development Corporation. We assumed the company was not involved in the drug dealing. But with your inquiry we're no longer so sure," Diaz said. Danny was shocked. He had never gotten this much information from a DEA agent or any other fed before. He was beginning to like Diaz but his cop instincts told him not to trust anyone.

"What we propose, Sergeant, is Moses continue his activities and you continue your homicide investigation. Any information will be traded equally. I mean equally. No games. No bullshit. If we can nail these guys for dope and homicide, we can be assured they spend more years in jail than their lawyers can stand. Can you agree with that?" Danny decided to trust this guy. He knew Moses Hammond was a straight up guy, he hoped working for the feds hadn't corrupted him.

"Okay. I can work with Moses. If we clash, we'll work it out between us. Deal?"

"Good for me," Moses said, holding out his hand to Danny. "I'll call you as soon as something develops. We're kind of in a holding pattern right now. The guy I'm hooked up with is out of town."

"Fine. I've got some leads to chase down as well." Danny rose and shook hands all around.

Danny dialed the number and waited for the phone to ring. He pondered his meeting with Diaz and Moses. He wondered how forthcoming they would be with their side of the deal. He would give them enough to assist in the case but not everything until he was sure he wasn't being played.

"Everglades Adventures." The woman who answered the phone sounded out of breath.

"Beth. What are you doing, running a marathon?" Danny asked.

"Daniel, is that you?" Beth Otter Killer squealed. "How are you. We haven't seen or heard from you in a long time. Too long."

"I know, Honey. It's gets crazy and I don't get to talk to the people who are important."

"Will we see you soon?" Beth asked.

"Very soon. We hope to come out for a week or more. I'm involved with a case that may take some time to clean up. But we'll be there soon." Beth was the wife of William Otter Killer, one of Danny's closest friends on the reservation. He had practically been adopted by William's parents when his parents died. Beth had been William's childhood sweetheart and they had been married right out of high school. "Is William around?" Danny wanted to ask William about the area around Sawgrass Camp. William knew everything that went on in the Everglades or knew someone who did. Even though the tribe no longer owned that area of the Everglades, they still knew every inch of it and kept abreast of the activity there.

"Just a sec," Beth said, putting the phone down.

"Hey. I don't know you but the name was familiar," William said, picking up the phone.

"Don't start on me. I know I've been absent but it will change." Danny chuckled.

"Heard that one before. That cop stuff is more important than family."

"You know that's not true. Listen. What can you tell me about the area of mile marker fifteen, specifically Sawgrass Camp?"

"This part of a case?" William asked.

"Yeah. Talk to me."

"Strange doings out there sometime. Lots of partying. They like to target practice, drink and screw. Sometimes they hunt. Not very discriminating either. Game Wardens would have a field day with those assholes."

"Any aircraft landing? Do you think they're using that airstrip to bring drugs in?"

"Naw. Planes sometimes land there but mostly bring fancy white people for parties."

"Thanks, William. I will be out to visit soon. Promise." Danny replied.

"Take her easy." William hung up. Danny felt even more guilty for not visiting more.

The phone rang almost as soon as Danny hung it up. It was Moses Hammond.

"Dan. I know how local cops feel about the Feds, but I can tell you Arturo Diaz is good people. He wants to put bad guys away any way he can. He was a street agent for years and still believes it's more important to make the case than who gets credit, Okay?" Moses waited for a reply.

"Okay, if you say so." Danny replied and wondered where this conversation was going.

"That said, I just got a call from the guy I've been dealing with. The people he works for are taking me one step further. They want to increase their profit margin and want me, with my supposed network, to help with the black ink on the financial line."

"Which means what to me?" Danny asked.

"Which means you get to play narc for awhile. Interested?"

"Depends. What will I be doing?" Danny waited for the screwing to commence. He could see the Feds taking the case already and his investigation taking a back seat.

"I have a meeting set up for night after tomorrow. They want me to join them for a night of play. We wondered if you would like to tag along on the surveillance van?" Moses replied.

BOHICA, Bend Over Here It Comes Again, Danny thought. He got to sit in a dark stuffy van while Moses did his thing and if they should happen to mention the murders, Danny would get the scraps.

"Look, Dan." Moses said, sensing Danny's hesitation, "I am a Deputy first, a Fed second. They don't own me. I am assigned to them but the Sheriff's Department is my home. This would be a good chance to see who they are and take some pictures. The pictures will help if you show them around to witnesses and associates. Might help to shake up the players and get some things moving on your case. Okay?"

Danny had to admit Moses was right. The case was bogging down. This might be it. "Okay. Tell me where and when."

Rich Martelli's stomach lurched again and he leaned over the side of the boat. The seas had turned choppy and he believed he was dying. Dying from seasickness. His mouth tasted like sulfur and old soup. He had emptied his stomach for an hour and now he dry heaved. He wished he could die, right now. He heard the boat captain as if in a fog, warning there was a police boat approaching. Martelli looked up and saw the blue gray boat with the flashing blue light bearing down on them. Oh God, now this, he thought.

The police boat drew alongside and Martelli squinted up at the gray uniform of a Florida Marine Patrol officer. He felt another retch coming and fought to gain control. The cop peered down at him.

"You okay, sir?" The officer asked. Martelli could only nod, his head hanging over the side of the boat. "Seasick, huh?" Martelli nodded again. He leaned back against the side of the boat and prayed for a breeze.

"Good afternoon, Captain," The cop addressed the boat captain. "Where you headed?"

"Just coming from a fishing trip to the Islands. My client is not doing too well. "Martelli stared at the captain. He spoke with no sign of an accent. The entire trip he had spoken with an obvious Spanish accent. Martelli was very confused, his head pounded.

"I need to see your registration and fishing licenses." The cop smiled pleasantly. He was a husky man with thinning hair and a good suntan from hours on the ocean.

"Yes sir," the captain replied, gathering up the requested documents. The first mate edged toward the cabin door. The cop inspected the documents and as he did so he sniffed the air. He looked up at the captain with hooded eyes, suspicion showed.

"Have you made recent repairs, Captain?" The cop looked around the boat. Oh God, Martelli thought, he smells the fiberglass. The bottom of the boat is full of dope. Oh Shit! He knows. I'm gonna lose everything. Shit! Shit! Shit! Martelli glanced at the first mate who edged closer to the cabin door. Martelli saw his right hand begin to move ever so slowly toward the inside of the cabin door where the semiautomatic handgun was hidden in a compartment just inside the door. Oh Fuck! They're gonna kill this cop. Shit! Oh God, No! Jesus Christ, let it go you stupid cop, They're gonna blow your brains out.! Go away! Martelli was in a near panic. Time seemed to freeze. Martelli could feel his heart pounding and broke out in a sweat. After an interminable pause, the Captain pointed toward a patch of fiberglass near the waterline.

"Hit a rock entering the port on Grand Cayman, almost sunk my boat." The captain smiled. The cop looked at the patch. He smiled suddenly and handed the documents back to the Captain. He glanced at Martelli and frowned.

"Drink some flat coke, it'll help settle your stomach," he said, shifting into reverse and backing his boat slowly away. Martelli could only nod. The first mate's hand moved back to his side as the police boat swung away and accelerated. Martelli realized he was holding his breath. He let the air out slowly. Jesus Christ! This isn't worth it, he thought. There isn't enough money in the world to be worth this. He should get out of this deal. Sure, he and Trevor were friends but Martelli was no killer. This business was getting too dangerous. Somebody murdered Gina and none of them knew who or why. Too many people in this dope business had no feeling for human life. None. He didn't need this. The real estate business was lucrative enough. He'd had enough. Suddenly, nausea washed over him and he bolted for the side of the boat. What a lousy fucking trip, he thought, as the first spasm racked him.

Trevor Daniels sipped his drink and watched the fishing pole beside him. It was a beautiful day, a little choppy but Trevor didn't mind. The end of the pole twitched once then twice. Suddenly, the line screamed from the reel. Trevor dropped his drink and grabbed the rod from the holder. He slammed the pole into the rod holder in the seat between his legs. He locked the straps to the pole and leaned back. He could feel the fish pull against him. He yanked the pole hard to set the hook. Instantly, a sailfish rocketed out of the water and danced across the surface on its tail, its iridescent blue body gleamed in the sunlight. The fish crashed back into the water and dove for the bottom. Trevor strained to hold the pole as the fish sounded. He could feel the vibration of the fish through the rod. The Captain eased back on the throttle to keep pace with the fish. The line went slack and Trevor reeled furiously to keep the line taut. The fish was coming back up. It crashed to the surface again, shaking its head, trying to dislodge the hook. The long pointed snout sliced the water. Trevor reeled as the fish swam toward the boat. It sounded again and Trevor allowed the reel to scream as the line played out. I love this, he thought. A million dollars worth of profit hidden under the deck and a sail on the line. What a great way to get rich. Too smart for the cops and lots of money. Yeah, this is good stuff.

Trevor watched as the first mate leaned over the side to grab the snout of the fish. He glanced at Trevor. He grinned at the mate and drew his finger across his throat. The mate shrugged and sank a gaff into the fish's side. He heaved the fish over the side and into the boat. It twitched four times and lay still. Trevor was excited. Fuck the conservationists! He wanted the fish to show his friends. Catch and release, my ass. Trevor wanted to show it off. Afterwards he would throw it into the canal behind his house. He hated the taste of fish. Never could eat the stuff. It was good for a few pictures and that was it.

He glanced at the bare breasted blond lying in the sun on the front deck and smiled. Certain things were good for certain purposes. His father taught him the best way to get ahead in the world was to use what was necessary to get where you wanted to be. He had married his wife because she was in the right social circles and she came from money. He thought he was in love when they started, but he realized later they were just comfortable with each other. In the social group they traveled in, you had to have a family to be considered stable and in big business you had to be stable. Thus, they had two children and his wife had the responsibility to raise them properly. Trevor's responsibility was to make the money, and his dalliances with other women were overlooked as long as they didn't become public knowledge and bring disgrace to the supposedly perfect family.

No one would ever suspect Trevor was involved in a side business considered taboo. Not even the cops would suspect him. He even used his friends. They were necessary to keep the Sawgrass Development Corporation legitimate. Trevor never really felt close to them, they were just necessary. The only one he cared about acceptance from was his father.

He had tried all his life to impress his father and get him to acknowledge his presence, but his father was more interested in the bank and his business and his money. Well, Trevor would show him. If his father ever knew they were involved in smuggling drugs he would have a stroke. Serve him right. That would get his attention.

Trevor remembered the first time he met Ricky. Gina had introduced them at a party. Ricky seemed fascinated with the fact Trevor was the head of a bank. After they became acquainted, Ricky had approached him about laundering drug profits through the bank. The Development Corporation was Trevor's brainchild. He convinced Ricky to abandon his current system and work exclusively through the bank. Trevor eventually become the boss and Ricky the employee. He would like to find the son of a bitch who killed her and have Ricky cut his throat.

Ricky still hadn't found out who killed her. He said it was an accident. She went to Naples to see friends for the evening and had too much to drink. She parked on the side of the road and fell asleep. The fire was accidental. The grass was dry and the muffler or something on her car caught fire and she died. Even the cops seemed to believe the death was an accident. Trevor had to accept it. Besides, he couldn't really order Ricky to kill anybody. He didn't have the guts for it. He liked the money and the thrill of thinking he was like some kind of secret agent. The double life excited him. Besides, it was the ultimate FUCK YOU to his father and the kids he grew up with.

As a young man, Trevor had been overweight and not very handsome. He had been teased as a student in elementary school and middle school by cruel classmates.

When he reached high school, he was large enough to try out for the football team, but he was not a star player. He wanted to be accepted in the right social circles but the cliques were made up of the cheerleaders and football stars didn't want him around. Although they were of the same financial and social status, Trevor was an outsider. He hurt from the emotional pain of being teased and not a part of the group. He even considered suicide once. Then Michael had died. Michael was a star player but not from the right social group so he was not accepted either. He had been the only one in school who was physically mature enough to grow a beard. And he was a phenomenal athlete, starring in football and baseball. But he wasn't accepted so he and Trevor had become friends. Trevor never realized Michael had been hurting too. Trevor was jealous of Michael because of his ability and Michael had lots of girlfriends. But Michael killed himself. The first day of senior year they met in the hallway and Michael said he was doing great and would be playing football that year.

That night he had taken his father's pistol and gone in the bathroom, put it in his mouth and blown his brains out. Not being accepted by your peers was a very painful thing to a teenager. After Michael's death, Trevor decided he would be so rich his classmates would be jealous and he could tell them all to go to hell.

The sun was beginning to set as the boat eased between the jetties and into the canal, headed toward the marina. The sky was painted with shades of orange, red and purple. The air was beginning to cool but Rich Martelli didn't care about any of it. He just wanted to be on dry land. The flat soda had helped settle his stomach a little. The Marine cop had been right. Martelli prayed they would dock soon. Please hurry and get me home, he thought. He dreamed of air conditioning and his apartment.

As soon as the boat backed into the slip and the mate tied it to the piling, Martelli grabbed his bag and raced off of the boat. As he stepped up on the dock, his knees wobbled, causing him to grab a railing until the spots in front of his eyes went away. His stomach did flip flops again and he thought he would vomit. His head pounded and the taste in his mouth had changed to old brass. He wobbled to his car. The heat blasted from the interior when he opened the door, causing him to stumble backward. He dropped into the front seat and started the engine, turning the air conditioning control on full blast. He held his face in front of the air vents as the cold air blasted at him. Ah! Sweet Jesus that felt good. He sat for fifteen minutes with his face in the vent until his head cleared.

Martelli lay on the couch and held the cold glass to his forehead. He thought about his future. Since arriving home he had picked up the phone half a dozen times then thought better of it. If he called the cops and Ricky found out, he was sure Ricky would cut his throat and feed him to the fish. Besides, Trevor was his friend and he would understand if he wanted out of the deal. He had let Gina go. Martelli thought about the incident with the Marine cop. He had no doubt they would have killed that cop. He had never been so scared in his life. He shuddered from the thought. He was in this for the money, nothing more. He would talk to Trevor. He would tell him he couldn't go on the boats any more. He would claim he just got too sick every time. The captain and the mate would verify his seasickness. He decided that was the only way.

Trevor opened the front door and could hear the kids laughing in the back of the house. He found his wife in the kitchen and walked up behind her. She turned on him before he could touch her.

"Did you have a good time?" she asked, searching his face.

"Yeah, I caught a big sailfish. It's out in the garage." He dropped his bag on the floor. Pouring himself a drink, he turned and watched her cutting up vegetables. "What did you do while I was gone?"

"I took the kids to the club a few times. We had takeout last night and watched a movie." And you were probably screwing some bimbo, she thought. "Go shower and clean up. Dinner will be ready soon."

"I've got a business meeting tomorrow night, so don't plan on me for dinner."

"Fine." She watched him walk from the kitchen. And fuck you, she said to herself.

CHAPTER 14

Danny waited for the coffee to perk and mulled over his options. He could send members of his squad to the funeral or he could go himself. He hated funerals. It always reminded him of his own mortality. At least this one wouldn't be a full police funeral. He considered that and the anger sprang up in him again. Gus Conrad deserved full honors. He had spent most of his adult life protecting the citizens of this community and they owed him at least that much. When Danny heard about it, he had gone directly to his boss and raised a stink. Of course, Major Dick had reminded him that Conrad had died under questionable circumstances and there was the question of him being crooked. Danny had pretty much shot down the suicide theory and at least Major Dick hadn't brought that up again. But Conrad's wife was still waiting for the city to pay death benefits and they were trying to claim he wasn't killed in the line of duty, which cut the life insurance payoff to about one third. Of course, Major Dick's wife was in charge of that department for the city and it would be difficult to win those benefits for Conrad without solving his death. And Danny intended to do just that. When he proved Conrad died as a direct result of his police duties, the city could shove it where the sun didn't shine and Mrs. Conrad could at least survive financially. Danny wished he had already solved the case so Conrad could have the funeral he deserved. Danny figured if Major Dick died of lockjaw from a paper cut he would get a full honors funeral. The Good 'ol Boys club would see to that. They would also make sure he got full death benefits. But Gus Conrad, who had been a street cop, all his life, would get nothing. Major Dick had put it clearly when he said, "crooked cops don't deserve an honorable funeral." What an Asshole, Danny thought.

Danny decided to take Mike Richards and Marshall Grimes with him and go to the funeral. They would be able to point out who was who to him. He was interested to see who would attend. He wondered if there would be any interesting faces there, someone involved with the case, like Trevor Daniels maybe. That would clarify things considerably.

Danny slipped the bedroom door open quietly and stood looking at his wife. She was lying on her back breathing softly. He loved to watch her sleep. He loved everything about her. After all these years, he still felt the same twinge when he held her. She still excited him. He thought about how nice it felt to be snuggled up to her, her soft warm skin against him, her breath against his neck. Someone once said there was someone for everyone. He had been lucky to find his soul mate in this life. Few people were that lucky. He bent and kissed her gently on the cheek, feeling the warm flesh against his lips. She stirred and stretched her back. She opened her eyes sleepily and looked into his eyes. She wrapped her arms around his neck and pulled him to her. He held her for a few seconds until she released her grip. She searched his face and realized what day it was. She knew how he hated funerals.

"Are you going today?" she whispered. He nodded sadly. She hugged him again and said "I'm sorry, Baby."

He shrugged and kissed her forehead. "Time to get up, darlin'." She stretched her back and raised her arms over her head.

"I don't want to," she groaned.

"I know, but you have to, you have to support me in this lavish lifestyle. "He grinned at her. He straightened and left the bedroom.

Danny dialed Mike Richards' number and listened while the phone rang five, six, seven times. Richard's voice answered with a gruff, "Hello?"

"Are you conscious yet?" Danny grinned at the receiver.

"No! And I don't want to be either," Richards replied.

"Too damn bad," Danny chuckled. "You and Marshal and I are going to the service today."

"Ah Daddy, do I have to?" Richards whined.

"Yes you do. So dress appropriately. The service starts at nine. I'll meet you guys at the office and we'll take one car."

"Do I have to wear a shirt?" Richards asked.

"Yes, and a tie." Danny replied. He knew Richards would never shirk the funeral, even if Danny didn't attend. Richards' attitude reflected the fact he was angry that Conrad wasn't getting a full honors funeral either. Danny remembered Richard's reaction when he told him about the funeral. Danny wasn't sure the chip in the wall could be patched where Richards had thrown his coffee cup against it.

Danny arrived at the office and found Kay Matthews and Raphael Fernandez already there. Matthews was dressed in a dark mid-calf length dress and Fernandez was wearing a black suit. They were obviously planning to attend the funeral. Danny smiled. At least Conrad had the respect of his fellow cops. Marshall Grimes and Leon Carter arrived together and both were dressed for the funeral. Leon Carter looked at Danny and shrugged sheepishly.

"Is it okay if we all attend today?" he asked quietly. He knew with the whole squad at the funeral, there would be no work done in the homicide unit today.

"Absolutely," Danny smiled. "If they need us they can page us."

When they arrived at the church, Danny was pleasantly surprised. There were rows upon rows of marked and unmarked police cars parked around the church. All of the cars were from surrounding agencies. The local cops had at least decided to attend a brother officer's funeral despite the cloud hanging over his reputation. Without the cloud, a teletype message would have been sent to all agencies nationwide and officers from across the country would have attended. There would have been over a thousand. As it was, they still had to park a block from the church and walk. Danny insisted they arrive early to watch and see who showed up. They positioned themselves near the doors of the church and watched the arrivals. Danny watched a black limousine arrive, followed by a black hearse. The door to the limousine opened and a burly, dark bearded man emerged, then leaned into the open door and helped Mrs. Conrad step out. Danny recognized Dominic Basso. Next, Mrs. Conrad's sister emerged. Danny waited and no one else emerged. He wondered where Gus Junior was. Surely the Department Of Corrections would have allowed him to attend, at least under guard. Danny watched as the casket was removed from the back of the hearse. Uniformed police officers from the city acted as pallbearers. The casket was wheeled into the church and the family followed. The police officers filed in after the family was seated.

Danny and his team stood in the back since the church was too small to seat all of the police officers. Danny scanned the crowd and noticed there was no police brass, anywhere, not from the city or the county. Just lower level officers. That figured. They would want to be politically correct. Not dare to be seen at the funeral of a questionable cop. The lower level officers attended funerals no matter what. They figured they had a duty to attend. They all hoped if they ever fell in the line of duty, at least they would have earned enough respect of their peers for them to attend the funeral. Cops who didn't even know the deceased attended, because they figured 'there but for the grace of God go I.'

Danny noticed a blond haired man who slipped into the church at the last minute and took a seat with the other narcs from Conrad's unit. Conrad's boss Sergeant Johannsen. Bet he'll catch some shit from the brass for being here, Danny thought.

After the service, Danny and his team gathered outside and waited for the casket to be wheeled back to the hearse. All the uniformed officers returned to their cars to go to the cemetery for the burial. Danny knew there would be no need to go to the burial.

If this had been a full honors funeral, there would be a graveside service. Mrs. Conrad would be given the flag that draped the casket. There would be a twenty-one gun salute and a flyover by police helicopters. This day, there would be no such ceremony. Danny was disappointed that he had seen no one who looked out of place. He had hoped he would see someone who raised his interest. But all he saw was cops. He turned to Richards.

"Ride with Marshall. I need to go back to the office and check something out." Richards nodded. He and the rest of the team would attend the burial.

The office was quiet with the team gone. Danny drummed his fingers on the desk and waited with the phone cradled on his shoulder. He had been on hold for fifteen minutes. Finally a gruff voice came on the line.

"Captain Gordon," The man growled.

"Good morning, Captain. This is Sergeant Quinn from Homicide. I'm investigating the death of Gus Conrad." Danny waited.

"What can I do for you, Sergeant?" Captain Gordon asked.

"You have an inmate there, Gus Conrad Junior. His father's funeral was today and he didn't attend. I was wondering why. Was he denied a furlough?"

"No, the Corrections Board granted the furlough at his mother's request. Conrad refused the furlough."

"Any idea why he refused?" Danny asked.

"He didn't say why," Gordon replied.

"Okay thanks." Danny hung up. Why would Gus Junior refuse? Didn't he care how much his mother would need him there? Did he hate his father so much he would hurt his mother to avoid the funeral? Danny decided he needed to find out the answer to that question. It might explain some things. He called Moses and told him he would not be able to attend the surveillance that night. What a shame. He was going to miss sitting in the surveillance van. A thrill he could do without. He found Mike Richards and let him know he would be gone the rest of the day.

The drive to the prison was boring and Danny got stranded in a traffic jam for over an hour. It gave him time to think. He needed to find a motive for this whole thing. He still couldn't put the reasons together. The drug thing was connected but he didn't see how it fit with Conrad. Gina Morelli made sense. It wasn't unusual for drug runners to terminate their own if they became a liability. But why Conrad? There was nothing to indicate Conrad was dirty and working for Sawgrass Development and nothing to indicate he was investigating them. Trevor Daniels did not seem the type to be ruthless enough to kill a cop. Sure there was probably a lot of money at stake. Probably millions. Did Conrad know Gina Morelli? Could there be another reason for Conrad? Somebody sure as hell put the phony account in Conrad's name. Was it Gina? Trevor Daniels? He hoped Moses' meeting would introduce him to all the players. Somebody ruthless and cold hearted enough to kill two people. Especially a cop. They must know the heat for a cop killing would be tremendous. That was obviously the reason for the attempt to make it look like suicide. They had been sloppy. Somebody thought they knew police procedure and how to fake a death. Same with Gina. They tried to make it look like an accident but didn't quite get it right. There was enough to prove murder if Danny could find a suspect.

Danny dialed the cell phone in his car and waited for Richards to answer. He dropped the phone to swerve around a car that suddenly screeched to a stop in front of him. He could hear Richards' voice from the floor saying "Hello, hello?" Danny finally found the phone under the seat.

"Mike. Do we still have Conrad's car impounded?" he asked.

"Yeah, I think so. Why?" Richards asked.

"Call the Crime Scene boys and make sure they vacuumed the car for hair, fibers and such. If they did, see if you can light a fire under them to get us the results."

"Okay. Anything else?"

"I'll let you know if I think of anything."

"You know you are wasting the county's money using the cell for long distance. Haven't you heard about the budget constraints?"

"Screw you," Danny replied and hung up.

Danny thought about Gus Junior. It was obvious from their last meeting Gus Junior had something to hide. Danny wondered how to break him in this interview. Guilt? Pride? He needed to get inside him and make him open up. Gus Junior had been interrogated all his life. Cop's kids had that burden. Their parent always knew they were lying to them. It was cop's instinct to see through the bullshit. Danny would see where to go with the discussion when they met.

He pulled into the gate and parked in front of the Administration building. He hadn't called ahead. He didn't want Gus Junior to be ready for him. Keep him off balance. Danny met the lieutenant in charge in his office.

"Lieutenant. Sergeant Danny Quinn," Danny smiled as they shook hands. "I need to see Gus Conrad. I'm investigating his father's murder."

"Do you have an appointment, Sergeant? " The Corrections Lieutenant frowned.

"No. This is a surprise visit. I have a reason for that. I need some answers."

The Corrections Lieutenant shrugged and picked up the phone.

"Bring Conrad down to the interview room. He has a visitor." The Lieutenant looked up at Danny with a questioning look. Danny shook his head.

"Don't tell him who is here. Just escort him down," The Lieutenant said to the phone. Danny thanked him and was led to the same interview room he used before. He settled in a chair and put his feet up on the desk. Start out casual and see where it goes. Try to put Conrad at ease to start with.

Ten minutes later the door opened and Gus Junior stepped in. He saw Danny and muttered, "Motherfucker!" Danny motioned toward a chair and told him to sit down. Danny noticed a fresh, raw tattoo on his shoulder.

He slid carefully in the chair, looking like a cat ready to pounce or bolt. Danny noticed he looked bigger and more muscular. Obviously, he had been spending time in the weight room. Danny never understood the reasoning behind providing weights to inmates. In prison, they had nothing to look forward to, nothing to relieve their frustration, so they lifted weights. A lot. They were fed three times a day and lifted weights. The end result was an inmate that was bigger and stronger when they were released. It was not uncommon for some inmate to go back on the street and the first time a cop confronted them, they tried to stuff the cop up the tailpipe of the patrol car rather than go back to jail. Since most cops didn't have the time or the energy to work out much because of work schedules, family time and the like, the end result sometimes was tragic. The excuse was it allowed the guards in prison to control the inmates better. If they committed an infraction, they lost their weight room privileges. Danny thought they should take away the weights and make the inmates run laps around the yard. That way, when they got out, they could only run from the cops. Besides, cops would prefer a suspect ran from them and got away rather than beat the shit out of the cop.

Danny sat quietly and studied Gus Junior's face. He saw the resentment hiding just below the surface. This kid had a lot of hate. Danny waited and let Conrad make the first statement. He saw the uncertainty start to creep in and he waited. Finally, Conrad couldn't stand it anymore.

"So what the fuck you want, asshole?" Conrad burst out. Danny waited. He let the silence hang in the room. He wanted Conrad's mind to start to panic.

"Don't play this game with me, muthafucka, "Conrad snarled, trying a show of bravado. Danny showed no emotion and continued to watch.

"Why the fuck are you here?" Conrad was starting to lose some of his bluster. A slight pleading crept into his voice.

"Your father's funeral was today. I wondered why you didn't go," Danny said softly.

"I didn't feel like it." Conrad said sullenly. Suddenly averting his gaze, he studied the wall behind Danny's head. Gotcha, Danny thought.

"I don't understand you, Gus. You were given a furlough to go. Why didn't you? Do you hate your father that much?"

"Yeah. Fuck that asshole." Conrad replied. Danny could see the facade. Conrad's answer had been a bluster but Danny could see the uncertainty. Just like a child who lies to his father and hopes he believes the lie. Danny decided to use that child to get Gus to talk to him. He decided a gentle approach was best. He kept his voice soft and gentle.

"Tell me why you hate your father so much. Did he beat you? Did he beat your mother? Drink too much? What?"

"He was an asshole. Mister high and mighty cop. Did you know he had me busted the first time? I was fifteen fucking years old and he found some pot in my room. He called some of his buddies and they busted me."

"What happened? You were a juvenile. The penalty couldn't have been too severe. "

"The judge let me go with a warning. He and the old man were friends and the old man talked him into it." Conrad looked at the floor.

"Sounds to me like your dad was trying to prove a point. Sounds like he was trying to make you see that what you were doing was wrong," Danny replied.

"Fuck that. Couldn't he just chew me out? Dump the shit?"

"Maybe. But I'm sure he did what he thought was right. Didn't you two ever have some good times. Go fishing and things?" Danny waited and could see in Conrad's eyes he was remembering other times. Conrad looked at the ceiling. His eyes scanned the room. He glanced at the small window, high up on the wall.

"Yeah. Sometimes. When I was little, he used to take me fishing. One time, I caught a huge bass and he had to help me reel it in."

"Don't you think that was important? Didn't that show you he cared about you?"

"Later, he was never around. He was always working. He didn't care about my mom and me. If he did, he would have been there."

"Did your mother have a problem with that? Don't you think she knew it was necessary so you could have the things you needed?" Danny asked.

"We needed him," Conrad whispered.

"What about your mom? How were things with her?"

"Mom's cool. She was always around and we could talk about things."

"Why did you get involved with drugs, Gus?" Danny asked softly, like a father asking his son.

"Friends. We used to go to parties and everyone was smoking. I just went along. Besides, I knew it would frost my old man's ass if he knew," Conrad answered.

"How did the dealing start. Your friends get you started in that too?"

"Dude I hung with. He was making good cash. I decided I wanted the good life. So I got him to front me. I did good too. Made lots of green," Conrad said proudly. "Then I got busted. Sold to an undercover Five-O. That made the old man really pissed. After that we didn't talk much."

"How many times you been busted?"

"Five."

"Tell me about it," Danny said firmly.

"I was working for a guy. He calls me one night and tells me to pick up a truck and deliver it to a warehouse. So I did." Conrad slumped in his chair and folded his arms. He stared at the floor. Danny could see him deciding whether to tell it all. He suddenly straightened, making the decision. "They were late. While I was waiting, a police car came by. They jacked me up, wanting to know why I was there. I didn't know how much was in there. The dope dog came and he smelled the truck. They opened it up and that was that."

"Who were you working for?"

Conrad lurched from the chair and paced around the room. He swung his arms back and forth. He ran both hands across his face and over his head. He suddenly stopped and glared at Danny.

"Man. Fuck you. I can't tell you nothing." He hollered. He started to pace like a caged cat. Danny decided to be firm and push him a little.

"Gus. You got to tell me what you know. Other people could die. These people don't mess around."

"Yeah? No shit! I seen it! I know what they can do." Conrad spat.

"Look! They killed your father. Who's gonna be next unless I stop it? Now!" Danny crossed the room and grabbed Conrad's arm and spun him around. They stood face to face and Conrad glared at him.

"I can't tell you. Don't you understand. He'll kill her too!" Conrad yanked his arm away and fled to the other side of the room. Danny pursued him.

"Who'll kill her. Her who? Talk to me goddammit!"

Conrad spun and punched the wall. He began to sob. "My mom! They'll kill my mom!"

Danny put his hand on Conrad's shoulder and guided him to his chair. He waited for a moment to let Conrad stop sobbing. Finally, Conrad looked up at him, tears streaming down his face. Conrad composed himself.

"Talk to me, Gus. Let me help you and your mom." Danny leaned close and put a hand on Conrad's arm. Conrad leaned back and sucked in a big breath. He let it out slowly. He seemed to deflate before Danny's eyes.

"Right after I got busted the last time, I got a phone call. I was in the county jail and they found me. They said if I ever tried to talk they would make it so my father was ruined. They told me they set it up so he would get fired and busted. I was scared. I loved him even though it don't show. So I kept my mouth shut. Nothing happened for a while. Then the old man called while I was in here. I hadn't heard from him in a long time. He didn't come to the trial or nothing. He wanted to know who I worked for. I couldn't help him. I tried to tell him that, but he wouldn't listen. He said he was going to get the people responsible, as he put it. I tried to make him let it go. After that he died. I thought it was suicide, like they said. Until you came along and told me different. But my old man would never kill himself. We talked about suicide once. A friend of his had done it. He said it was weak and cowardly. He was like that. Did you know he was a Marine? Served in Vietnam." Danny didn't know that. "After you came to see me, I got another message. That if I talk to anyone, my mom will be next. That's why I didn't go to the funeral. I didn't want to be seen around her in case they thought I told her anything."

"Who sent you the message?" Danny prayed for a name.

"Just a voice on the phone, didn't recognize it."

"Do you know how they planned to ruin your father?" Danny asked.

"I didn't. But when you told me about the account, with the money in it, I figured it out. They must have put the money in there. I guess they would have tried to make it look like he was taking money or working for a drug ring."

"Who were you working for? Gimme a name."

"All I know is a dude named Ricky. He's Colombian or something. Wears a ponytail," Conrad replied.

"What else do you know about him? Where he lives or anything else?" Danny asked.

"No. That's all. He always called me to come work and met me at the place."

Danny was disappointed. He had hoped to get more. But at least now he had a motive. It should help move in a direction. He hoped Moses Hammond would be able to develop Ricky's identity. Danny stood and placed a hand on Conrad's shoulder.

"Thank you, Gus, " He said quietly. Conrad looked up at him with a pleading look.

"You gotta protect my mom," Conrad begged. "Ricky's cold-blooded. I seen him slash a guy's face just for sassing him."

"I'll take care of it. Don't worry." Danny smiled. If he messes with your mother, I'll kill him myself, Danny promised to himself.

The house was dark when Danny arrived home. He slipped the key in the lock slowly and eased the lock open. He stepped inside and waited for his eyes to adjust to the total darkness. He slid the bedroom door closed so as not to disturb his wife. He was tired from the drive but his mind was too busy to sleep. He knew he would just toss and turn, so there was no point. He undressed in the kitchen and laid his clothes over a chair. He stretched out on the couch and began flipping channels on the television. There was nothing on to capture his interest, so he settled on one of the mundane late night shows. The host had just begun his monologue and Danny half listened to the political satire. He thought about Gus Jr.

The poor kid had it rough. The emotional turmoil he must have felt not being able to go to his father's funeral, out of fear, must have been gut-wrenching. Danny knew Gus Jr. was in danger now and so was his mother. Danny knew he had to convince Mrs. Conrad to go away for awhile, maybe to her sister's house. Just until this case was solved and all the assholes were in jail. He needed Gus Jr. moved too. Arturo Diaz and the DEA would have to help with that. They could pull some federal strings and maybe get Gus Jr. moved to a federal facility. Maybe they could put him under an assumed name.

Danny thought about what Gus Jr. told him. It answered the big question of why. Why the money was under Gus Conrad's name. Why he was killed. And Danny had a name. Ricky, with a ponytail. Colombian maybe. Danny realized he wanted Ricky with the ponytail. Wanted him bad. Now that the decision had been made, he felt he could sleep. He crept into the bedroom and could hear his wife's soft breathing. He slipped into bed carefully and was instantly asleep.

Danny parked next to the fence and climbed over the gate. The day was not quite hot. He walked between the rows of orange trees to where Conrad's car had been found. Danny stood in the shade and looked around. The grass was still tall under the trees and showed no sign of all the police vehicles and cops traipsing around. Mother Nature cleans up after man.

Danny looked down the row of trees and could see a tractor parked ten rows down. He walked toward the tractor and came to another fence. The tractor was on the other side of the fence in a different section of trees. The paint of the tractor was faded and peeling in places, like a tourist who stayed out in the sun too long. The tractor looked old. Danny realized the grass around the base of the trees in this section was mashed and trampled. The trees were bare of fruit. He turned and studied the trees in his section. Large green fruit hung from the trees, not yet ripe. This new section had been recently picked. That meant somebody had been in there working.

The grove business had, at one time, been booming in this part of Florida. Progress and population had driven out the groves in order to make way for houses and subdivisions. Most of the oranges in the grocery stores were from California and the oranges from Florida were shipped to other parts of the country. Farther upstate, the groves were still a big business. This grove was one of the few left and had succumbed to the need of the tourist trade. Still a working grove, it was also a tourist attraction. There was a tour tram that took visitors around the grounds. A gift shop and an alligator show. Next to the gift shop were long sorting tables used to pick out the good fruit from the load. The sorting tables were under a roof but open to the public like the tables at an outdoor flea market. Beyond the sorting shed Danny could see three large green trailers with wire mesh enclosing the back storage space. The trailers were brimming with bright green oranges. The new harvest. At the sorting tables, ten black men and women stood sorting the fruit, shuffling them around according to size.

In the corner of the sorting shed, Danny spied a tall white man seated in a lawn chair watching the sorters work. He clenched an old pipe between his teeth. His skin was tan and leathery from years in the sun. He stood when Danny approached and watched him curiously. His white t-shirt was stained and he wore blue jeans that had faded white with a rip in the left knee. He had close cropped black hair, matted from sweat.

"Can I hep ya?" the man asked.

"Maybe," Danny replied showing the man his badge. "I'm Danny Quinn. Sheriff's Department Homicide."

The man nodded and sat back down in his chair, motioning Danny to sit in the chair next to him. He held out a calloused hand. "Woodrow Bates."

Danny shook the hand that felt like the bark of an old tree. "I'd like to ask you some questions if it'd be alright."

"Sure. What'cha need to know.?"

"It's about the body they found in your grove."

Bates nodded. "Sad thing about that man. Baking in his car out there for a week in this heat. Heard he was one of you boys."

"City police. Different department," Danny replied.

"Same thing. Cop's a cop," Bates snorted.

"Sounds like you don't like cops much."

"Don't like 'em or dislike 'em," Bates replied with a sidelong glance at Danny's face.

"Can you tell me anything about the car or if you saw anything unusual out in the grove during that week?"

"Didn't see the car 'til they towed it out of there. Didn't see the dead man neither." Bates chewed on the pipe he held in his teeth.

"How is it you work in those groves every day and didn't see the car out there?" Danny asked.

"Wasn't working in that section of the grove. See Officer, we pick different sections at different times. Each section comes ripe at different times and we pick each section when it's ready. That way there's always fresh fruit for all these damn Yankees who come down here to visit."

Bates glanced at Danny as if he might be one of 'those damn Yankees'. Danny chuckled to show him he wasn't. Satisfied, Bates continued. "Them bastards come down here with their New Yawk accents and their fat little wives with the dyed hair and their white skin, whiter than a bass's belly most of 'em. They spend money and come here and pick through my fruit and act like the good lord made 'em special. All's they do is bitch and complain. Pain in the ass, most of 'em. That section of trees won't be ready 'til we get some cooler weather to sweeten the juice."

"When was the last time you worked that section?"

"'bout two weeks before they done found that man."

"Did you see anything unusual around that time? You must ride around the grove quite a bit."

"Well sir. I did see one car round about that time. Driving out of the grove. Black job, small."

Danny pulse quickened. " Do you know what kind of car. Did you see who was in it?"

"Naw. I can't tell them newer cars apart. Didn't see who was in it. Had them dark tinted windows."

Danny could relate to that. He had a hard time telling new cars from each other, they all looked the same to him too.

"Ever see the car before?"

"Ain't never seen it before nor since," Bates replied. "Just figured it was some developer scoutin' around lookin' for more land to buy up to put up more damn houses. Too many damn houses 'round here now. Be okay if them snowbirds would spend their money and leave. Too damn many of them decide to stay. All they're doing is ruining the place. Too many people 'round here anymore."

Bates leaned back in his chair so far Danny was afraid he would fall over backward. Danny knew this interview was over . He thanked Bates and walked toward his car.

"Take a bag of fruit with ya!" Bates hollered after him. Danny just waved and continued walking.

Danny called the crime lab and waited for the information he requested. He doodled on the notepad in front of him. He listed the information he had obtained from Gus Jr. Next, he wrote what Bates told him. A small dark car with tinted windows. Some guy named Ricky, Spanish maybe, with a ponytail. Gina part of the Sawgrass Development group. How had they discovered Conrad was looking into their activities?

"Sarge, you there?" the voice asked on the phone, breaking his thoughts.

"Yeah, go ahead," he replied.

"We found a lot of hair and fibers in the car. We matched some of them to Conrad and the rest are outstanding, unknowns. It appears there are two people in the mix. Both male, one blonde, one very dark brunette. We also found some green carpet fibers that don't belong in the car. It's small tight ply, similar to indoor outdoor carpet. Probably from an office or some space that see lots of foot traffic. What we did not find, were any orange blossoms or other vegetative debris that would indicate the occupants stepped out of the car in the orange grove and got back into the car. That indicates the occupants got into the car somewhere else and drove to the grove, killed Conrad and got out, walked away, and never returned."

"Any footprints around the car that could be traced?" Danny asked, hoping.

"Sorry. Too many cops walked around the car. No discernible footprints."

Danny thanked the lab tech and hung up. He added the information to his doodling. Conrad picked up two people, males, somewhere else and drove to the grove. One blond, one brunette. Had to be someone he trusted enough to let into the car. He must not have suspected anything. The question was, did he drive to the grove voluntarily or did they have a gun to his head? Trevor Daniels had blond hair. This Ricky person had dark hair. Would Conrad trust either one of them enough to let them into the car and drive to the grove? Danny doubted it. He needed to get a sample of Daniels' hair for comparison. He could get a court order but that would put Daniels and Ricky on alert. Had to be another way. He wished he could push the DEA case along so he had some leverage. He hoped Moses was getting close to making some arrests.

Danny glanced up from his pad as Lieutenant Green stepped into the cubicle. Green slid into a chair across from his and smiled wearily. Danny knew the look.

"Well, how goes it with Conrad?" Green asked. Danny filled him in. He told him about the threats to Gus Jr. He led him through the connection to Sawgrass Development, the death of Gina Morelli and the connection to the same group. He finished with the forensic information he had just received. Green nodded when Danny finished.

"The pressure is getting intense. We need a resolution soon, if you get my drift," Green replied. Danny said he understood. Shit, he thought, now the bosses, who wouldn't know how to conduct a homicide investigation if it bit them, were getting anxious. Green left and Danny called Moses. He was told Moses was not available. Danny hated relying on someone else in his cases. He knew drug cases took time, but something better break soon. Danny was getting frustrated and when he got frustrated, he figured out a way to shake something loose. This time he couldn't. He thought about it for awhile and made a decision. Moses wouldn't like it.

CHAPTER 15

M oses felt like the music was pounding through his body. It pulsed into him and his whole body was vibrating with it. The music was so loud, conversation was impossible. Moses wondered if it was just the music or the music combined with the alcohol. He was on his second scotch. He knew he needed to slow down because three would make him drunk and he needed his wits about him. Moses rarely drank and when he did, he hated the feeling of being out of control. He tried to act drunker than he was. Not that the others would notice. Trevor Daniels was on his fifth or sixth drink. Moses noticed he looked a little bleary-eyed. Rich Martelli seemed pensive, almost nervous. He glanced around the bar every few seconds and kept looking at the door, as if waiting for the devil himself to walk in. Moses made a mental note that Martelli would be easy to crack in an interrogation.

Jeff Grayson yelled loudly and banged his empty beer bottle on the table. He glanced wildly around the room, looking for the waitress. Moses figured he was on his tenth beer. Moses studied Grayson carefully. He was a large, big chested man. His hands were huge and callused. His complexion was red and Moses wondered if it was the booze or spending all day in the sun. He looked like a typical construction worker, big and hard and mean. Moses figured he would be the toughest to crack. The bouncers had already asked him three times to behave himself. Grayson tried to grab the rear ends of every woman who passed close enough. Grayson looked like he would enjoy a good fight. The only reason he hadn't been escorted out yet was the amount of money he stuffed in the women's garters.

A tall blond glided up to Moses' side and had to holler in his ear to ask him if he wanted a table dance. The bouncer stood expectantly behind her, holding a small round pedestal. Moses nodded and the bouncer plopped the pedestal in front of him. The blond, wearing only a G-string and skimpy top, stepped onto the pedestal and began to slink and gyrate in front of him. Moss couldn't help but admire her moves. He wondered how they learned to make their bodies undulate that way. She removed her top and Moses could see she had large breasts and figured she'd had them enlarged. It seemed all the women in the bar had large breasts. This place was a gold mine for plastic surgeons. Around the room, naked and half naked women gyrated for the customers. On the center stage, two identical twins, dark-haired and sultry, rubbed and entwined their bodies together. The blond in front of him turned away and bent in front of him, swaying her hips back and forth inches from his face. Moses was getting bored. He wished the evening would end and they could get down to business. Jeff Grayson solved the problem for him. He lunged forward drunkenly and grabbed the blonde's left breast. Moses saw the bouncer coming and slid his chair quickly out of the way. Grayson was propelled out of his chair and two bouncers grabbed him by the shoulders, launching him toward the door. Grayson would have fought back if he had the chance. The door flew open and Grayson was standing outside. He spun to swing on them but they were already back inside, the door slamming shut behind them. Moses admired their moves too.

The manager approached and apologized to Trevor Daniels and told them they'd had all the fun they were going to get and would they please leave with their friend. Daniels paid the bill and they joined the still confused Grayson outside. Grayson ranted and raved about his rough treatment, saying he could kick the asses of everyone in the place. Daniels signaled for the limousine and they piled in, pulling Grayson in with them.

"You guys get thrown out of these places all the time?" Moses asked Daniels.

"Only when we bring Jeff along," Daniels chuckled. Grayson was already dozing in his seat, head back and mouth open.

"Not a good idea to bring attention to yourselves, don't you agree?" Moses asked. " What if the cops get involved? Things could get sticky."

"Fuck the cops," Daniels replied. "Let's talk business."

Moses nodded. He glanced at Rich Martelli, who looked as if he wanted to dive out of the car and run away.

"Here's what we have to offer you. We supply the product and you distribute it to your people statewide. We take a cut off of the top of twenty percent. You keep the rest. The more product you move the more you make. And the more we make. We are looking for a quantity market. Supply and demand. You provide the supply and we fill the demand. With

Andre's group and your group we figure we can up our profit margin by forty or fifty percent."

"Why do I need you guys? I get to keep all the profit if I stay independent," Moses asked.

"True. However you have to buy your product and the markup is pretty high. We supply the product and keep twenty percent of your profit. You can lower your price to increase the amount of customers, and therefore you realize a larger profit," Daniels answered. Moses felt like he was discussing the stock market. Daniels ran this like any good bank president would. Moses had to admit if he was a real drug dealer this would be a pretty good deal. He decided to see how much more he could get Daniels to tell him.

"How do you plan on getting that much product in?" Moses asked.

"Don't worry. We have ways." Daniels smiled.

"What. Boats, planes how do you do it?" Moses asked.

"Don't ask too many questions, my friend. It could be unhealthy. You just worry about getting it distributed. Do I ask you who you work with? Or how your organization functions?" Daniels frowned. Moses decided he had pushed too hard and decided to let it lie. Well Andre, get ready, it's your turn in the barrel. He hoped they could crack Andre. If not, all this work would go down the toilet and they would lose this game. They would end up with Andre and nothing else.

Danny Quinn sat across the desk from Arturo Diaz. Diaz had just finished filling Danny in on the game plan. He asked if Danny had any questions. Danny shook his head. He really didn't have much say in the matter. It was their show until they allowed Danny in. At least they would let him watch the interrogation. Danny followed Diaz down the hall to the briefing room. The room was filled with agents. Moses was there. Agents Danny had never seen before milled about, drinking coffee and talking in small groups. Diaz guided him by the arm to a group in the corner.

This group was dressed in black SWAT type uniforms. They were the D.E.A.'s SWAT team, called the CLET team, Clandestine Lab Enforcement Team. They wore black flak vests and had submachine guns slung across their chests. They were all very physically fit with the intense look of men used to being on the edge. They reminded Danny of his team in Vietnam. People who faced the worst and knew they could handle whatever came.

"Manny Quintana. Sergeant Danny Quinn. Sheriff's Office Homicide." Diaz introduced them and they shook hands. "Manny is the leader of the CLET team in this region of operations."

"Welcome to the show, Sergeant." Quintana looked deep into Danny's eyes. He appeared satisfied with what he saw. He recognized Danny as someone who had been there. "Vietnam?" Quintana asked. Danny nodded.

"You?" Danny asked.

"SEALS." Quintana replied.

"All right. Let's get started." Diaz announced, stepping into the center of the room.

The street was quiet and dark. There were no lights showing in the houses. Somewhere in the distance a dog barked as the side door of the black van slid open silently. Black clad CLET agents slipped down the sidewalk and gathered in front of the house next to Andre's. The lead agent carried a black Halligan tool, a long handled pole with a hook, shaped like a parrot's beak, on the end. The second agent carried a large sledge hammer. Behind them, two agents carried small armored shields. The agents with the shields slipped into the front yard of Andre's house and knelt down behind the shields, weapons trained on the front windows. At the same time, agents with shields slipped over the fence in the rear yard and took up positions, weapons covering windows. The hook and hammer team slipped soundlessly to the front door and the hook was inserted in the door jamb. The rest of the team lined up behind them, weapons ready. Hearts pounded and muscles tensed in anticipation. Quintana tapped the hammer agent on the shoulder and he swung the hammer against the head of the Halligan tool with a clang. With the sound of ripping wood, the door crashed open and the team entered the opening as one body, like a big deadly snake, each one screaming, 'POLICE SEARCH WARRANT!'

Andre Baptiste was startled awake by someone yelling in his house. He jumped out of bed and reached for the bedroom doorknob, forgetting to grab the handgun on the nightstand. The bedroom door exploded toward him and he was blinded by a light in his eyes. Suddenly, he was knocked to the floor by two black clad, helmeted creatures who screamed POLICE in his face. His arms were wrenched behind his back and handcuffs clicked on his wrists. Andre was jerked to his feet and hustled out the front door in his boxer shorts. He was guided to a car at the curb and shoved inside. In the front seat were two men wearing jackets with the letters DEA printed on the back. The car screeched from the curb and Andre shook his head to clear it. *What the hell is going on? What time is it? Who the fuck are these guys? Where are we going?* Andre struggled to wake up and make sense of what had just happened.

The car entered an underground garage and he was pulled from the back seat. He was hustled to an elevator and bracketed by two more men in blue DEA jackets. He finally found his voice and glanced at the men.

"Who the fuck are you guys. Where are you taking me? Somebody answer me goddamn it." Andre demanded. The men stared straight ahead and didn't answer.

Danny stood beside Moses and watched Andre enter the room on the other side of the glass. Andre was still full of bluster and demanded to know why he was kidnapped out of bed and who the fuck was in charge here. The agent left him in the room and closed the door. Alone in the room Andre began to pace. Danny was reminded of an animal in a cage. Andre walked around the room and studied the walls. He walked to the one way glass and tried to see through it. They let him sit for about fifteen minutes. Suddenly the door burst open and Arturo Diaz strolled into the room with a file under his arm. Behind Diaz was Clancy Grainger of Immigration. He too had a file under his arm.

"What the fock gwan on here Mon?" Andre asked in his best Jamaican accent. Diaz sat at the table in front of Andre and opened the file folder. He glanced up at Andre and said one word, a command really. "Sit!"

"Hey Mon. Who the fock you tink you talkin' too?" Andre demanded but sat anyway.

"Mister Baptiste, my name is Arturo Diaz. Special Agent United States Drug Enforcement Administration. You are under arrest for possession of dangerous drugs, possession of a firearm in connection with drug dealing, conspiracy to smuggle illegal drugs into the United States, delivery of cocaine and numerous other federal charges. I can continue with the entire list if you'd like but it's not really necessary. "Diaz closed the file and stared at Andre. Andre tried to stare back but couldn't maintain it for long.

"Fock ya, Mon," Andre glanced away.

"Mister Baptiste, you don't seem to understand the gravity of your situation. Any one of these charges is punishable by life in a federal prison. You have been charged under the Drug Kingpin statute. Some of these charges could carry the death penalty. You need to help yourself here," Diaz said.

"I don' know what the hell you talking 'bout. You got notting on me Mon. I ain't deal no drugs Mon," Andre snarled. Diaz sighed and stood up. He walked to the one way window and winked at it. Moses took his cue and headed to the interrogation room. Danny watched through the glass. It wasn't his turn yet. He saw Moses enter the interrogation room and almost laughed at Andre's surprise. Andre stared and his mouth dropped open. He blinked rapidly and his mouth moved but nothing came out. His eyes got so round, Danny thought they would cover his whole face. Andre seemed to dissolve into his chair. He glanced wildly at the three agents.

"Hello Andre." Moses said.

"Damn. Mothafucka," Andre sputtered.

"Mister Baptiste, may I introduce Special Agent Moses Hammond. I believe you know each other." Diaz gloated. He enjoyed this. "Oh yes," Diaz continued, "This other gentleman is Agent Clancy Grainger of The U.S. Immigration and Naturalization Service."

"What you want Mon?" Andre stared at Moses.

"Well. We have you by the nuts, as it were, and can put you away for a long, long time. Or you can help yourself. We are prepared to offer you a chance to leave the country and avoid prison. In exchange you provide what we call Substantial Assistance."

"No way Mon." Andre said. Diaz nodded imperceptibly at Grainger.

"You don't seem to understand, Andre," Grainger said. "You have a chance here to walk on these charges and go back to Jamaica. If you help. If not you can always go to Haiti. They would love to have you."

"What you mean,. Haiti?" Andre asked.

"You see Andre, we know about your father fleeing Haiti. You were born in Haiti, before your parents fled to Jamaica. So technically, you are a Haitian citizen. Meaning, we deport you to Haiti, the poorest country in this hemisphere. Not to mention there are probably people in Haiti who remember your father and carry a grudge. You would be fair game for them. Not much money in Haiti to buy drugs so the market is pretty slim. You would have a tough time making any money. Now, in Jamaica you might have a better chance of living well. Your choice." Grainger stood and walked to the corner of the room. Andre sat and stared at the floor. Moses decided to help him decide.

"You're pretty much fucked Andre. Take the deal."

Andre nodded in resignation. He looked up at Diaz and whispered," What you want from me?"

"I want it all. I want your people. I want the people in charge of the operation. And I want Sawgrass Development and its members. In exchange, you're on a plane to Jamaica in four hours. We seize your assets in this country and you get to start over in another country," Diaz said.

Two hours later Andre was finished. His notes took up ten pages of a legal pad. He outlined the operation and its people. He gave them the names of his employees. He gave them addresses of the stash houses and the names of the boats and where they were docked. He finished with the names of members of Sawgrass Development. When he finished, he pushed the legal pad toward Diaz. Diaz studied the pad and nodded in satisfaction. He had everything he needed.

"Tell me about these people here." Diaz pointed at the names of Trevor Daniels and his friends.

"Fucking playboys. Don' know notting about the business. All they want is to have lots of money and women. Ain't serious bout it. Just want to pretend they big players," Andre answered. Diaz waved his hand toward the glass and Danny walked into the room. He was excited. It was about to come together. He picked up the legal pad and read it, flipping through the pages. Nobody named Ricky. Where the hell was the one name he needed? He slapped the pad in front of Andre.

"This is Sergeant Quinn of the Sheriffs Homicide, Andre. He has a few questions for you," Diaz said by way of introduction.

"Tell me about the murders of Gina Morelli and Gus Conrad, " Danny said, trying to control his anger.

"I don't know bout that," Andre replied.

"Tell me who Ricky is."

"I don' know nobody named Ricky," Andre answered. He glanced at them with an innocent look. Danny stormed out of the room followed by Diaz and Moses.

"That son of a bitch knows. He fucking knows," Danny growled.

"Sorry, Danny. It seems that if he gave us everything else, he would have given us this guy Ricky. Do you really think if he gave up his whole operation he would leave that part out?" Diaz asked.

"Maybe not. Goddamn it! I thought we had it. "Danny glanced at Moses who just shrugged. Diaz went back into the room and glared at Andre.

"This better be all you know. I can still reach out to you in Jamaica," Diaz said. Andre just looked back it him, emotionless. "You call Trevor Daniels and tell him you have to leave for Jamaica suddenly. That way he won't be suspicious. Tell him your mother is dying or something."

Two hours later, Andre was delivered to two US Marshals at the Miami airport. He was escorted onto a plane with US MARSHAL painted on the side. As the plane taxied from the terminal, Diaz turned toward Danny and smiled.

"Too bad we lied to him."

"What does that mean?" Danny asked.

"When our friend lands in Kingston, he will be met by officials of the DEA and Jamaican police. Starting over won't be as easy as he thinks. He will be closely watched. If he ever tries to come back to the U.S., his ass will be done. He will spend a long time in jail." Diaz chuckled. Danny was really starting to like Diaz.

Danny and Diaz stopped for breakfast at a local diner that advertised home cooking. Diaz ordered the egg and bacon special. Danny had toast and coffee.

Danny suddenly realized he was tired. He still had a full day ahead. He wondered if he should confide his plans for the day to Diaz and decided against it. Diaz wouldn't like it and Moses would like it even less. Danny decided to let them find out for themselves after it was over.

"So what's next for you guys?" Danny asked, wiping crumbs from his mouth.

"Next we figure out how the money is worked. How they launder it and how to prove everything they own is drug proceeds so we can seize it. I suspect, as Andre said, this is not a long term thing with this group. They haven't been in business long and they don't have strong ties to the cartels. If we were dealing with a true cartel, there would be so many layers we would not have been so lucky to bag them this early. This is a fringe group. They get their dope from a supplier, probably through a middle man, and peddle it on the street through Andre. The cartels usually have the whole set up to themselves. From growing the dope, to producing the product, to distribution and the rest of it. These kinds of groups are easy. That's why we won't ever stop the flow. We only get the small streams. The river keeps flowing in."

"Sounds like you're fighting a useless battle. Why bother?" Danny asked.

"Same reason any cop does his job. The job is full of bullshit bureaucracy and over management. They cater to the people who complain a cop wrote them a ticket, or he wasn't polite enough or he was too polite and they think the cop was being snotty. On top of all the stress and crap cops live with every day, we are the only ones who worry about the victims. And that's because we see them. The accused has all the rights in this country and the victim gets fucked. I do it for every kid who might try dope for the first time and get hooked. I sleep at night because I hope the dope I took off the street tonight is the one hit that kid would have used for the first time. And maybe I kept one kid from getting hooked by keeping it away from him in the first place. Sounds pretty stupid, doesn't it? I protect the people from themselves and they don't really want to be protected."

Danny knew the feeling. The administrators of police agencies entertained complaints about cops because they didn't say sir to some dirtbag who just robbed and beat some little old lady. But nobody took any action against the guy who spits in a cop's face or calls him names or threatens the cop's family. No wonder cops tend to develop an "us versus them" mentality.

Danny said good-bye to Diaz in the parking lot of the DEA building and got in his own car. The appointment was in an hour and Danny wanted to be in the office ahead of time to collect his thoughts.

Moses sat in his undercover car and wished Trevor Daniels would do something. He should have left the house long before now. Moses had been parked down the street since leaving Andre in the interrogation room. He had enjoyed the look of utter defeat on Andre's face. The best part was having them dead to rights and watching them lose.

Moses wondered how long it would take for the police to show up. A black man in this neighborhood stood out. Especially since the old guy in the house next door had walked out in his silk bathrobe to get the morning paper. He looked at Moses long and hard. Moses figured he had called the police about the stranger in the neighborhood. Rich people lived in a paranoid fear of losing their possessions. But the police hadn't shown yet and Moses hoped Trevor would make a move before they did.

A black Jaguar turned onto the block and pulled into the driveway at the Daniels' house. At last. The car sat in the driveway and in a few minutes Trevor Daniels emerged from the house. He was dressed in what appeared to be a very expensive suit. A leather briefcase swung from his hand. He opened the passenger door of the Jaguar and slid in. Moses caught a glimpse of a head of gun metal gray hair on a white male seated at the wheel. The Jaguar left the house with Moses following.

Edgar Jerome Gould led the way up the escalator for his client. They stopped at the desk of the Homicide secretary.

"Trevor Daniels and counsel to see Sergeant Quinn," Gould stated as if addressing the court. The secretary led them to one of the interview rooms in the corner. She showed them inside and asked if they would like anything , coffee or tea. Gould surveyed the room and sniffed the air as if there was a foul odor he couldn't identify. They refused refreshments. The secretary informed them Sergeant Quinn would be with them shortly and closed the door.

Danny let them wait for fifteen minutes, then breezed into the room. He apologized for the delay and sat at the table facing Daniels.

"I am sorry to interrupt your busy schedule, Mister Daniels," Danny began. Gould snorted as if he didn't buy it. "I am investigating the death of Gina Morelli and have just a few questions."

Gould glanced at his watch and Danny noticed it was a diamond-studded watch. He figured Gould wanted him to see it, as if to say "We're above you and don't need to be here."

"My client has numerous appointments, Sergeant. Let's get this concluded, shall we?" Gould said.

"Fine. Mister Daniels, I understand you are the president of the Sawgrass Development Corporation, " Danny said.

"Is that a question or a statement Sergeant?" Gould asked. Danny wanted to throw him out the window.

"That is a question of clarification, counselor," Danny replied.

"My client is the president of that corporation. So?" Gould asked.

"And Gina Morelli was an employee of that corporation?" Danny asked.

"Miss Morelli was a low level employee for the corporation," Gould replied. Danny wondered if Daniels had suddenly become a mute in his sleep. Gould certainly took the term 'Mouthpiece' to new heights. Daniels absently brushed lint from his thigh.

"What exactly did Miss Morelli do for the company?" Danny asked.

"Miss Morelli arranged certain social gatherings and assisted in corporate meetings," Gould replied.

"Do you have any idea why someone would want to kill Miss Morelli?"

"We were under the impression Miss Morelli's death was an accident." Gould answered.

"Did you know fifty thousand dollars in cash and a large amount of cocaine were found in Miss Morelli's apartment?" Danny asked. He thought he saw a glimmer of surprise in Daniels' eyes but it disappeared instantly.

"Miss Morelli's personal life has no bearing on her work and is of no interest to Mister Daniels or his associates," Gould replied. Danny was getting bored with this asshole. He thought about asking Gould about the open marriage his wife described.

Danny decided to try a new tact. "Do you know Gus Conrad?"

"That name is not familiar to Mister Daniels," Gould replied. Danny was impressed. He hadn't even seen Daniel's mouth move.

"Gus Conrad is a narcotics officer who was murdered. There is an account in Mister Daniels' bank under a fictitious name, but Conrad's social security number. Any idea how that came about?"

"If some crooked cop deposited money in Mister Daniels' bank, it is not his responsibility. Lots of people have money in that bank," Gould replied. Danny could see he was getting nowhere. He decided to have a little fun with this prick.

"Gina Morelli was good friends with Karen Gould. How intimate are you with Mrs. Gould, Mister Daniels?"

"This bullshit is over," Gould huffed. Danny could see the anger in his eyes. He saw a flicker of hatred there too. Fuck you too Counselor, Danny thought. Gould and Daniels left the building.

Danny found it interesting Gould was Daniels' attorney. With Gould's reputation and Daniels' involvement in narcotics, they made a perfect match. Gould's presence only strengthened Danny's belief Daniels was up to his neck in the deaths. He just didn't know how yet. He wanted to throw the name Ricky at him and see if there was any reaction but Gould had hustled him out too quickly.

Danny wondered if Karen Gould had summoned her husband from Washington after their meeting or if Daniels had called him after he was summoned to the Homicide office. He wondered how long it would take for Moses to find out Daniels had been there. Moses would blow his stack. Danny knew the backlash would be severe. But what the hell, everything about this case had been a tightrope walk because of Conrad's benefits.

Moses considered charging into Danny's office and punching his lights out. Danny had known he would get his information from Moses. That hard-nosed son of a bitch had to push. Moses followed Daniels and Gould back to Daniels' house. He watched as Daniels went inside alone. There was only one car in the driveway. That meant Mrs. Daniels had left with the kids for the day. Maybe Daniels intended to work at home today. Moses decided to wait and see what happened. He called Diaz on the cellular and told him about Daniels going to the Sheriffs Homicide office with his attorney. Diaz sputtered and cursed and referred to Danny as a Fucking Idiot and said he would take care of it. Moses settled back to wait. He disliked surveillance. Especially in summer. He started to bake in the heat in minutes.

Luckily, he didn't have to wait long. He watched the Corvette turn into Daniels' drive and grabbed the camera from the seat next to him. He quickly focused the telephoto lens on the blond man as he walked to the front door. He shot as many pictures as he could before the blond entered the house. That guy looked familiar, Moses thought. Where have I seen him before? He zoomed in on the license plate and read the numbers. He called the office and ran a registration check on the plates. It was a confidential tag. No record in the computer. Son of a bitch! The only people who could get confidential tags were government agencies.

Usually narcs had confidential tags., so no one could find out who they were. Was another agency working a case on these guys? Was this blond guy inside the organization undercover? The check on NERD had shown only Quinn's inquiry. What the hell was going on now?

"Look Glen, I want some answers. I just got dragged down to the Sheriffs Office and interrogated about Gina and your cop that died. I want to know who the fuck killed her." Trevor Daniels paced the room.

"I don't know," Sgt. Glen Johannsen replied. He lounged in the big armchair and watched Trevor carefully. This guy is a fool, he thought.

"What have you and Ricky found out?" Daniels asked.

"Not much. The Homicide guys have been keeping everything quiet. Conrad and Gina were accidental deaths as far as we knew until the Sheriffs boys started asking questions and told the city Conrad was murdered and started pushing for his benefits for the widow." Johannsen replied.

"Luckily for us you're doing that broad in the city personnel office. Make sure that relationship stays friendly so we know what they know. Understand?" Daniels growled. Johannsen nodded. He hated taking orders from this little prick. This rich boy thought he was Al Fucking Capone or something. Only he didn't have the balls to run a real organization. He was beginning to be sorry Ricky ever got him into this deal. But the money was good, and he had no intention of being a cop all his life.

He had started out wanting to do a good job and put the bad guys in jail. Then, he learned the system didn't want him to put the bad guys in jail. The old saying was true, society gets the police it wants and deserves. Johannsen realized he was dismissed and let himself out. Daniels stayed in the study, pacing angrily.

Moses decided to follow the Corvette. He followed it back to Johannsen's house. Nice place, he thought. Whoever this guy was, he had some bucks. Most cops couldn't afford a house like this. He decided to wait and see who showed up now. The players in this deal were multiplying like rabbits.

The blond woman parked her car in the driveway and turned the rearview mirror to check her hair and makeup. She brushed her hair carefully. Moses wrote down the license plate and had the camera ready when she stepped out. Looks like a date, Moses thought. Women usually fixed themselves up when they went to meet their man. So, Johannsen has a lunch fling going. Moses couldn't remember the last time he had a fling at any time of the day. Moses decided Johannsen and the woman would be occupied for a awhile. He decided to drive to the Sheriffs Office and confront Danny. Think I'll get this film developed first, he decided.

Moses could hear Diaz's rage ten feet from the door. He was yelling at the top of his lungs. Moses almost felt sorry for Quinn. He knew how mad Diaz could get. He had the unique ability to make you feel two inches tall and then feel as if you were crushed under his shoe. He could hear Quinn yelling back and he seemed to be holding his own with Diaz. Moses quietly stepped into the room.

"Look, Quinn. I am in charge of this case and I don't want some local Homicide cop screwing it up. Not only have you jeopardized this case, but you have jeopardized the safety of Agent Hammond. His ass is on the line with these people. We had it set up so he was covered. We got Andre out with a good cover story so they wouldn't suspect anything if he disappeared for awhile. But no! As soon as Andre leaves you start shaking the tree to see what falls out. These people aren't stupid. They are going to wonder why Hammond suddenly gets brought in by Andre and then Andre disappears. Then the cops start sniffing around them. They might figure it out and realize Hammond is a cop and whack him too!" Diaz dropped in a chair, his anger spent.

"I didn't give them any reason to suspect Moses. I convinced them this was just the next phase of my investigation. The only reason, as far as they know, is because Gina was an employee." Danny countered.

"We had a fucking timetable. All laid out nice and neat but now we'll have to push the timetable up and start rounding them up. You fucked up our case." Diaz snarled. Diaz noticed Moses for the first time. "What have you got Moses?"

"Something interesting," Moses answered dropping the pictures on the table. "Right after Daniels attorney left, this guy showed up." He pointed at the pictures. " He looks vaguely familiar. And he has a confidential tag. Don't know who he is."

Danny picked up the picture and glanced at it. His heart skipped a beat. He held his breath, wondering how to approach this one with them.

"That is Sergeant Glen Johannsen. Conrad's supervisor," he breathed.

"What!" Diaz exclaimed and grabbed the picture. " Are you sure?" Danny nodded.

"He was at the funeral. Sat right in the front row. Comforted the widow ." Danny picked up the next set of pictures and laughed out loud. Moses leaned over his shoulder and looked at the picture.

"You know her too?" He asked. Danny nodded and sat back with a big grin.

"Mrs. Richard Stevens. Mrs. Major Dick Stevens. She is director of personnel for the city," he replied.

"Do you know what this means?" Danny asked, glancing at them. "This is how they got Conrad's social security number." He noticed their blank looks. "We found a bank account in Daniels' bank under Conrad's social security number but a different name. Conrad's son told me he was warned to keep his mouth shut or they would take the old man down by making him look dirty. Hence, the bank account. But I couldn't figure out how they got his social security number, unless he was involved with them and he really opened the account himself. But the kid says Conrad was a straight shooter. Even asked the kid to help him bring these assholes down. This is how they got the number. From his personnel file. Johannsen is dirty and Mrs. Stevens is at least involved with Johannsen."

"I would say involved is a good word. From what I saw, she was going to Johannsen's house for a rendezvous," Moses said.

"You mean she's having an affair with Johannsen? Shit, I wonder if Major Dick knows," Danny wondered out loud. He would love to take this picture straight up to Major Dick's office and shove it in his face. Show him while he was screwing the troops, his wife was screwing somebody else. Danny was enjoying this.

"All right. Moses, where do we go from here?" Diaz asked.

"Well. Because of Danny's screw up today, we need to start picking these assholes up soon. Before they get suspicious of me. We squeeze them to see what they'll give us. We've got a good drug conspiracy case. At this point, we drag them in here and see if we can solve Quinn's homicides. If that's okay with him?" Moses glanced at Danny. He nodded.

"But first, there's something I want to do first. Just to have some leverage." Danny said.

Danny watched as the Jeep Cherokee turned into the gas station. He glanced at Mike Richards seated next to him. Richards nodded solemnly. He had been forced to tell Dominic Basso the reason they needed the paperwork. The Jeep parked next to them. Basso slid into the back seat of Danny's car.

"I don't like this one bit," Basso grumbled.

"I don't like it either, Dominic. But I have no choice. If Johannsen is involved then we need to know. If not, then we need to know that too," Danny said.

"How you gonna know for sure?" Basso asked as he handed the envelope over the seat.

"Handwriting analysis. We compare Johannsen's handwriting to the the bank paperwork. Then, we know." Danny opened the envelope and slid the papers out. "You're sure Johannsen won't know you took this?"

"Not a chance. He wasn't in the office and I copied the original. The original is back where it was. Man! I can't believe Johannsen is dirty. Motherfucker hid his tracks well. There was no sign. But I guess trust makes you blind." Basso sighed.

"Yeah I know. When you depend on the person next to you to go through a door and cover your back, you hope he's on your side. Or you just accept he is," Danny answered.

"Well. Let me know what you find." Basso opened the door and got out. He walked to the Jeep and Danny noticed that his shoulders slumped. He looked like a man whose last faith in the world had just been trampled.

Danny glanced at Richards as they returned to the office. He looked a little pale and seemed to have lost weight. His jacket hung loosely on his shoulders.

"Everything all right with you, Mike?" he asked.

"Yeah. Been on a diet. Trying to regain my youthful figure," Richards replied. He changed the subject. "You ever known a dirty cop?" he asked. Danny shook his head. He thought about the question. He had known a lot of cops in his time. He had known some who got too physical with suspects, some who cheated on their wives and some that drank too much. But he had never known one that took money or planted evidence or did anything else dishonest. Even the ones that got physical. Danny knew when cops got physical, it was usually with a suspect who had violently resisted or tried to hurt the cop. He had never known one to hurt a prisoner out of maliciousness. He wouldn't have allowed it anyway. He looked at Richards.

"You ever known a crooked cop?" He asked. Richards nodded.

"I stayed away from them though. Never thought my badge could be bought. If I had ever seen a cop stealing or planting drugs, I'dve beat his ass," Richards replied.

"Would you turn 'em in?" Danny asked.

"No. But I would have made them real sorry they chose to go that way," he answered. The answer satisfied Danny. He knew the hell a cop could pay for being accused of being a rat. Richards' way was probably better.

Danny leaned against the counter and waited. He was getting impatient. The handwriting examiner leaned over his magnification screen and made notes with a marker. How long did it take to say yes or no, Danny wondered. Finally, the handwriting tech looked up at him.

"That's definitely your man. The handwriting is the same. Where did you get this sample?" he asked.

"I would rather not say," Danny replied. "You are sure and will testify in court that it is the same person?"

"Absolutely." The tech nodded. Danny had blacked out the signature to mask the author. Better not to let too many people know about this yet. He nodded at the tech and retrieved the paper from him. He slipped it back into the envelope. Now, you son of a bitch, your sorry ass is mine, he thought.

CHAPTER 16

R ose Hinton glanced at herself in the mirror. She thought she looked all right. Nothing special. Ever since Trevor Daniels had started touching her, she had tried to dress more conservatively. She wore no makeup to work and had started to wear baggier clothes. She thought maybe she had caused his attentions somehow. Every time he touched her she felt like screaming. Every time she felt as if she were covered with a oily film she couldn't scrub off. She had tried. In the shower she scrubbed her skin until it was bright red and almost raw. She noticed she was thinner. She had no appetite and was jumpy all the time. Every little noise made her start. She slept with the light on now. Always afraid he would show up at her house. He had never tried to approach her after work, but she didn't doubt he would. She rarely left the house anymore. She was afraid to go out. She went to the grocery store and hurried home, glancing over her shoulder every two seconds. The only time she dared to leave was to visit her grandmother in the nursing home. Like today. But today would be different.

She was scared but had resolved herself to do this thing. She considered a lawsuit, but after seeing an attorney and discovering she would have to bare all in front of strangers, she decided against it. The lawyer told her it would be her word against his. It would be tough to prove, even though juries were more inclined to believe this kind of thing went on in this day and age. Rose believed her way was better. She would destroy the sleazy bastard and she wouldn't ever have to appear in court, if she was lucky. She hoped they would find her a nice place to go. Maybe they would even let her take her grandmother. She worshipped the old woman. She was the toughest woman Rose had ever known. Even now, when she had nothing to look forward to, she bravely continued on. Lately though, she had been saying things that worried Rose. Things like, she was just waiting to die. She sometimes wondered out loud to Rose why God was waiting so long. She had been ready for quite a while. Rose always reassured her there must be a good reason.

Rose slammed the car door and made sure it was locked. Even here, where she knew she must be safe, she was frightened. She walked up the circular walk and admired the landscaping. She took in the manicured grounds and noticed the roses in the garden were starting to bloom. She smiled. Her grandmother loved roses. Her grandfather had grown magnificent roses.

She thought of him in his garden. His faded, old blue jeans with the hole in the knee. Her grandmother once threw the jeans away and he dug them out of the trash and washed them. He raged at her grandmother that the jeans were just getting broke in. She could see him in the garden. A pipe dangling from his mouth. The gray fringe of hair around the bald pate wet and stuck to his head. The bald spot always peeling from sunburn. His hands were huge and callused from a life of hard work. But they were gentle hands, holding and caressing the rose blossoms like delicate porcelain. It was her grandfather that convinced her mother to name her Rose. He once confided in her that he grew the roses so he could give them to his beloved wife as gifts every day. He said her name was Rose because she was a wondrous gift.

Rose opened the double glass doors and stepped aside to let a resident in a wheelchair pass. The old woman had a sweater around her shoulders, even in this heat. Her hair was patchy and stuck out wildly from her head. She stared straight ahead, unseeing. The nurse pushing the wheelchair smiled at Rose as they passed. Rose waved at the nurse behind the desk who waved and said, "She's in her room."

Rose crossed the dayroom and glanced at the old people who slumped in big armchairs facing the television. A game show was on. She walked down the hall toward her grandmother's room. The halls were sparkling clean. The entire place smelled stale. The smell of moth balls mingled with the smell of antiseptic. Rose hated that smell. She wondered why all nursing homes smelled the same way.

Her grandmother was facing the window when she entered. The sunlight lit her face and seemed to make her glow. Her white hair was neatly combed and she wore a flowered house dress. She smiled at Rose and held out her arms. Rose leaned down and kissed her on the forehead. The skin felt dry and brittle.

"Hi good looking," Rose smiled at her. "How ya doing?"

"Not bad for an old bird," her grandmother replied. Her crippled and bent hands fluttered at her knees as she smoothed her skirt.

"Are they treating you okay?" Rose asked.

"This place is miserable. Nothing but old farts waiting for something to happen," She giggled.

"Now dear. Don't be so hard on them. They're just not as fun loving as you," Rose laughed. She wondered how to tell her. She decided to wait until she was ready to leave.

Rose had a good time visiting with her grandmother. She wheeled her around the garden in her wheelchair. They admired the roses and the trees that had been planted recently. They reminisced about her grandfather and the old lady became misty-eyed. They even challenged an old man with a cane to a race around the grounds. Rose returned the old lady to her room and decided it was time to go. She dreaded telling her but knew she had to. In case, the old lady couldn't go with her.

"Grandma. I may have to go away for awhile," Rose said quietly.

"Go where dear? Why?" Her grandmother frowned.

"It's because of work. It'll only be for a little while. I'll keep in touch with you. Let you know where I am. I can't tell you any more because I don't know," Rose said. The old lady nodded in understanding. She wouldn't ask anymore.

"I'll be back Grandma. I promise." Rose touched her arm..

"Well. Maybe I'll be here when you get back." The old lady smiled.

"You will. I love you Grandma." Rose fought back tears.

"I love you too, dear. You do what you have to," her grandmother answered. Somehow she knew and understood. But then, she always did.

Rose fought back tears as she hurried from the building. In the hallway, she passed an old man huddled in a big chair. His skin was almost transparent, the veins visible. He looked like a skeleton with skin. He cried out." Oh-oh-oh-" over and over.

Rose almost turned and fled three times before she got to the federal building. And twice more when she entered the lobby. The only thing that stopped her was the guard behind the glass asking if he could help her. She braced herself by deciding her grandmother would have the strength to do this.

"Special Agent Bolton, please," Rose said, handing Bolton's card through the slot at the bottom of the glass. The guard nodded and picked up the phone. After a short conversation he looked up at Rose and said,

"Agent Bolton will be right with you."

A door in the corner buzzed and opened. Bolton stepped out and grinned when he spied her.

"I don't know if you remember me," Rose started. He cut her off.

"Of course, Miss Hinton. What can I do for you?" Bolton replied.

"I have something you should be interested in," she answered, silently praying for strength.

"Let's go to my office." He said ushering her though the door.

Rose took the chair he offered and opened her purse. Extracting four computer disks, she handed them to him.

"It's all there," she said, then noticing his quizzical look she continued. "Sawgrass Development. All the records. Business transactions. Payments. Everything." He took the disks and turned them over in his hands. He could hardly contain his excitement. This was a gold mine, if what she said were true. He had no doubt it was. He reached for the phone and waited.

"Moses. Greg Bolton. I think you better come to my office. Bring the boss with you if you can find him." He nodded and hung up. He turned to Rose.

"There are some other people in the office who need to see this too."

Moses and Diaz arrived minutes later and Bolton introduced them. Moses and Diaz shook her hand.

"Miss Hinton brought us the records from Sawgrass Development," Bolton said, holding up the disks.

"Should we call Quinn?" Moses asked. Diaz shook his head.

"Let's see what we've got first. "

Bolton inserted the first disk into the hard drive and the screen came alive. He pointed the cursor to the first entry and clicked the mouse. A list of companies and numbers were displayed. Bolton glanced at Rose and asked her to translate. She pointed at the screen.

"This is the way they hide the money," Rose began. "The money comes in and is immediately diverted to these companies' accounts. You'll notice they are construction companies, real estate and others. The money is used to purchase properties. After the property is purchased, it is developed by these construction companies, contractors, electricians, plumbing everything you need to build a mall, office building, housing developments and the like. After the property is developed, the profits are deposited into the account of Sawgrass Development. The members are then paid from the profits. At this point, the money is legitimate and clean. You know where the money comes from?"

"Why don't you tell us," Bolton replied.

"Drugs. They buy the drugs from a Colombian. They then smuggle the drugs in through their own people and sell it through this guy." She pointed at the name, Andre Baptiste. "These are the names of the people who are members of Sawgrass Development. Here are the names of the boats they use. These addresses are properties they own and rent out. Only, they don't rent them out. They're fakes. I think they keep the drugs there."

"How do you know all of this?" Diaz asked.

"I hear them talking and I know everything about the bank. Of course, I'm not sure about all of it. Some of it I am assuming."

"I think you're assuming right. My question is why are you here and why are you doing this?" Diaz asked.

"I can't take it anymore. Trevor Daniels is a pig." She looked at the floor. Diaz glanced at Bolton quizzically.

"Why don't you tell us about it?" Bolton soothed.

"He touches me. He fondles me." She began to cry softly. "I talked to a lawyer but they aren't any help. They try, but they have to tell you the whole thing. How bad it will be in court and the rest. I can't do that."

"Well, I think this way will be better." Diaz smiled at her. "We can do a lot more damage to Trevor Daniels than a lawsuit will. And maybe we can make it worth your while besides."

"Will I have to testify?" She looked up.

"You may have to tell a Federal Prosecutor how you got these disks. But we'll see what we can do about having to testify," Diaz replied. He pointed at the screen and asked, "Who is this guy here?"

"He's the Colombian. Enrique Madeira. They call him Ricky. That man scares me. He always has a guy with him. Big, evil-looking. His name's Jose something. I never heard his last name. What do I do now?" Rose asked, looking from one to the other.

"Miss Hinton," Diaz said, "I know this will be difficult for you, but we need you to stay where you are for a very short while. We need a little time to put this all together. Can you do that?"

"If I know Trevor is going to get his, I suppose I can. But then what?"

"Then we get you relocated and protected. The US Marshall's will get you into Witness Protection," Diaz answered.

"I have an elderly grandmother in a nursing home. She's all I have in this world. Can she go with me?" Rose pleaded.

"I'm sure we can take care of that too," Diaz reassured her. She smiled sadly and stood. Greg Bolton rose with her and escorted her out of the building.

"Well. I guess the next thing is to find out if this guy Madeira is Quinn's man Ricky?" Diaz asked Moses. He nodded.

"I'll call our office in Colombia and see if the locals have Madeira's record or prints on file."

Moses had been waiting for three hours. He paced, then sat. C'mon, he thought to himself, call dammit. The phone rang and he snatched it up. The agent on the other end had good news. Ricky Madeira was known to the local office and the police. His fingerprints were being faxed to Moses in five minutes. Moses thanked him and hung up. He called Quinn and was informed he was out of the office. Moses went to the fax machine and watched the finger print card scroll off the machine. He took the fingerprints and tucked them into his pocket.

Danny searched Dominic Basso's face. He would have liked to bring Johannsen in himself, but he didn't have enough to charge him with murder. He hoped he could get him to talk.

"Look, Dom. This is not easy for me to tell you, but it is necessary. We compared Johannsen's handwriting and it matches. He filled out the paperwork to open the account in Conrad's name. He's involved in this up to his ass," Danny spoke gently to Basso. He could only guess how hard it was for Basso to discover his boss and partner was dirty, maybe even killed one of his own. Basso had to be wondering what else Johannsen had done no one knew about.

"What do you want me to do?" Basso asked, looking at the floor.

"I want to get him to the office and see if we can get him to crack. What I don't want is for him to run or hole up. I also don't want him to scream for a lawyer or a PBA rep before we get what we need," Danny replied.

"What do I say to get him there?"

"Tell him we know who killed Conrad and we want to bring you two in to help with the arrest," Danny said.

Basso glanced up sharply. " Do you know who killed Gus?"

"Not yet. I'm hoping we can get Johannsen to give it up," Danny answered.

"You think Johannsen did it?" Basso asked.

"I hope not. Tell him we want a meet at six o'clock at my office. Think you can get him there?"

"How about if I just shoot the motherfucker myself and save us all the trouble?" Basso asked.

Danny smiled grimly. He understood the feeling. He wanted to shoot Johannsen himself. But it wouldn't solve anything. He wanted to watch him squirm, then crash.

"I don't think that would help. I know how you feel. Let's just get him in and see where he takes us?"

"I'd rather shoot him." Basso snarled as he left. Danny started the car and looked at Mike Richards seated beside him. Richards was deep in thought.

"I say we let him shoot the fuck," Richards mumbled. Danny nodded. Suddenly, his hip vibrated and he pulled the pager from his belt, glancing at the display. The office number was followed by 911. He handed the pager to Richards and asked him to call the office. He listened as Richards talked to the office on the cellular phone. He thought to himself how technology had made the job easier. Pagers, cell phones. Used to be you got messages late or not at all. Then you had to find a pay phone. Richards hung up and dropped the phone on the seat between them.

"Moses Hammond's waiting for us at the office. Says it's urgent," Richards said, then asked. "What's your read on this guy Hammond?"

"Seems to be decent cop. Pretty good narc too. Why?" Danny asked.

"I don't know. I have a hard time trusting feds, I guess. Never know whose agenda they are running," Richards answered.

"Well, don't forget, Moses is one of ours. He's just assigned to the Feds."

"That makes me more nervous. You gotta wonder if he's trying to impress the DEA so they'll take him away to bigger and better things," Richards grumbled.

"I really don't think that's the case. Damn! You are cynical."

"I learned everything I know from you, master." Richards laughed.

Moses was thumbing through a police supply catalog when Richards and Quinn entered the cubicle. He dropped the magazine back onto Danny's desk.

"What's so urgent?" Danny asked. Moses picked up a manila envelope from the chair beside him and handed it to Danny. Danny opened it and slid the fingerprints form out. He raised his eyebrows in question.

"Those are the fingerprints of one Enrique "Ricky" Madeira. You get the significance of the name Ricky. May be your phantom Colombian with the ponytail. You said you had prints from Conrad's car you couldn't identify. Maybe there's a match." Moses smiled. Danny handed the forms to Richards and sat down without saying a word. Richards hurried from the room. Danny looked at Moses quizzically.

"An informant turned up out of the blue. Works at the bank. In an attack of revenge she brought us computer disks of bank transactions and all of the doings of the Sawgrass Development Corporation. Seems that Trevor Daniels has been sexually harassing her for years. She wants payback. She is also familiar with the entire group, including Ricky Madeira. I called the DEA field office in Colombia and got the prints from the Colombian police. At this point, we have all we need to take down the entire operation for drug smuggling, money laundering and hopefully, if those prints match, Murder one." Moses sat back proudly.

"I don't know what we would do without you on this, Moses. We are this close," Danny held two fingers close to each other. "Since I talked to you, we have had some good fortune too. A handwriting analysis of Greg Johannsen's handwriting and the bank paperwork shows that Johannsen wrote the account request. He opened the account in Conrad's name. With the photographs and the analysis, I think we can get him to roll. He's coming here at six o'clock for a meeting. He thinks it's a case update. I would like you here with those photos in case we need them."

Moses nodded.

Mike Richards felt a knot in the pit of his stomach. He looked at the screen of the AFIS fingerprint comparison machine. The fingerprints of Ricky Madeira blended with the fingerprint from Gus Conrad's car. The technician smiled and punched some buttons on the computer keyboard. The computer marked the similarities of the two fingerprints. Twenty seven points were the same. Only fifteen were needed for court. The technician stroked more keys and the machine finished its work. There was no doubt the same person made both fingerprints.

Richards felt the anger well up inside of him. He wanted to find this motherfucker Madeira and put a bullet in his mouth like Madeira had done to Conrad. This son of a bitch was a cop killer and Richards wanted to make him pay. Cops were funny about a cop killer. They worked just as hard on every homicide, but when it was another cop, it meant something different. People got murdered for greed, rage jealousy, or fear. But with a cop, it was different. They died because they were a cop. Nothing more. Every cop looked into the eyes of a dead cop's family and saw their own family's eyes. They knew it could be them tomorrow if they weren't careful. Cops took it personally. Richards called Danny with the news.

CHAPTER 17

Dominic Basso had stifled his rage all day. Since his meeting with Quinn, he had avoided Johannsen, not sure he could contain his rage. He felt lost. He decided when this was over he would find a new profession. He had a fairly busy landscaping business on the side that he let his partner run. He decided he was done with police work once and for all. He had tried to do what he could but the system was broken and Dominic doubted it could be fixed. Criminals were walking away scot free every day for stupid legal technicalities and the cops were left holding a bag of shit. Everyone blamed the police for letting the criminals out. But the cops weren't to blame. The court system was completely fucked up and nobody cared. Now, cops were killing each other. Basso felt as if every thing he ever believed in was nothing but bullshit. Basso hesitated before entering the narcotics office. He took a deep breath just like when he was going into a drug deal. He shifted into character and pretended everything was normal. He found Johannsen in his office.

Johannsen looked up when Basso entered and glanced at his watch. It would take them twenty minutes to get to the Sheriffs Office. Basso hoped he could contain himself that long.

Danny, Moses, and Mike Richards waited in Danny's office. Danny forced himself not to be excited. Richards finally asked the question none of them had dared to pose.

"How are you going to play this guy?" he asked carefully.

"The way we play any suspect. Lie, terrify, crucify, then let them fry," Danny answered.

"What if he's armed? He is a cop." Moses asked.

"Let's just hope he's not." Danny had considered the possibility. If he was confronted and panicked, there could be a serious problem if Johannsen was carrying his gun. Danny had decided to see what happened when he and Basso arrived. He decided if Johannsen was armed, they would have him place his weapon in a gun locker by using the excuse there were other prisoners in the same unsecured area. Danny had his backup gun in the ankle holster. He suddenly wondered if he could shoot another cop. He decided he could.

Johannsen and Basso arrived and Danny led the way to a conference room in the corner of the detective division. The question had been posed that no weapons were permitted in the area. Johannsen had left his weapon at the office. Danny relaxed slightly after that. Danny had arranged for Moses to be out of sight when they entered the office.

"Sergeant Johannsen," Danny began when they were seated at the table. "I wanted to bring you up to date on this case so you know where we stand, since Conrad worked for you." Johannsen nodded. It was apparent he had no clue what was about to happen.

"What we know so far is this," Danny continued. "Conrad's social security number was used to open an account under a false name. Not unusual if you're dirty. On the day he was killed, Conrad was apparently lured by someone, someone he probably knew, to the area of the orange grove. Once there, he was attacked from behind and held to the seat by some kind of strap. His weapon was then used to kill him. It was supposed to look like suicide. But was actually a planned hit. Maybe over drugs, maybe money. However, the account was a dummy. Conrad had nothing to do with it. He was also not dirty. As you may know, his son is in prison for drug charges. Gus Junior was involved with a group of dopers. This group was run by a pony-tailed Colombian named Ricky." Danny watched for a reaction. Johannsen remained stone-faced. Danny wasn't surprised. This guy made his living acting out roles. Danny decided to drive the knife all the way in and see what happened. "What we want to know is how deep are you in this?"

The shock on Johannsen's face was immediate. He looked at Danny as if he had slapped him across the mouth, which is exactly what Danny wished he could do. Johannsen leapt from his chair, sputtering.

"What the fuck are you talking about? Have you completely lost your mind?" he raged. He glanced around wildly, looking like he was about to bolt from the room.

"Sit the fuck down, asshole," Dominic growled dangerously from behind Johannsen. Johannsen realized he was trapped in the room with them, with Basso, of whom he was terrified, between him and the door. Basso took a step toward him and Johannsen dropped in his chair. He looked wildly from Danny to Basso. He opened his mouth to speak but the words wouldn't come.

"Now Sergeant." Danny spoke quietly but menacingly," Suppose you tell us about it. See, we know your signature is on the bank paperwork. You opened the account to make Conrad look dirty. We also know you are part of a group called Sawgrass Development. We know about Trevor Daniels and your connection to him."

"You don't have anything. You're groping in the dark." Johannsen began to get his bravado back. "You can't solve this case so you fuck with me 'cause he worked with me. Conrad was dirty. The money proves it. His fucking kid is a user. The old man was helping the kid deal his dope. We just never knew it. Now you try to drag me into it. You're fucked up, man. If anybody was hooked with this guy Ricky, it was Conrad."

Danny glanced up at Richards who immediately left the room. He returned with Moses in tow. Danny almost burst out laughing when Johannsen saw Moses. He opened and closed his mouth silently like a fish out of water. He turned pale, then red crept in. Danny let him squirm for a minute.

"Glen. We know more than you think. This is Moses Hammond. DEA. He looks familiar to you, I'm sure. We got you by the balls. I'm trying to help you here. You're looking at some long time in prison. Not to mention the loss of your pension. All those years of risking your ass down the drain. Besides, we have a witness who identified you as one of the people in the car that left the orange grove when Conrad was killed," Danny lied. "We had your handwriting compared with the bank paperwork and the other written evidence in this case. You wrote it. There is no question. You need to save your ass right now. When we drag Trevor in here and the rest of them, they'll give you up. Especially Ricky. Maybe even Mrs. Stevens. Do you want that brought into the light?" Johannsen just stared at Danny. Moses opened the envelope he held and dropped the pictures of him and Mrs. Stevens in front of Johannsen.

He looked down at them and began to twitch. Moses dropped the pictures of Johannsen and Trevor Daniels on the desk next to the other pictures. Johannsen began to tremble. Everyone in the room seemed to be holding their breath. Danny wanted to scream at him to confess, but fought the feeling. They waited. Danny thought he could hear his heart beat. The air conditioner started up, humming somewhere in the ceiling. Johannsen sat and stared at the pictures. Danny saw tears begin to well up in Johannsen's eyes.

"I didn't kill Gus," he whispered. "I didn't know they were going to kill him. They were only going to make him a deal he couldn't refuse. Ricky had me open the account to keep Conrad out of our business. It didn't work. They had me set up a meeting. I didn't know it was going to go like that. Ricky said Conrad had been working a surveillance on them and saw something they didn't want him to see. I asked what, but they wouldn't tell me. We met Conrad at a mall and drove to the grove. Jose was in the back seat behind Conrad. He grabbed him with a strap. Ricky stuck Conrad's gun in his mouth and shot him." Johannsen shuddered. " My only job was to check out guys like Moses and see if they were cops. When a load came in, I was supposed to secure the landing sight to make sure there was no surveillance. I'm not a killer."

"Is there a load in now?" Moses asked. Johannsen nodded. "Will you give me the boats and the locations?" Johannsen nodded again.

"Do you know Gina Morelli?" Danny asked.

"She worked for Trevor. She was his main piece of ass. After Karen Gould. Gina would make the arrangements. Did social introductions, stuff like that. I don't know much about Daniels and the others. Ricky worked for them and I worked for Ricky. "

"Why was Gina killed?" Danny asked.

"I don't know. Ricky said not to worry about Gina. She was out of the group and he took care of the problem," Johannsen replied.

"You mean he killed her?" Danny asked.

"I guess so."

"You will be read your rights and I want a taped statement. All of it. Understand?" Danny said softly. Johannsen nodded. A tear drop dripped from his eyes and fell to the desktop.

Danny wanted to spit on him. Danny and Moses left the room and regrouped in the hallway. Danny was tired. The emotional fatigue had taken its toll. He knew he had a long night ahead. He knew it was time to round up Trevor, Ricky and the rest of them. He secretly hoped Ricky would try to resist.

Rich Martelli sipped the scotch in his hand and walked to the window. Trevor said nothing was wrong and not to worry. He couldn't help it. He turned off the stereo because the music was starting to get on his nerves. Johannsen had disappeared. Andre was gone to Jamaica. Martelli felt something was up. He wondered if he should pack his bags and grab the first plane to anywhere. He wished now he had never gotten into this mess. He was an honest businessman but the money had lured him in. He had to admit the excitement of a double life had been fun for awhile. But now, he felt his world crashing down on him. He should have just stayed with the real estate business. He would have been rich soon enough, but this way was quicker. Besides, Trevor had been very convincing.

The first time, the money had shocked Martelli. He had never seen so much money and it was tax free. Martelli was from a small town in Ohio and grew up on a farm. He watched his father work his hands to the bone. Out of bed hours before the sun came up and fall into bed at midnight. He remembered the day his father had been diagnosed with cancer. He was devastated with the possibility that his father would die. His father had always been so big and strong. Rich never thought his father could be struck down. He watched his father waste away to one hundred and twenty pounds. The doctors said he could be treated and have more time to live. But Martelli Senior refused and kept working on the farm. There were cows to be tended and crops to plant.

Martelli shuddered as he remembered the day his father slumped over in the seat of the tractor and had to be carried to the house. It hadn't taken long after that. The endless hours sitting by his father's bed as the cancer ate away at him. He thought of the day his mother had woken him up in the morning to tell him his father had gone during the night. She had tears in her eyes. It was the first time Rich Martelli had seen any sadness in his mother's eyes. She tried to be strong for Rich and his younger brother, but Martelli heard her through the closed bedroom door, crying softly, late in the night. He had decided then and there that he would be rich and take care of her. But she had gone two years after his father. The doctors said it was her heart and it had just given out. But Martelli believed it had been broken and never healed.

He had let them both down now and he was probably going to prison for a long time. Maybe the rest of his life. He stood at the window and looked down on a yacht passing by in the Intracoastal waterway below. He thought how beautiful the city looked at night. It seemed cleaner somehow, the ugliness hidden by the darkness.

Martelli loved his condo. It had cost him half a million dollars. Just beyond the building across the Intracoastal was the ocean. He loved the ocean, having grown up so far from any water. He walked to the beach every evening and stood with his feet in the surf and closed his eyes, letting the ocean breeze cool his face. Now, he probably would never feel the breeze again. Maybe he was overreacting. There was no sign the cops knew about them. The fact Johannsen was not to be found wasn't unusual. He had gone incognito before, when he was working a case for the police department. Maybe Andre's' grandmother really was sick. Trevor said he was a worrier and he should relax. Trevor said they had covered their tracks too well. But Trevor always was too sure of himself.

Martelli wished he could be more like Trevor, more of a leader. He had never been the type to take charge. In school, he stood in the back of the group when the team captains were picked so no one would pick him, fearing he would fail as a leader. He even let his younger brother run things when they played. His brother picked the game and Rich just went along. He started to relax, Trevor would take care of everything. Trevor and Ricky. Martelli was more frightened of Ricky than anyone he had ever met. Something in his eyes. They seemed to be looking into your soul, searching for weakness. Martelli believed Ricky could see into him and see the weakness huddled there.

Martelli turned at the sound of a knock on the door. He set his drink on the window sill and crossed the room. He wondered who it could be. Probably some delivery man. The security guard downstairs wouldn't let anyone into the building without checking them out first. He opened the door and his heart stopped.

The man at the door wore a blue jacket with DEA stenciled on the right breast and a badge stenciled on the left. His companion had a pistol pointed at Martelli's eyes. He froze as the man with the jacket stated, "Federal Agents, Mister Martelli, you're under arrest. Raise your hands very slowly and turn around." Martelli didn't move. The man repeated his command and Martelli felt the room tilt. The image swam before his eyes and he raised his hands slowly. The men stepped into the room and the jacketed agent yanked his hands behind his back, clicking handcuffs on his wrists. Martelli felt nausea well up inside him and his eyes burned with tears. He gasped for air and his knees were weak. Oh God. Momma help me, he pleaded silently. The agent spun him around and frisked him roughly. He was escorted by the arms to the elevator and directed into it. The doors slid closed silently and Martelli heard the muzak begin to play. He felt like his heart would burst through his chest. He began to cry softly. The agent glanced at him with a look of disgust but remained rigid and silent.

Trevor Daniels pulled on his slacks. He reached for his shoes in the corner and slipped them on. The door to the bedroom opened and his wife stood in the doorway, arms folded, glaring at him. She wore a satin robe and fuzzy slippers. He glanced up at her. " What?" he asked.

"Where are you going ?" she asked.

"Out," he replied with a grunt.

"You always go out. I thought maybe we could spend some time together tonight. The kids are asleep. I bought a bottle of wine," she said wistfully.

"Not tonight. I'm going with the guys for a while. Don't wait up." He had no interest in spending the evening with his wife.

The marriage had become boring to him long ago. Since the kids were born he had found no excitement with her. They met in college and she had been in the right social circle. He had been in the debate club and the rowing team. She had been in a sorority and traveled in the same elite circles. The relationship had blossomed in the back of a fraternity house one night after a big homecoming party when they had sex for the first time. After that they just seemed to be together, expected to be a couple by all of their friends. Trevor knew immediately his father would approve of her. She was " their kind of people." Her father was a very wealthy stock broker who owned his own brokerage house and seemed to have more money than God himself. Now they sort of just co-existed. This fight had happened before, when he told her there was no spark left and no matter how hard she tried, she couldn't re-ignite it. The last time they had argued about this he had informed her he would do what he chose and her job was to raise the kids. Besides, he told her, didn't she have a very comfortable life with all his money, so she shouldn't complain.

She thought about going home to her parents that last time but knew her father wouldn't understand, telling her it was her job to raise the kids and a man had the right to do what he wanted. Her mother put up with it so why shouldn't she? She decided not to fight about it this time and left the room as he finished dressing.

Danny sat motionless in the passenger seat as Diaz fidgeted behind the wheel. Diaz was tense. They had discussed making the arrest in the house but Danny convinced him to wait and see what developed. He hated to arrest a man in his own house if it could be avoided. It was always uncomfortable with the pleading wife and the crying children begging for their daddy not to be arrested. He always felt sorry for the wife and kids. The kids especially. They would be traumatized for years because their father was a criminal.

Another mosquito buzzed through the open window and bit Danny's arm but he ignored it. He blocked them out of his mind, just like he had done in Vietnam. He had once lain in a rice paddy for three days, waiting for the right victim to come within range of his rifle. Vietnam had more bugs than Danny had ever seen. They seemed to be crawling on one's body constantly. The other soldiers had swatted and slapped at them endlessly. Danny ignored them. He knew if you slapped at a bug at the wrong time, the enemy would hear you and you could end up dead. Besides, the Everglades had lots of bugs too and he had learned to ignore them growing up. Unlike his buddies in 'Nam he hadn't hated the place. The heat and the bugs and the rain hadn't bothered him much. Vietnam was a lot like the Everglades. To Danny it felt like home.

Diaz stiffened beside him and pointed towards the Daniels' house. Danny saw a sudden flicker of light as the front door opened and closed. They watched as a figure walked down the drive towards Trevor's car. Danny caught a full view of the face as the streetlight shone full on the figure. Trevor!

Diaz reached for the microphone under the seat as the Jaguar backed out of the drive.

"One seven one to all units. Target is moving. Black Jaguar, southbound." The other agents acknowledged the transmission and Diaz replaced the microphone. He turned to Danny as he shifted into drive. "Looks like it's gonna go your way," Diaz said.

They followed Daniels for several blocks until Danny was sure none of his neighbors would see the arrest. Diaz keyed the microphone and announced, "One seven one. Take him down." Two unmarked cars, blue lights flashing on their dashboards, zoomed up to Daniels' vehicle. Another car cut in front of him, blocking his path. Agents in the front car leapt out, guns pointed at the windshield of Daniels' car, and began barking orders. Daniels stepped out and was ordered to lay on the ground. When he was prone, one agent moved in and handcuffed Daniels' hands behind his back. The agents pulled him to his feet as Danny approached. Daniels glared at Danny.

"You again! You motherfucker, I told you not to mess with me. I'm gonna own your ass!" Daniels snarled. Danny smiled at him.

"Not this time." Danny growled.

Rich Martelli sobbed softly, sitting in the chair, looking at the ceiling. He wanted to crawl in a hole somewhere. He tried to warn Trevor, but he wouldn't listen. Now, he was going to jail for a long time. He was glad his parents were dead and wouldn't know the humiliation. The room was empty except for three chairs and a wooden table. He had tried to talk to the agents on the ride into the DEA office but they sat silently and refused to acknowledge his presence. He wondered what would happen next. He had never had so much as a traffic ticket. Now this. Sweet Jesus, he was scared. He tried to stop crying but had no luck. He was afraid he would piss his pants.

Danny joined the agents in the hallway. One of the arresting agents was chuckling at Martelli's discomfort.

"This chicken shit. He traffics all that dope, sells it to kids and when he gets busted he cries like a schoolgirl. I would have more respect for him if he acted tough like they usually do."

"You think he'll talk?" Danny asked.

"Oh yeah. He tried to confess to us on the way in. He's so scared of jail he'll give up anything we want. Fucking wimp," the agent replied.

"He say anything about the murders?" Danny asked.

"Nope. But he tried to give us the entire smuggling setup. I told him to save it until we asked for it." The agent laughed.

"He's had his rights and waived?" Danny queried. The agent handed him the rights form.

"Signed, sealed and delivered," he answered. "Doesn't want a lawyer or any counsel."

"That'll work," Danny answered, taking the rights form.

He opened the door and stepped into the room. Martelli's head jerked up. Danny sat across from him. He studied the rights form for a few seconds to let Martelli worry. Finally, he cleared his throat and sat back, looking Martelli directly in the eye.

"Mister Martelli, I'm Sergeant Daniel Quinn. I'm with the Sheriff's Office. You understand why you're here?" he asked. Martelli nodded sadly. "You understand your rights and do not wish a lawyer at this time. Is that correct?" Martelli nodded again.

"Sir, you have to answer verbally. A nod is not sufficient," Danny said coldly.

"Yes." Martelli squeaked out.

"Yes, you understand your rights and do not wish a lawyer at this time?" Danny coached.

"Yes, I understand my rights and do not wish a lawyer at this time," Martelli mimicked.

"Do you understand that I am a police officer and am empowered to take an oath," Danny stated.

"Yes, I understand."

"Sir. I am going to swear you to tell the truth and this statement will be recorded on an audio tape for future prosecution. Do you understand?" Danny asked.

"Yes." Martelli answered. Danny administered the oath and turned on the tape recorder.

"Mister Martelli, you are under arrest for the crimes of trafficking in controlled substances. Importation of controlled substances, conspiracy to sell, manufacture or distribute dangerous drugs. Do you understand?" Danny monotoned.

"Yes, I do." Martelli squeaked.

"Mister Martelli. I am a homicide investigator for the county Sheriffs Office. I am not here to question you about the smuggling charges. I am here to ask you about some murders." At the word murder, Martelli's head jerked up. He stared at Danny.

"Murders? What murders?" Martelli stammered.

"Specifically the murder of officer Augustus Conrad and the murder of Gina Morrelli." Danny searched Martelli's face for a reaction. Martelli tried to reply but no words came out.

"Mister Martelli. Tell me what you know about these murders," Danny continued.

"I don't know anything. We don't know anything. We've been trying to find out what happened to Gina. I never heard of this Conrad person," Martelli replied, incredulous.

"What do you mean, we have been trying to find out about Gina?" Danny pressed.

"We don't know what happened. Trevor had Ricky checking into it. He hasn't found out anything, though. Trevor said it must have been an accident. She fell asleep on the Alley in her car and the muffler or something caught fire and burned up. You mean she was murdered? Somebody killed her? Like on purpose?" Martelli asked. Danny wondered if this guy was a good liar or he really didn't know anything. He was about to find out.

"Don't play with me Martelli. You know damn good and well she was murdered. You guys planned it and had her killed. Right?" Danny growled.

"No! No! I would never kill another human being. Trevor would never do that either. He's not that way," Martelli replied. " We don't know what happened to Gina. We loved Gina. She was part of us. Why would we kill her?"

"Because she wanted out and you were afraid she would turn you all in, maybe?" Danny asked.

"I don't believe Gina wanted out. She thrived on it. She liked the game as much as Trevor. That and the money. "

"Maybe because Gina ripped you off? We found a large amount of cash and some cocaine in her house. What about that?"

"There is so much money involved, so much coke floating around, Gina could take whatever she wanted and who would care?" Martelli replied. Danny had to admit he had a point.

"What if I told you I have a witness who says Ricky Madeira killed Gus Conrad and Gina? What would you say about that?" The shock registered on Martelli's face. It was real and genuine. Danny could tell this was news to him.

"Dear God. What have we become? I didn't honestly know anything about that. I swear. Look Sergeant, this was business. We did it for the money, nothing more. We're not killers," Martelli whispered.

"Not killers, huh? You bring drugs in and sell them on the streets so kids and adults get so hooked, they would kill their own families and you're not killers? Bullshit!" Danny rose to leave. He was disgusted with this asshole. Just did it for the money. That was the sickest part of all. The human destruction didn't matter, just the almighty buck. Danny changed his mind and sat back down. He studied Rich Martelli for a long time, staring at him. Danny waited. Martelli fidgeted in his chair. He glanced around the room. He suddenly looked at Danny with the look of a lost child.

"Honestly Sergeant. We didn't kill anybody. If you say you have a witness that Ricky killed those two, I believe it. Ricky is an evil man. He has a look that goes right through you. He scares the hell out of me. I heard he killed people before."

"Killed who?" Danny asked.

"Not here, but in Colombia. Supposedly he knifed a few competitors. He has a heart of stone," Martelli whispered.

"Tell me how you and Trevor and the others got started in this business. And how did Ricky get into the picture?"

"I met Trevor at a dinner party. A fund raiser for some group. A child's shelter I think. You know how it goes. I had a small real estate office and wanted to get bigger. So, you learn how to travel in the right social circles. Attend fundraisers. Meet the politicians. Get your picture in the social section of the newspaper. After you make a few friends the contacts start coming in. The wealthy clients start trickling in, they heard about you from a friend of a friend. It's all a game. I made friends with Trevor and his friends. We played golf together. Started spending time together. Going to clubs. We hunted and fished together out at the camp. I really didn't care for the clubs but the camp I like. I grew up in the country and felt like a kid again, out there. After a while, Trevor started talking about how we could make big money and not pay taxes. He said he had met a guy through Gina who would set us up. All we had to do was put the money together for the first investment and the profit would pour in. And it did. The guy he met was Ricky. He started coming around with us, clubs, the camp. The deal sounded too good to pass up. So I joined in. I didn't think about the human damage we might be doing. Just the cash. I didn't have much growing up and I guess I let it get hold of me. When that much money starts to flow, your conscience goes to hell."

"Gina brought Ricky to you? Where did she meet Ricky and did Trevor know Ricky beforehand?" Danny asked.

"I don't know how Ricky and Gina met. I'm pretty sure Trevor and Ricky didn't know each other before, but I'm not sure. He may have been planning this for some time. He suddenly started talking about this deal he heard about. We fell right in line." Martelli sighed and looked at the floor. Danny rose and looked down at Martelli. He was thoughtful as Martelli looked up at him pleadingly.

"I tend to believe you, Martelli. You are going to jail for a long time for the smuggling charge. But I believe you didn't know about Gina and Conrad. That's one point in your favor."

Danny could hear Trevor Daniel's voice fifteen feet from the room. He was yelling at the top of his lungs for his lawyer. Mike Richards frowned at Danny and handed him the Miranda rights form. Danny didn't have to look at it. He knew Daniels' style.

"We'll get nothing from him. He demanded his lawyer fifty times so far." Richards glanced at the door to the interrogation room. "I'd like ten minutes in a dark alley with this pompous fuck."

Danny smiled slightly. He pushed the door to the room open and stood in front of Daniels. Daniels glared up at him.

"Do you have any idea who you're fucking with?" Daniels growled at Danny. "My father is one of the most powerful men in this state. He knows the Governor, the Sheriff, and everybody in between."

"Mister Daniels," Danny said quietly, keeping his voice monotone. "I understand you don't wish to make a statement at this time, without your lawyer present. "

"You're fucking right," Daniels snarled.

"You understand you are facing charges of drug smuggling, conspiracy and others? Charges that could put you in prison for a long time?"

"Fuck you!" Daniels replied.

"Your cooperation in my investigation could be beneficial to your situation. These are heavy charges. If you assist in the murder investigation, that may help you with the judge."

"Talk to my lawyer. You remember him. Edgar Gould," Daniels replied.

"Oh yes. The lawyer whose wife you slept with. That should be interesting." Danny couldn't resist the personal dig.

"Fuck you asshole," Daniels spat. Danny left the room with a satisfied smile. Let Daniels chew on how much Danny knew about him and Mrs. Gould. And wonder how much he would tell Daniels' lawyer. Maybe Gould already knew. Karen Gould did say they had an open relationship. Maybe Daniels and his lawyer were swapping spit. Danny wouldn't be surprised anymore.

Danny waited until Daniels and Martelli were taken to the county jail. He decided to forego the interrogation of the other members of Sawgrass Development. He let them go directly to jail and not collect two hundred dollars. Maybe they would be more willing to cooperate after a night in the county jail. He didn't think they could tell him anything.

It seemed the Conrad setup and the murder of Gina Morelli was a mystery to them too. They were just greedy dope smugglers with no dangerous tendencies. Danny didn't even think Trevor knew about the murders. He wondered if Ricky acted alone.

The black van parked in a space at the marina and sat silent. The driver peered through the windshield and studied the yachts and sailboats moored in neat rows. He counted the boats, starting with the one closest to the parking spaces and counting toward the Intracoastal. His eyes stopped at the tenth boat and watched. No movement. Someone in the back of the van shuffled his feet on the metal floor, making a hollow sound. Someone else cleared his throat. The occupants were getting impatient but they knew the watching was necessary. The driver studied the boat some more. A thirty foot fisherman, upper deck with a captain's chair and steering wheel. It looked like every other fishing boat in South Florida. That was the point, blend in. The driver watched a man, Latin looking, climb up on deck and stretch. He had a large belly from too much beer and a large black mustache. He glanced around and seemed to be studying the van. The front seat passenger of the van watched through binoculars. He read the registration number on the bow and compared it to the sheet of paper in his lap.

"That's the one," the passenger whispered to the driver, who nodded. The driver calculated the distance from the van to the boat. About two hundred feet. The walkway along the dock was lined with bright lights. Too much light. They would have to move fast. The Latin on the boat disappeared into the cabin. The front passenger shifted the submachine gun resting across his lap.

"Let's go," the driver said tensely. The side door of the van slid open immediately and the six men in back slipped out. They shifted guns to shoulders and ran quickly in a line down the dock toward the boat. Two stopped at the stern and aimed their submachine guns at the cabin door. The other four slipped onto the deck as the first man hollered,

"Federal Agents. Search warrant!"

They kicked open the door of the cabin and caught the Latin man standing in the head with the door open. His pants were around his ankles. A stream of urine stopped instantly. Rough hands yanked him from the bathroom and shoved him to the floor. The rest of the boat was searched quickly. No one else inside. The captain was handcuffed and yanked to his feet. Someone pulled up his pants and rushed him from the boat to the dock. The curious were already flowing onto the dock as the captain was whisked to the van and shoved inside. One of the black clad DEA agents shooed the curious away and they retreated to the decks of their boats to watch .

Two uniformed US Customs agents approached with a large black Labrador Retriever between them. The dog tugged at the leash. The dog leapt onto the boat and immediately started scratching and biting at the sides of the boat. One of the Customs agents produced a small electric saw and cut a square in the gunwale of the fishing boat. A tightly wrapped package was visible in the hole. It was tugged out. A Customs agents knelt at the hole and peered into it with a flashlight. He looked up at the cluster of agents on the dock.

"Big load." He grinned.

Arturo Diaz couldn't help but smile. The raid teams had just reported to him all the boats had been accounted for. The captains and crew had been arrested and booked. Ten in custody, over two hundred kilos of cocaine and still counting. Not a bad night's work. The only one left was Ricky. They just didn't know where the hell he was. Diaz had teams out on the streets all over town and no Ricky. They had checked every hangout Ricky had been known to frequent. All of the local nude bars had turned up empty. The dockside lounges where drug runners were known to frequent. Nothing.

Diaz glanced at his watch, almost one in the morning. How long had they been at this? He could barely remember the last time he had slept. His eyes burned and ached. He rubbed them furiously but it didn't help. His vision clouded over for a second and he blinked hard to clear it. He stood from the desk and stretched as high as he could. He felt a pop in his back and felt better. He reached to the desk and retrieved his coffee cup, taking a sip. The dark brown liquid was ice cold and left a foul taste in his mouth. He couldn't understand how anyone could drink iced coffee.

Diaz headed down the hallway to the coffee pot, hoping someone made coffee. The office was empty and the desks sat silent as he passed between them. The teams were either out looking for Ricky or gone for the night. The office seemed strange to him when it was empty. There was usually so much activity he felt a wave of loneliness at night, here by himself. Diaz thrived on the bustle of the job.

He found the coffee pot in the conference room, crouching empty and clean on the hot plate. Damn! He changed course and walked to the night duty office. There was always a night agent in case someone needed something after hours. The night duty officer sat with his feet on the desk watching a small portable television. The communications was quiet in front of him. Diaz poured a cup of coffee and sat on the edge of the console.

"Anything yet?" he asked the duty officer hopefully.

"Sorry, boss. They haven't found him yet," the duty officer replied. Diaz nodded, stood and left the room.

Diaz couldn't fathom the fact none of the members of the Sawgrass Development knew where Ricky lived. Daniels probably knew, but he wasn't talking. Ricky was a phantom to the rest of the group, a dangerous specter that loomed over the operation and they were afraid of him. Very afraid. Diaz wondered if Ricky would kill one of them. They certainly seemed to believe it.

Every muscle in Danny's body was stiff and sore. He yawned uncontrollably. His stomach felt like a blowtorch was burning the inside of his stomach and he had a headache that wouldn't go away. He knew the other detectives were just as tired as he was but they couldn't stop now. If they gave up and went home for the night, they would give Ricky the chance to slip out of the country and he would be gone. Danny wasn't about to let that happen.

He parked the car in front of the sign reading, VALET PARKING, under the neon orange canopy. A valet in black pants and white shirt jogged toward them as he and Richards closed the car doors.

"Hey pal. You can't park there." The valet barked at them. Danny held up his badge, causing the valet to stop in his tracks.

"Yes I can," Danny replied. He was too tired to take any crap from the snot nosed kid. The parking lot was full of BMWs, Porsches and other expensive sports cars. A line of classy dressed men stood in line at the door, accompanied by very beautiful women, whose outfits showed lots of leg and cleavage. All of the women looked the same. Danny wondered if there was a factory somewhere that made these women for the rich men who favored them. Many of them were strippers or professional escorts. Many of the men were middle-aged, but wearing very expensive watches and chains, perpetually caught in a mid-life crisis. They spent lots of money on these women for their company just to appear to have some sex appeal left. They reminded Danny of roosters in a barnyard.

A huge, black man stood at the door of the bar and controlled entry. Danny guessed he weighed three hundred and fifty pounds. His tuxedo struggled to keep from splitting under the strain of covering his bulk. He eyed Danny and Richards warily as they approached. Danny smiled at him and held up his badge.

"Police. Official business. We need to see the manager." The black mountain picked up the receiver of a nearby phone mounted on the wall. He spoke quietly for a minute, then opened the door to the bar, waving them through.

Inside, the music thumped and pulsed so loud Danny could feel his heart palpitate with the rhythm. It was dark inside and Danny waited for his eyes to adjust. Lights flashed in time to the music. Danny wondered if all bars were dark to make the women look prettier and the men less desperate. A short, dark-complexioned man approached. His hair was slicked back and was jet black. His flowered shirt was unbuttoned half way down his torso, revealing a hairy chest. Three very thick gold chains hung around his neck. He leaned toward Danny and yelled in his ear.

"What can I do for you, Officer?"

"Let's go to your office. I can't hear myself think," Danny yelled back. He led them through the crowd on the dance floor and into a small office. He closed the door behind them and the music became a dull vibration.

"Okay Officer. What's up?" The manager smiled at them. Danny produced the photo of Ricky from his pocket and handed it to the manager.

"This guy. He's known to hang around these kinds of places. Have you seen him?" Danny asked. The manager took the picture and Danny could tell he was miffed about the 'these kinds of places' crack. Danny didn't care.

"Yeah, I've seen him. He dated one of our waitresses for awhile." The manager handed the picture back. Danny felt hope rise in him. If Ricky dated the waitress maybe he took her to his house. He tried not to let his excitement show.

"Is that waitress working here?" Danny asked hopefully.

"Yeah, in fact she's here tonight." The manager replied. "You want to talk to her, I suppose?"

"Yes, please." The manager nodded and left the office. Danny glanced at Richards.

"I've got my fingers crossed," Richards said quietly.

The manager returned with the waitress in tow. Her dark, curly hair hung to her waist and she had the deepest brown eyes Danny believed he had ever seen. She was clad in a bikini top that barely covered her small, firm breasts. The bottoms consisted of a thong bathing suit that covered next to nothing. The outfit was completed by black lace stockings and high heels.

"I'm Sergeant Daniel Quinn. This is Detective Richards." Danny introduced them. "And your name is?"

"Carla Mann. Am I in trouble?" she asked.

"No Carla. We're looking for this man and we understand you know him." Danny handed her the picture. He saw a flash of anger.

"Yeah. I know him, or should I say, knew him." She handed the picture back. "What did he do?"

"I'm afraid I can't tell you that," Danny replied. "How well do you know him?"

"I went out with him for a short time. He took me out to nice places, we slept together a few times, then he disappeared. He turned into a real asshole," she answered.

"Do you know where he lives or where we can find him?" Danny asked.

"Sure. I went by the house a few times after he dumped me but he wouldn't see me. You want the address?"

"You know the address?" Danny was surprised.

"Yeah. I sent him a card when he wouldn't see me. I memorized the address when I was at the house. Big, expensive place on the Intracoastal. He has a real nice boat. Fast as hell." She removed a napkin from the serving tray she held and wrote the address, handing it to Danny. He wanted to kiss her.

Mike Richards parked the car at the end of the street. They surveyed the house which loomed at the end of the street. The house was large, two storied and had a circular, tiled driveway. The front doors were smoked glass with an Egret etched in them. On each side of the doors were glass windows that reached to the second floor. The garage doors were closed and made of a thick wood with a carved design in them Danny couldn't distinguish from this distance. There were no cars in the driveway but that didn't mean they weren't in the garage. There were lights shining in the foyer behind the etched glass doors. Lights also shone in an upstairs window. Danny couldn't tell what other lights were on. He decided to look around while they waited for the rest of the team.

He slid out of the passenger door and leaned in the window.

"I'll be back. Wanna take a little look," Danny told Richards.

"Well, don't be a hero. Wait for the rest of us," Richards said softly. Danny nodded.

He walked nonchalantly down the street, staring at the house, watching for any sign that someone was looking, watching. Nothing. He glanced at the houses he passed. Typical homes with families and children and dogs. He wondered if they knew a drug smuggler and murderer lived in their midst. Probably not. He slowed as he approached the house and slipped into the yard next door. He eased along a hedge separating the properties.

Every nerve in his body jangled, his eyes were wide to let in as much light as possible. He slipped the automatic from his holster silently, just in case he should surprise Ricky in the yard. He walked carefully, putting his heel down first then easing his weight completely onto his foot to keep from making any sound . He had used this trick many times in Vietnam to slip past the enemy.

He followed the hedge until the property met the seawall, separating it from a canal. The hedge went all the way to the water. No way around the end. He eased back along the hedge until he found a sparse patch and eased into it, holding the branches to keep them from snapping back and making noise. He pushed himself into the hedge and stood still, scanning the house. No movement. The rear of the house was made of large floor to ceiling windows. He could see a large leather couch and glass coffee tables. A man-sized ceramic giraffe stood in a corner of the room. He could see past the couch to the kitchen. Still no movement. Maybe the bastard was upstairs. He eased through the hedge and followed the side of the house to the rear. He stayed in the shadows, listening for any sound from inside the house, straining for the slightest bump or vibration. He pressed his face to the concrete wall and put his ear to the warm rough surface. He placed his hand on the stucco next to his face, feeling for any vibration. Nothing. Suddenly, Danny heard a loud hissing noise at his feet. He pressed away from the wall. Sprinklers! Shit! Water erupted around him as the sprinklers spewed to full strength. He slipped quickly through the spray to the hedge, ducking quickly through it. Dammit! It never failed. He couldn't remember the number of times he had been soaked by sprinklers while slinking around in the dark. The sprinkler manufacturers must design them to come on when a cop is sneaking around.

His pants were wet from the hips down. His boots were soaked. He shook the water off of the gun in his hand. He stepped carefully into the street and watched Madeira's house in case he had been observed. He forced himself to walk nonchalantly back down the street. His pants were glued to his legs.

There were three unmarked cars parked behind his when he returned. Richards, Diaz, Moses and four DEA agents were huddled around the rear of Danny's car. Richards looked at Danny's pants and burst out laughing. Two of the DEA agents joined in.

"Did you find some sprinklers?" Richards gasped between laughs. This caused the others to start laughing. Danny grimaced at Richards. He waited for them to stop. They had all been victims of automatic sprinklers before. The laughter died to snickers then stopped.

"See anyone?" Diaz asked Danny when they had regained their composure.

"No. It's lit up like somebody's home but I didn't see anybody," Danny replied. Diaz pulled a folded sheet of paper from his pocket and handed it to Danny. Danny opened it.

"Federal arrest warrants. For Madeira and his buddy Jose. The judge wasn't happy to get woken up for those but I worked my charm on him. Now, we can go in and get the son of a bitch. Legally." Diaz smiled. Danny tucked the warrants in his pocket and grinned. He briefed the team on the layout of the house and what he had seen. He turned to Diaz.

"I think a quiet entry is best. Like to surprise the asshole to keep from having to shoot anybody if we can." Danny said. Diaz nodded and pointed at one of the DEA agents.

"That's his specialty. He'll pick the lock in under ten seconds."

They moved slowly down the street so as not to attract attention. They stopped at the corner of the house and the DEA agent with the lock picks slipped up to the door. He knelt beside it and reached up to try the knob.

Danny knew a lot of cops who had broken down unlocked doors because they didn't try the knob first. The door was locked. The agent reached up again and four seconds later he signaled the rest of them to join him. They slipped in the house silently, guns ready. Danny's heart pounded in his ears. He breathed slowly and evenly to slow his heart down. The team separated and began a careful check of the house.

Danny and Richards climbed the stairs slowly, their guns held in front of them, ready to shoot if necessary. The stairway ended at a long hallway. Danny motioned Richards to take the first door. He eased to the door and gently turned the knob. Richards pushed the door open carefully and slipped into the room. He quickly scanned the bedroom. Nothing.

He stepped back into the hallway and signaled Danny to go to the next door. Danny eased the next door open and entered another bedroom. He checked the bathroom and the closet. Men's clothes were hung neatly in the closet. The rest of the upstairs was searched without finding anyone. They rejoined the rest downstairs.

"He's gone. There's clothes in the closet. He must have heard Daniels was in custody and split," Danny mused.

"The garage is empty. No cars. The boats still tied up out back. They left by car." One of the DEA agents added.

"I've got people at the airport here and in Bogota. We'll get 'im. Maybe not right away but we will," Diaz assured them. They returned to their cars and Diaz said he was sending his agents home for the night. He and Danny shook hands and agreed to meet at the office in the morning.

Richards drove toward the office. Danny sat beside him silently. Suddenly, he slammed his hand against the dashboard in anger. Damn! He wanted Madeira and now he may not get him. His wet pants were cold against his legs, making his mood darker.

The cellular phone rang and Danny snatched it up. He pressed the button and put it to his ear.

"Yeah, Quinn."

"Hey brother," William Otter Killer said, "Got something for you. You wanted that house on the alley watched. "

"Yeah, William, I did." Danny waited breathlessly.

"Somebody there. Two guys. Spanish looking. Driving a black BMW. Looks like they're waiting for something."

"William, you are a life saver. What the hell are you doing out there at this time of night?" Danny asked.

"Hunting," William replied. More like poaching, Danny thought. He couldn't care less.

"Can you hang for awhile?" Danny asked. " I want those two. We'll be there as soon as we can."

"No problem. Hunting sucks anyway."

"William. Don't let them see you. These guys are killers."

"No shit. Since you work homicide I didn't figure they were shoplifters. Besides, I got my rifle. They won't know I'm here. I'm an Indian, remember?" William replied.

Danny chuckled and hung up. He dialed Diaz's cell phone. No answer. He called Moses and got an answer on the first ring. He told Moses to meet them at the toll plaza at the east end of Alligator Alley. Richards was already on the radio calling the Homicide squad to meet them there. Danny hung up with Moses and called the Sergeant in charge of the night shift in the Everglades District. He requested two marked cars and uniformed deputies to meet at the toll plaza.

"Haul your ass," Danny said to Richards as he turned on the blue light and siren.

CHAPTER 18

Trevor Daniels removed his jail-issued pants, peeked out the cell door and scanned the hallway. Empty. He tied the cuffs of the pants together and hooked the pant's legs over the corner of the top bunk. Plead guilty and take your chances, my ass! Lawyers What the fuck did they know? He couldn't stand the thought of being dragged through a trial. The disappointment in his father's eyes. The old man would be publicly ruined. He could hear him now. Let down again. Trevor refused to hear how he had screwed up, again. Not anymore. His ego wouldn't let him be humiliated by his father again.

He slipped the pants over his head so the crotch was under his chin. He turned in a circle three times until his neck was trapped in the crotch. Trevor sat on the edge of the bunk, took a deep breath and pushed off.

He landed in a sitting position. His legs thrashed and darkness enveloped him. Then, he was still.

When Danny and Richards arrived, the rest of the team was already waiting, including Moses Hammond. None of the DEA agents were there, having all gone home and turned off their pagers. Richard's screeched the car to a halt and Danny leapt out. The grim faces of his team told the story. They knew this was serious business, going after a man like Ricky Madeira. Two marked sheriff's cars arrived and the group grew by three, two uniformed deputies and the sergeant from the Everglades District. The toll booth attendant leaned out of her booth, craning her neck to watch.

Danny passed out pictures of Ricky and explained the situation. The conversation was interrupted by the ringing of Danny's cellular phone. It was William Otter Killer.

"Something's going down out here. A small twin engine plane just landed on the strip out back. Looks like they're about to fly the coop.

Better hurry," William said quickly. The deputies and detectives sprinted for their cars.

The wind whistled through Danny's partially opened window as they raced for Sawgrass Camp. Danny prayed they wouldn't be too late. He kept William on the phone in case things changed.

Ten minutes later they parked behind William's truck on the shoulder of the road. Danny could barely make out the light mounted on the top of the gate at the camp. William leaned against his truck with a scoped rifle resting over his shoulder. Danny shook William's hand firmly. He realized how much he missed his old friend.

"They're still there," William nodded toward the camp. Danny studied the light on the gatepost. It was going to make an undetected approach unlikely. He decided that he would go first and unscrew the bulb so they could slip into the grounds without being seen. The team had orders to make a quiet approach as soon as the light went out.

Danny slipped silently along the fence that bordered the front of the property. He crouched and stayed below the tops of the hedge along the fence. He could hear muffled voices from inside the house. In the distance, an owl hooted a mournful warning. An approaching car flashed its bright headlights and Danny melted into the bushes. The car whizzed past him and he could feel the wind from its passing brush across his face. Another car approached and Danny waited, crouched below the light. He raised his pistol and punched it against the bulb as the car passed, the noise covering the sound of the bulb popping. Danny was shrouded in darkness. The team joined him, Moses first in line, and they crept through the gate. Danny motioned for them to spread out. A mosquito landed on his cheek and began to bite. He ignored it.

Danny heard an airplane engine suddenly cough to life at the back of the property. The back door of the house slammed. Two men appeared and began to walk toward the back of the property.

"Police! Freeze!" yelled a uniformed deputy.

Not yet. Not yet! Danny screamed silently. They were caught in the open. Flashlights came on and illuminated Ricky and Jose. Jose spun and raised a small Uzi machine gun toward the flashlights and ripped off a burst of automatic fire. The flashlights wavered crazily and went dark. Danny dove for the corner of the house. He pointed his .45 in Jose's direction. The gun roared in his hand and he closed his eyes against the muzzle flash to keep from being blinded. Jose fired again and bullets whacked off the building above Danny's head. Danny's pulse pounded in his head. He peeked around the corner and saw two figures fleeing in the darkness toward the sound of the airplane. Danny rose and sprinted after them. He glanced back and saw two detectives crouched next to a figure face down in the darkness. Shit! Goddamn it! Danny cursed as he sprinted after Ricky and Jose. The engine noise grew louder.

Suddenly, he burst into the clearing. In the center, a dark twin engine airplane raced its engine. Ricky and Jose sprinted toward it. Danny pointed his gun at Jose's back and it roared twice. Jose stumbled and fell then rolled into a seated position next to the plane. He raised up and fired another burst from the Uzi. Bullets ripped past Danny's side. He dove to the ground. He fired twice more and Jose flopped onto his back.

Two figures leapt from the airplane and began firing pistols in Danny's direction A uniformed Deputy along with Kay Matthews appeared beside Danny. The uniformed deputy fired a shotgun at the men as they ducked behind the plane. Danny saw Ricky's white shirt veer away from the plane and fade into the darkness beyond.

Danny mentally marked the spot. He pushed off of the ground and sprinted after him. The engine noise died behind him as he followed the white shirt bobbing in the dark. He heard more shotgun blasts and handgun fire behind him. Then it was quiet. Danny strained his ears and listened for Ricky's footsteps. He heard splashing footsteps ahead and sprinted after them.

Danny's lungs burned from exertion and adrenaline. It was suddenly quiet ahead. He stopped and held his ragged breath, listening. There. Not far in front, he heard a splash then sloshing footsteps. He sprinted forward, his boots slipping in wet mud. He was immediately in a stand of sawgrass and knee deep water. The blades of grass slashed his face, cutting bloody furrows. His feet found muddy ground and he slipped and fell. Cursing, he jumped to his feet and slipped forward. He was in a stand of cypress trees.

Ricky slipped behind a cypress tree and waited. He clutched a large cypress limb and waited. His hands trembled and he fought gasping breaths. He wished he still had his gun. He heard running sloshing footsteps approach and strained his eyes in the darkness to see his pursuer. The footsteps got louder and Ricky tensed, ready to swing.

Suddenly, Danny realized the footsteps in front had stopped. He tried to stop but slid in the wet mud. A flash of white shirt and a tree limb streaked at his head in the dark. Too off balance to duck, he started to fall when the limb cracked into his forehead just below his hairline. His feet shot from under him and he saw a blinding red and yellow light in his head. He landed on his back with a splash, mud erupting around him, covering his face.

Danny opened his eyes and the world tilted crazily. His head was buzzing and bile rose in his throat. He swallowed hard to keep from vomiting. He moved his eyes and could see nothing but darkness. He rolled to his side and pushed to a kneeling posture. He fought nausea again. His neck was stiff but he could feel his arms and legs, a good sign. He closed his right hand into a fist and realized it was empty. He groped in the mud for his gun but it had vanished in the mire. His forehead burned like it was covered with a million fire ants. He reached up and gingerly touched it. He could feel something hanging loose but couldn't tell what it was. He remained motionless and listened. The buzzing in his head was intense but he heard faint footsteps retreating.

Danny pushed himself slowly to his feet. The world tilted again and he almost passed out. Stumbling sideways, he propped his hand against the rough trunk of a cypress tree. He fought to slow his breathing until the dizziness passed. He reached down and raised his pant leg, digging in his boot for his backup gun. Gripping the little revolver, he plunged off in the direction of the footsteps.

Ricky Madeira heard splashing coming closer. Son of a bitch, the bastard was still coming. Ricky decided on a different ambush. He leaned over and gasped for air, hands propped on his knees. Danny heard the footsteps stop again and slowed, not about to be surprised twice. Something wet flowed down his forehead and he tasted blood in his mouth, mixed with mud. He raised the revolver and held it in front of him. A voice close in front of him said,

"Okay man. I give up."

Danny could barely make out a white shirt in front of him, arms raised. He stopped and pointed the gun at the center of the shirt.

"Don't you fucking move," Danny growled, squinting in the darkness.

"No problem," the white shirt answered. Danny stepped closer and examined the man in front of him. Dizziness washed over him and he fought to stay upright.

"Turn around," Danny rasped. The shirt turned. "Hands behind your back."

Ricky lowered his hands behind his back. His right hand slipped into his waistband and he gripped the handle of the knife. Danny moved toward Ricky, reaching for his handcuffs. Suddenly, Ricky spun toward him. Danny saw a flash of metal and felt a punch in the chest, a red hot flame shooting through his upper chest. He felt the blade of the knife grind against bone and he stumbled backward. Ricky charged and stabbed with the knife again. Danny couldn't raise the gun to fire. He sidestepped and blocked the arm with the knife. Ricky stepped past him and Danny launched a sidekick that struck the outside of Ricky's knee. Danny felt and heard a loud snap. Ricky went down on one knee, the knife flying from his hand. Danny swung the gun at Ricky's face, hitting him in the mouth. He felt teeth crack and Ricky flipped on his back. Danny fell on top of him. White hot pain flashed in his chest and down his left arm. He couldn't raise it.

Danny crawled on top of Madeira and sat on his chest. He looked into Ricky's eyes. They were half open, unseeing. His teeth were missing in the front. Danny shoved the barrel of the gun in Ricky's mouth and drew the hammer back. He wanted to blow his head off. It would be easy. No witnesses. Scum like this deserved to die. Do society a favor. Save the taxpayers some money. It was certainly justified. He would just say he shot Ricky when he was stabbed. But this wasn't Viet Nam. It was a war but a different kind. The good guys had rules and were overwhelmed since the bad guys had no rules. But Danny believed in right and wrong. And this would be wrong. He carefully lowered the hammer.

Danny heard sloshing footsteps approaching. He tried to turn his head but it wouldn't respond. He heard Mike Richards familiar voice calling his name.

"Over here," Danny croaked. Richards and Kay Matthews materialized besides him. Danny raised his eyes to Richards' face. " Arrest this asshole for me," he whispered. Danny pitched face down in the mud and lay still.

Danny Quinn opened his eyes and was immediately seized with a massive headache. He was on his back and could see white ceiling tiles. He tried to turn his head to look around but something held his head in place. He felt rough material rubbing tight under his chin. He realized he had a cervical collar on. He rolled his eyes around and saw his wife glide to the bed as if in a fog. He blinked and his sight cleared. She leaned over him and stroked his face.

"Where ya been Quinn?" She smiled at him.

"I give up?" Danny croaked out. Richards appeared over him and frowned down at him.

"You look like shit, boss." Richards grinned.

"Is it that bad?" Danny asked quietly. Richard's and Danny's wife exchanged glances. She looked deep in his eyes.

"You have a concussion. Your hair was almost ripped off your head. The wound is probably infected from mud and dirty water. A deep stab wound in the left side of your chest that probably severed the nerves to your arm, they don't know yet. Other than that it's not too bad." Her eyes were moist.

"Get me a mirror," Danny requested.

Richards held a mirror in front of him. His forehead was grotesquely swollen and a row of shiny staples held the skin together along the hairline. Both of his eyes were swollen and bruised. His skin was ghostly pale.

"Not as pretty as I used to be. Will you still love me?" Danny asked his wife.

"You're stuck with me Quinn," she replied, leaning down and kissing his cheek. Danny remembered the shoot-out and someone had gone down.

"I saw somebody go down. Who was it?" Danny asked Richards. Richards took a deep breath.

"Moses. He didn't make it Dan, I'm sorry," Richards replied sadly. Danny closed his eyes. Dammit! He should have killed Madeira when he had the chance. He drifted back to sleep.

CHAPTER 19

Trevor Daniels Senior stared at the wall. He could hear his daughter-in-law and his wife talking softly in the next room. He took another gulp of his drink and it seared its way down his throat. Things had really gone to shit. He thought of his wife's reaction when the cops told her Trevor hung himself. The look of utter contempt, like it was his fault. He had no way of knowing this would happen. When he recruited Gina to entice Trevor to get into the business he thought the kid could handle it. Apparently, he was wrong. Daniels Senior and Ricky had tried to scare Conrad off the case. When he told Ricky to waste Conrad he figured that would be the end of the problem. Then Gina decided to take up with that cop. She wanted to leave the group to run off with a cop. Ricky was afraid of pillow talk exposing them. Daniels Senior disagreed but Ricky convinced him Gina was a liability. Ricky had been careless. It was all supposed to look accidental. Now, there was dead DEA agent and a seriously injured Homicide Sergeant to contend with. That incompetent fuck, Madeira, had really made a mess. Now he was in custody and might talk. And that might expose Daniels Senior. Ricky was the only one who knew he was behind the whole operation, even his own son didn't know. Maybe Ricky had already talked. He didn't think so but better not to take chances.

Daniels reached for the phone and dialed the number in Colombia. Miguel would not be pleased but it had to be done. Madeira had to be silenced. He and Miguel had run this operation for twenty years without problems. Now this. Never leave a kid in charge of a man's business. Shouldn't be too hard to find some inmate to stick a shiv in Madeira in the showers.

He heard the phone ring on the other end.

ABOUT THE AUTHOR

The author is a native of South Florida and still lives there with the love of his life. Married to his wife of twenty five years, he is the father of a grown son, who is one of his greatest achievements and his best friend.

The author is an avid outdoorsman who grew up hunting and fishing in the Everglades. He is a veteran of thirty years of law enforcement and is still serving as a Deputy Sheriff in Broward County. He is a respected police tactical instructor and has extensive training in the martial arts.

The author has been widely published in law enforcement periodicals along with Karate International and Skin Diver magazines.

This is his first novel.

Printed in the United States
22662LVS00003B/163-171

9 781418 492250